WOMAN OF GOD

JAMES PATTERSON is one of the best-known and biggest-selling writers of all time. His books have sold in excess of 325 million copies worldwide and he has been the most borrowed autho̵ ̵ ̵ ̵ ̵ries for the past nine years in̵ ̵ ̵ ̵ ̵ ̵ ̵of some of the ̵ ̵ ̵ ̵ ̵ ̵ ̵ ̵ decades – th̵ ̵ ̵ Detective Mic̵ ̵ he has written ̵ ̵ ̵ ̵ ̵ ̵ ̵ ̵sellers including roma̵ ̵ ̵ ̵ ̵ ̵ ̵̵d-alone thrillers.

James is passionate about encouraging children to read. Inspired by his own son who was a reluctant reader, he also writes a range of books for young readers including the Middle School, I Funny, Treasure Hunters, House of Robots, Confessions, and Maximum Ride series. James is the proud sponsor of the World Book Day Award and has donated millions in grants to independent bookshops. He lives in Florida with his wife and son.

Also by James Patterson

STAND-ALONE THRILLERS

Sail (*with Howard Roughan*)
Swimsuit (*with Maxine Paetro*)
Don't Blink (*with Howard Roughan*)
Postcard Killers (*with Liza Marklund*)
Toys (*with Neil McMahon*)
Now You See Her (*with Michael Ledwidge*)
Kill Me If You Can (*with Marshall Karp*)
Guilty Wives (*with David Ellis*)
Zoo (*with Michael Ledwidge*)
Second Honeymoon (*with Howard Roughan*)
Mistress (*with David Ellis*)
Invisible (*with David Ellis*)
The Thomas Berryman Number
Truth or Die (*with Howard Roughan*)
Murder House (*with David Ellis*)
Never Never (*with Candice Fox*)

A list of more titles by James Patterson
is printed at the back of this book

JAMES PATTERSON
& MAXINE PAETRO
WOMAN OF GOD

arrow books

1 3 5 7 9 10 8 6 4 2

Arrow Books
20 Vauxhall Bridge Road
London SW1V 2SA

Arrow Books is part of the Penguin Random House group of companies
whose addresses can be found at global.penguinrandomhouse.com.

Penguin
Random House
UK

First published by Century in 2016
First published in paperback by Arrow Books in 2017

www.penguin.co.uk

A CIP catalogue record for this book is available from the British Library.

ISBN 9781784753849
ISBN 9781784753856 (export edition)

Printed and bound in Great Britain by Clays Ltd, St Ives Plc

*Dedicated to the selfless doctors and humanitarians
who travel to the world's most dangerous places to help
those in need.*

PROLOGUE

TWENTY YEARS FROM NOW

ONE

—

THE STORY had begun deep inside the Vatican, had leaked out into the city of Rome, and within days had whipped around the globe with the momentum of a biblical prophecy. If true, it would transform not only the Roman Catholic Church but all of Christianity, and possibly history.

Today was Easter Sunday. The sun was bright, almost blinding, as it glanced off the ancient and sacred buildings of Vatican City.

A tall, dark-haired man stood between towering statues on the colonnade, the overlook above St. Peter's Square. He wore Ray-Bans under the bill of his cap, a casual blue jacket, a denim shirt, workaday jeans, and combat boots. The press corps milled and chatted behind him, but writer Zachary Graham was transfixed by the hundreds of thousands of people packed together in the square below like one enormous single-cell organism.

The sight both moved him and made him sick with worry. Terrifying, unprecedented events were happening around the world: famines and floods and violent weather patterns, compounded by wars and other untethered forms of human destruction.

The *New York Times* had flown Graham to Rome to cover Easter in

3

the Vatican and what might be the last days in the life of an aging Pope Gregory XVII. The pope was a kind and pious man, beloved everywhere, but since Graham's arrival in Rome four days ago, he had seen the sadness over the pope's imminent passing and, not long after, his death eclipsed by a provocative rumor, which if true would be not just the turning point in one of the world's great religions and the explosion of a media bomb, but, to Zachary Graham, a deeply personal event.

Graham had been born in Minnesota forty-five years before. He was the eldest son of a middle school teacher and a Baptist minister. He was no fan of organized religion, but he was fair minded. He was a brilliant writer, highly respected by his peers, and clearly the right person for this job—which was why the *Times,* still the preeminent news machine of the twenty-first century, had sent him.

Now, as he stood in the shadows of Bernini's massive statuary, watching the crowd show signs of panic, Graham knew it was time to go to ground.

He walked twenty yards along the overlook, stopping at the small, cagelike lift. Other reporters followed him, cramming themselves into the rickety elevator. The doors screeched shut. Graham pressed the Down button, and the car jiggled and lurched toward the plaza below.

From there, Graham walked north through the colonnade, the harsh light throwing contrasting blocks of sharp shadow onto the worn stones. Moving quickly, he exited through the shifting crowd in St. Peter's Square and headed toward an alley off Via della Conciliazione, where the mobile production trucks were behind barricades, tightly parked in a bumper-to-bumper scrum.

Graham flashed his credentials to get through security, then opened one of the rear doors of a white panel van.

He peered over a sound man's shoulder at the large monitor and read so many expressions on the faces in the crowd: fear, desperation, and fervent hope that the new pope would bring much-needed change.

From the election of the very first "vicar of Christ," to the current Holy See, the pope had always been God's representative on earth—a man. Could it be true that Gregory's successor would be a *woman?* The provocative, unsettling story that had once been just a whisper was taking on more certainty by the moment: the next pope would be an American lay priest by the name of Brigid Fitzgerald.

The possibility of a woman pope was extraordinary, astounding, and if it happened, the consequences would be profound.

Zachary Graham had done his homework.

Legend has it that in the year AD 855, a woman who had disguised herself as a man was elected pope. Three years later, while in a processional through Rome, this pope had gone into labor and given birth. She was immediately tied to the tail of a horse, dragged through the streets to her death. Her baby was also murdered, and the two of them were buried beneath the street where they died.

Given the absence of physical artifacts, this story had been officially dismissed by the Catholic Church as a Protestant story concocted to embarrass the Church and the Papacy. Yet there were etchings of Pope Joan and footnotes in a hundred ancient, illuminated manuscripts. There was even a small, disfigured shrine to Pope Joan on a small street not far from St. Peter's Square.

This old story troubled Graham's soul. It was why he was afraid for Brigid when people spoke of her as "miraculous," and why for so long he had been unable to find satisfaction or love or even sleep.

Graham took a chair in front of the screen displaying those rapt, excited, tormented faces and carefully considered his options.

Should he wait, observe, and report the facts that were unfolding before him? Should he do his job? Or should he commit journalism's greatest sin by interfering in this true epic drama? If he did that, he might very well change the outcome.

TWO

CAMBRIDGE, MASSACHUSETTS

I WAS trying to get my seven-year-old, Gillian, ready for the day. She is a funny little girl, bratty and bright. And clever. And slippery. She's the apple, peach, and plum of my eye, and I love her to pieces. Thank you, God.

It was Easter Sunday, and Gilly was in the closet trying on various articles of clothing, some of which were actually hers, and she was telling me about her dream.

"I finally found out where the polar bears went."

"Oh. So, where did they go?"

She leaned out of the closet, showing me her darling face, her bouncing curls, and her bony shoulders.

"Gilly, you have to get dressed. Come on, now."

"They were on the *moon*, Mom. They were on the *moon*. And I was there. I had a special car with skis instead of wheels, and, even though it was nighttime, it was soooo bright that I could see the bears *everywhere*. You know why they're on the moon?"

"Why?" I said, lacing up my shoes.

"Because the moon is made of *ice*. The *ice* covers the oceans of the moon."

People had been talking about colonizing the moon for the better part of a hundred years. It was still an impossible hope. A total fantasy. But there it was every night, right up there, pristine, visible, and with historic human footprints still in the moon dust. And now Gilly's dreamed-up polar bears were not facing earthly extinction. They were partying on the moon.

As Gilly, now back in the closet, told me, "the man in the moon" provided the bears with food and volleyball.

I laughed, thinking about that, and she said, "I'm not kidding, Mom."

I was folding up the discarded clothes Gilly had flung all over the room when I heard her cry out for me.

"Honey, what is it? What?"

She came out of the closet showing me the blood coming from the web between her thumb and forefinger of her left hand. She still held a piece of broken lightbulb.

"It just rolled off the shelf and *broke*."

"Let me see."

She showed me the glass, with its sharp edges.

"No, silly, show me your *cut*."

She held out her hand, and droplets of blood fell on the front of her chosen Easter dress, a froth of ruffled pink with an overskirt of spangled tulle. It was excruciating, the sweetness and the vulnerability of this little girl. I stifled my urge to cry and said, "Let's fix this. Okay?"

A few minutes later, Gilly's finger was washed and bandaged, the glass shards were in a box in the trash; and now I was focused again on the time.

Gilly wriggled into her second-best dress, a blue one with a sash of embroidered daisies.

"Gorgeous," I said.

I stepped into my clean, white surplice, and, peering into a small mirror propped on the bookcase, I finger combed my unruly ginger hair.

"You look beautiful, Mom," she said, wrapping her arms around my waist.

I grinned down at her. "Thank you. Now, put on your shoes."

"We're not late, you know."

"Not yet, anyway. Let's go, silly Gilly. Let's go."

THREE

I BRACED myself, then Gilly and I stepped out onto the stoop.

The shifting crowd filling the street *roared*. Communicants, neighbors, people who had come here to catch a glimpse of me, ordinary people of every age and description, reached out their hands, lifted their babies, and chanted my name.

"Bri-gid! Bri-gid!"

I'd seen this outpouring of passion before, and still I wasn't sure how to act. Sometimes the mood of a crowd turned dark. I'd seen that, too.

Gilly said, "Mom. You'll be all right."

She waved, and the crowd went wild again.

And then they pushed forward, toward the stoop. News broadcasters, megabloggers, televangelists, and entertainment-TV hosts pointed their microphones toward me, asking, "Brigid, are the rumors true? Have you gotten the call? Are you ready to go?"

I had answered their questions in the past but was always asked for more, and by now, I didn't have any more. Gilly was too small to walk through this groundswell, so I hoisted her up, and with her arms around my neck and her legs around my waist, I stepped carefully down to the street, where the crowd was at eye level.

"Hey, everyone," I said as I waded into the river of people. "Beautiful Easter Sunday, isn't it? I would stop to talk, but we have to get going. We'll be late."

"Just one question," shouted Jason Beans, a reporter from the *Boston Globe* who liked to be called Papa. He was wearing a button on his lapel, the single letter *Y*, which stood for the all-inclusive, universal question about everything: the heat waves, the long, frigid winters, the eerily brilliant sunsets, and ever-warming, rising seas. *Why?*

"We can walk and talk," Beans was saying. He was standing between me and other reporters who were angling for their "just one question."

I kind of liked the somewhat annoying Jason Beans, but Gilly and I couldn't risk getting swallowed up by this crowd. We had to move.

"Have you gotten the call from the Vatican?" Beans asked.

"Aww, Papa. It's a rumor, nothing more. And that's the really big scoop. Now, pleeease pardon me. I have to go to church. I have a Mass to say."

"Bri-gid! Bri-gid!"

Flowers flew at me, and hands grabbed at my skirts, and Jason Beans stepped in front of us and wedged open a path. Gilly and I drafted behind him. We crossed the street, and there, midblock, stood the grand brick church that had anchored this neighborhood for a century.

People crowded us from all directions, calling out, "We love you, Brigid. Brigid, will you remember us when you're living in Rome?"

"I remember you right here and now, Luann. See you in church."

By the time we reached the entrance to St. Paul's, thousands were being funneled through the narrow streets, toward the entrance, and they understood that only a few hundred would fit inside the small neighborhood church. The panic was starting. They all wanted to see me.

Gilly was twisting in my arms, waving, laughing into the crook of my neck. "Mom, this is so great."

With Beans acting as the tip of the spear, I entered the sacristy with my daughter still in my arms. I thanked the reporter, who shot his last, desperate questions at me.

I told him, "I'll see you after Mass, Papa, I promise," and closed the door.

I let Gilly down, and she fed our pet tabby cat, Birdie. Then my little girl ran out to the nave and squeezed her way into a front pew. I crossed myself, and, hoping that I would find the right words, I walked out to the altar.

The air was supercharged with expectation.

I looped the stole around my neck and stepped up to the altar. But instead of beginning the Mass in the traditional manner, I spoke to the congregation in the most personal way I knew how.

"That was a pretty rough scene out there on the Street," I said to the congregants. "But I'm glad we're all together now on this momentous Easter Sunday. We have a lot to reflect upon and much to pray for."

A bearded man jumped to his feet at the rear of the church and called my name, *demanding* my attention.

"Look here, Brigid. Look at me."

Did I know him? I couldn't make out his face from where I stood, but then he walked up the aisle, crossed himself, and slipped his hand into his jacket.

In front of me, Gilly shouted, *"Mom!"* her face contorted in fear. But before I could speak to my precious daughter, I heard a cracking sound and felt a punch to my shoulder. I reached my hand out to Gilly.

There was another *crack*, and I staggered back and grabbed at the altar cloth, pulling it and everything on the altar down around me.

I fought hard to stay in the present. I tried to get to my feet, but I was powerless. The light dimmed. The screams faded, and I was dropping down into a bottomless blackness, and I couldn't break my fall.

PART ONE

PRESENT DAY

South Sudan, Africa

CHAPTER I

JEMILLA WAS beside my bed, yelling into my face, "Come, Doctor. They're calling for you. Didn't you hear?"

No, I hadn't heard the squeal of the P.A. calling doctors to the O.R. I had only *just* fallen asleep. I pulled on my scrubs and splashed cold water on my face, saying, "What's happening? Who else is on duty? Got coffee?"

Jemilla answered my questions. "Got new wounded, of course. You're the last one up. How do you want your coffee? Cream? Sugar? Or the usual, we have no coffee at all?"

"You're tough," I said to the young girl standing *right there*.

She grinned and kept me in her sights while I stepped into my shoes. Then she ran out in front of me, yelling, "She's coming, she's coming now," as I trotted down the dusty dirt path to the O.R.

We were in South Sudan in the drought season, in a hospital outpost in a settlement camp in the middle of a senseless and bloody civil war. The hospital was the product of an NGO organization called Kind Hands, and we were doing what we could in a desperate situation to keep bucking the tide of hopelessness.

The hospital compound was made up of eight shoddy concrete buildings roofed with corrugated tin or tarps or hay. The female staff lived in one building, the men in another. We ate and showered in the third when it wasn't filled with the wounded and dying. We had the most primitive operating theater possible, a laughable closet of a lab, and three wards: Isolation, Maternity, and Recovery.

The professional staff was constantly changing as doctors went home and new ones came, and we were assisted by local volunteers, many of whom were internally displaced persons, IDPs, themselves.

Our current roster consisted of six doctors, a dozen nurses, and a dozen aides responsible for the emergency care of the eighty thousand residents of this camp. Yes, eight zero, followed by three more zeros.

All the doctors here had had to compete for an assignment with Kind Hands. We wanted to do good in the world, and yet very few doctors signed up for a second tour. It took only a couple of weeks for the enormity and the futility of the job to set in.

Ten minutes after being roused by Jemilla, I was in the operating room, scrubbed in and gloved up. The sole light source was a halogen lamp hanging from chains over the operating table, powered by the battery in Colin's Land Rover.

The boy on the table was a very small four-year-old who, according to his mother, had wandered too close to the chain-link boundary and had been struck by a bullet to his chest.

Sabeena, our irascible and irreplaceable head nurse, her long braids tied up in a colorful head scarf, was wearing scrubs and pink Skechers left to her by a doctor who'd gone back to Rio.

By the time I arrived, she had efficiently swabbed the child down, anesthetized him, and laid out clean instruments for me in a tray. As I looked him over, Sabeena gave me a rundown on his vitals.

The child was bleeding like crazy, and, given his small size, he could barely afford blood loss at all. I saw that the bullet had gone in under his right nipple and had exited through his back, just under his right shoulder blade. The boy's mother was standing there with a tiny new baby in

CHAPTER 1

her arms, her tears plopping onto the contractor's garbage bag she wore as a sterilized poncho over her rags.

English was the official language here, and, although probably sixty tribal languages were in use, plain English was understood.

I asked, "Mother, what's his name? Tell me his name."

"Nuru," the woman said. "My God. My little son."

I said to the unconscious child, "Nuru, I'm your doctor. My name is Brigid. Your mommy is here, too. Hang tough, little guy."

Sabeena wrote Nuru's name on a strip of tape, wrapped it around the boy's wrist while I did a FAST exam with our portable ultrasound. There was so much blood still coming from this small boy, I had to find out if the bullet had gone through only his chest or if he also had an intra-abdominal injury.

I looked at the ultrasound.

"There's no blood in his stomach. That's one good thing, anyway," I said to our head nurse. "Maybe the only good thing."

Sabeena clucked her tongue and shook her head. Then she hung a bag of blood and threaded an IV needle into the boy's vein while I considered what to do.

It was my call. It was all up to me.

I had recently finished my residency at Johns Hopkins and had volunteered with Kind Hands thinking, like almost everyone here, that I knew what to expect. But the books and documentaries that had inspired me to come here had given me only the slightest inkling of the reality of South Sudan.

Since 1983, the normally dire, antithetical-to-life conditions had gotten worse, with the country now divided and its people and their villages, families, and livelihoods shredded by genocide.

The number of displaced persons in South Sudan continued to swell. Food shortages, a lack of potable water and medicine, contagious disease, killing floods, and droughts had been compounded by gangs of murderous teenage boys and actual army militias doling out unspeakable violence.

And now I stood in an operating room that was bare to the bone. We had two standard operating tables, six beds, a few shelves of expired medical supplies. Instruments were sterilized in pots of boiling water hanging from bicycle handlebars positioned over the fire pit outside the back door. Along with the car battery, we had a small, noisy generator.

We made medical equipment with tire pumps, duct tape, and cotton jersey. I could do a lot with an empty coffee can and a length of plastic tubing.

This was it, the real hell on earth.

Everything here was desperate and chaotic. Except that right now, the radio was plugged into the generator. The Red Sox and Yankees were playing at Fenway. David Ortiz was stepping to the plate with two outs in the bottom of the ninth. The score was tied, 3–3. If Ortiz could somehow get hold of one, maybe Nuru, too, could go deep.

I had hope.

CHAPTER 2

ONLY MINUTES had passed since I met my young patient, Nuru. Sabeena was bagging the child, and I had determined my course of action, when my colleague, Colin, came up from behind, saying, "Step aside, Brigid. This kid could drown in his blood."

Dr. Colin Whitehead was a late thirty-something, tireless, bright, frequently cranky surgeon who had left his practice in Manchester, England, to come here.

Why? It was commonly believed that we were all running away from something, whether we knew it or not.

Colin had ten years on me and was in his fourth month of doing what he called meatball surgery. Nuru was *my* patient, but I handed the scalpel to Colin. It was always exciting to learn from this man.

Colin held a penlight between his teeth and made his incision on the right side of Nuru's chest. He followed up the incision by using a hand retractor to spread open a space between the boy's ribs. Then he put in a tube to drain the blood that just kept coming.

I saw what Colin saw: plenty of blood and no clear source of the bleeding. And so Colin reached into Nuru's chest and twisted the child's lung, a brilliant move that I understood might temporarily stanch the flow.

I had clamps in hand and was ready to take Colin's direction when we were interrupted by the awful clamor of people charging into the O.R.

Our settlement was poorly guarded, and outlaw gangs constantly roamed outside the fences. Everyone on the medical staff had been given a death sentence by the outlaws. Our pictures were posted in the nearby villages. Colin wore a T-shirt under his gown with a target on the front and back.

He had a very black sense of humor, my mentor, Colin Whitehead.

Maybe that darkness in him was what brought him here, and maybe it was why he stayed. Colin didn't look up. He shouted over his shoulder at the intruders.

"If you're here to kill us, get it over with. Otherwise, get the hell out of my surgery!"

A man called out, "Help, Doctor. My daughter is dying."

Just then, Nuru's mother tugged on my arm. To her, I was still her son's doctor. I was the one in charge.

I said to her, "Mother, please. Nuru is getting the best care. He'll be okay."

I turned back to little Nuru as Colin threw his scalpel into a metal bowl and stripped off his gloves.

That quickly, Nuru had stopped breathing.

The little boy was gone.

CHAPTER 3

COLIN SAID, "Well, that's it, then," and headed off to the new patient on the second table.

Nuru's mother screamed, "Noooooooooo!"

Her days-old infant wailed. Her little boy was dead, and already flies were circling. Sabeena started to cover him with a scrap of a sheet, but I just couldn't stand to lose another child.

I said, "Nope, stop right there, Sabeena. I'm not done here. I'm opening his left side."

Sabeena looked at me like, *Yeah, right.*

I said, "Can't hurt, could help, get me?"

"Yes, I do, Doctor, dear. Better hurry."

"Berna, Rafi. Someone take care of Mommy and the baby. *Please.*"

The procedure Colin had performed is called a limited or anterior lateral thoracotomy, a cut into the chest cavity through the side of the rib cage. Colin had opened Nuru's right side. And now, although it was highly unlikely that I would find a torn artery in the side of the chest opposite the bullet hole, we hadn't found the leak. And there had to be one.

Meanwhile, Nuru wasn't breathing, and his heart had stopped. The technical term for this is "dead."

But in my mind, he wasn't *too* dead.

"Stay with me, Nuru. I know you can hear me."

I made my incision on his left side and used the hand retractor, and as Sabeena held a penlight for me, I peered inside. The heart wasn't beating, but blood was still filling the chest cavity from the force of gravity.

Where was the leak? Where?

Sabeena wasn't looking at me, and I knew why.

One of the things that you started to get after a week or two in this place was that you could not save everyone. Not even close. Fifty percent was a good score, and then half those patients died in recovery.

Still, Nuru was *my* patient.

My responsibility.

As the flies descended on her child's face, Nuru's mother howled and crowded back up to the table, crying out, "*No, no, you said, Doctor. You said.*"

Normally, it would be insane to have parents in the O.R., but here, it was necessary for the closest kin to see what we did, the decisions we made, even to help us make the decisions. So Nuru's mom had to be here, but I needed every one of the seconds that were racing by.

"Please give me room, Mother," I said. "I'm sorry, but you're in my light."

She did what I asked. She stepped back but stood at my right arm, crying and praying, the sound of her voice cutting into my ability to concentrate like a machete to my forehead. Other people were screaming, too. Colin yelled at his patient, who was shrieking in agony. He blasted the patient's father and cursed at our poor orderly, who had been working for a day and a half straight. I had to block it all out.

I focused my attention on the little boy and began sponging down his still-oozing left lung.

"Where is your leak, little man? Help me out."

And that was when I *felt* something with my fingertips. Something hard. I pinched and extracted a scrap of metal from the child's lung—and now it made sense. The bullet must have hit the fence and fractured before it ricocheted into Nuru. The core of the bullet had gone through and through, but a bit of the copper jacket had taken a hard left once inside Nuru's chest.

Sabeena said, "Well done, Brigid. Damned good catch."

If only. If only we had found it ten minutes before. Nuru's mother was pleading, "You *must* save him. You *must.*"

The heart wasn't beating, but I wasn't letting that stop me. I sutured the tear in the lung, opened the pericardium, and began direct cardiac massage. And then, I felt it—the flutter of Nuru's heart as it started to catch. *Oh, God, thank you.*

But what can a pump do when there's no fuel in the tank?

I had an idea, a desperate one.

The IV drip was still in Nuru's arm. I took the needle and inserted it directly into his ventricle. Blood was now filling his empty heart, priming the pump.

Sabeena was whispering in her native Hindi. I was talking to God in my mind. Nuru's mother had her hands on her son's forehead, and she was speaking to him, asking him to come back.

And then, the little boy *moved.* He tried to speak.

"Mother" *screamed.* And Colin was back at the table.

"Jesus Christ."

"Amen," I said, giving him a sidelong grin.

Nuru's mother grabbed for me, and then she simply swooned. Sabeena caught her and her baby before they hit the floor. When they were lying safely on a bed, Sabeena gave me the highest of fives.

"Oh, my *God,* Brigid. That was kind of a miracle, you know?"

"Meatball-surgery-variety miracle," Colin growled as he finished closing Nuru's wounds. "But, still. Very good job."

That was another high five, but even without the actual hand slap, it felt good. I respected the hell out of Colin and was a little bit crazy about him, too. Sometimes I thought he might be a little bit crazy about me.

I said, "Thanks, Doc."

I ripped off my mask and cap, handmade out of a T-shirt, and tuned back into the radio. All I could hear was a staticky roar many thousands of miles away.

Then, the voice of the announcer: "Well, he did it, Red Sox fans. David Ortiz just launched an Andrew Miller slider into the stunned Yankee bull pen. The Sox have just swept the series, and the Yankees are retreating to the Bronx."

Jemilla, my little gal pal, grabbed me around the waist, and we did a funny little dance, part native to Sudan, part cha-cha slide—which was sharply interrupted by the loud chatter of automatic gunfire at the gates.

Oh, God. It was starting again.

CHAPTER 4

ATTACKS OFTEN happened at this time, just before dawn, when people were sleeping, when the marauders still had the cover of night.

Now the call to battle stations came as a wordless siren over the P.A. system. The men and boys with weapons went to the walls, the fences, the front gates. At the same time, a handful of boys, none older than twelve, took up posts outside the hospital compound.

Jemilla pushed a handgun at me, and I took it reluctantly, stuck it into the waistband of my trousers.

This little darling was twelve. She'd been gang-raped, had had an ear sliced off by an attacker, and she'd seen her parents murdered when her village had fallen to the gang of thugs. She walked for a week to get here, by herself, and we "adopted" her at Kind Hands. She would live here for as long as we remained, but the thing was, this was not a permanent hospital. We survived here on charity, and we were vulnerable to terror attacks. We could get orders to pack up and leave at any time.

What would happen to Jemilla then? How would she survive?

"I'm not going to be able to kill anyone," I said to this brave and irrepressible young girl. She grabbed my hands and said quite seriously, "You can, Dr. Brigid. If you have to, you can. There's no such a thing as a warning shot."

Outside the O.R., men were shouting as they raced up the dirt track that ran between our compound and the *tukuls*, the round, thatched huts where the refugees lived.

Colin clicked off his walkie-talkie, saying to all of us, "We're needed at the gate."

Surgeons Pete Bailey, Jimmy "Flyboy" Wuster, and Jup Vander armed themselves and followed Colin out to his vehicle and into the lethal, crackling predawn.

With help from nurses Sabeena and Toni, I shoved the patients in their beds into the center of the floor, stubbing the wheels on the buckling planks, and I tucked little Nuru, now bandaged in clean cloth and duct tape, into a laundry basket. Nurse Berna administered knockout anesthesia to the patient who'd been moaning since she came in, and gave a gun to the patient's father. Nurse Toni chucked our instruments into boiling water, and I shut down the generator.

And then we sat in the dark with our backs against the beds. And some of us prayed.

I visualized our attackers. They were known as the Gray Army because when those men were cattle herders, they rubbed gray clay into their skin to ward off insects. Now, as a rampaging militia, they dressed in camouflage with bloodred head scarves. Their ghostly skin added another layer of terror to their attacks.

We were in the massacre zone of a long-standing dispute in Sudan and South Sudan that had roots along ethnic, geographic, and religious lines. After the autonomy of South Sudan was official, internal fighting began between the Gamba and the Gray Army rebels. The fighting defined the expression "take no prisoners."

The Grays, as they were also known, re-formed into a rogue militia avenging those deaths, the work of the Gamba. And within weeks, thousands more were dead, and the living had fled. Now, 1.8 million people were displaced, and, although the Gamba had been decimated, the Gray

Army, twenty-five to fifty-thousand strong, and drunk with bloodlust and power, kept crossing and recrossing the country, their only objective to destroy it in wave after murderous wave.

Colonel Dage Zuberi was the head of the Grays.

The atrocities this evil man had left behind him in Darfur have all been documented. The mass killing of the men and rape of the women, the torture and looting, the kidnapping of young girls, and the total obliteration of villages all form part of his legacy. And now he had turned to South Sudan.

Throughout this period, IDPs had only one option, the Kind Hands settlement located outside Nimule, though by now, our hands were full. Ironically, just when it seemed completely hopeless, as we were weighing scrapping our mission, a message was relayed by an ambulance driver. He said that twenty thousand volunteer soldiers—all military veterans— were on the way to protect us.

Was this true? And, if true, would they arrive in time?

As I sat against a bed pondering all of this, Aziza, another of our little orphan runners, burst breathlessly into the O.R.

"They're here, Dr. Brigid. Our army has arrived, and they're shooting at the Grays."

"You're sure, darling?"

"Oh, yes. It's true."

Oh, thank you, God.

But Aziza hadn't finished her report.

"The Grays have so many. Our new army is too...too *small*."

"How many?" I asked, although I knew full well that Aziza could not count.

"Like, three cups full of pebbles. The Grays are shooting them as they try to save us."

CHAPTER 5

SABEENA FLEW through the operating-room door, running directly to me as my patient was being removed from my table.

"We've got incoming. Some of our new fighters have been shot. Brigid. They're all black."

"Say that again?"

"Our new army. They're all black. Men and women. Europeans and Americans, too. Dr. Jimmy is bringing in a boy from New Jersey. He's conscious but bleeding profusely from a head wound."

The ambulance and other vehicles roared up to the O.R., and as our volunteers unloaded the patients, I did triage, sending those with bullets that could be dug out with a knife tip to Maternity.

We kept the rest.

Our instruments had been sterilized before the shooting began, but we had no place for the wounded except on empty grain sacks laid out on the floor.

We had to work faster and more efficiently than ever. The generator was back on, charging up our mini X-ray and ultrasound machines. Runners carried blood samples to our so-called lab for typing. Sabeena and I marked treatment notes on dressings and directly on the patients' bodies. And throughout it all, the gunfire continued.

Dr. Jimmy Wuster was working feverishly on the volunteer soldier from New Jersey. As Sabeena had said, the young man was bleeding profusely. He had gunshot wounds to his head and chest, and we didn't have enough blood to perfuse him. Of course, Dr. Jimmy still tried to keep the boy alive, until Jup pulled him away from the body.

Jimmy yelled, "*Fuck!* Get away from me."

Jup persisted until Jimmy stormed out of the O.R. I followed him and found the reed-thin thoracic surgeon leaning against a parched tree, his chest heaving.

He said to me, "That kid is from West Orange. I grew up there. I told him I would keep him alive."

"We all do that, Jimmy. What else can you do?"

"He's wearing a dog tag. His name is Henry Webb. His unit is called BLM."

"What does it mean?"

"Black Like Me. A solidarity movement, I suppose. *Damn* it."

"I'm sorry," I said.

"Do you have a cigarette?"

I shook my head no.

He said, "I stink like rat shit in a meatpacking plant, but I need a hug."

I needed one, too. I took him into my arms.

He was sobbing when Colin's Land Rover returned from the gates and our aides unloaded the freshly wounded. I squeezed Jimmy's hand, and then we went back to the O.R. I helped Colin do a bloody leg amputation with a Gigli saw, but after our patient endured the surgery, he died from cardiac arrest.

Colin walked to the sink and put his head under the trickle of cold water. I handed him a dry rag, and when he looked at me, he saw the blank shock on my face.

"Brigid. Surgery here is life-or-death. We're not going to have miracles every day. Get used to it."

"I won't. I'm not like you."

Colin reached into his pants pocket and pulled out a nut-and-grain bar laced with chocolate. He handed it to me.

"Take this before I change my mind. And don't give it to anyone. Stand right there so I can watch you."

My hands were shaking so hard, I couldn't tear the wrapper. Colin pulled the cellophane apart and watched me eat and cry at the same time.

Then he went to the next table and started a new life-or-death surgery on a patient he was seeing for the first time.

That this was a desperately bad place was indisputable, and the badness never stopped. I'd fought for a position and won it over hundreds of applicants. I was twenty-seven, idealistic, and also an optimist. Two years into this mission, I was asking myself how much more I could take. Another week? Another day?

I imagined dressing in street clothes, returning to Boston, where I could have had a bedroom with a real bed and a window, a bathroom with hot water, a kitchen with a refrigerator and, inside it, bottles of cold drinks.

But I *couldn't* imagine leaving these people. I loved them. And the idea of not working with Colin—I couldn't bear the thought.

Two teenage boys entered the O.R. and wrangled a writhing soldier onto the surgical table. It was a safe bet that she was from a clean, sane place and had come here with an aspiration and a plan. Now that she'd been shot to pieces, there were fresh odds on her surviving another hour. Fifty-fifty.

Colin yelled in my general direction, "Break's over!"

I wanted to scream, loudly and for a long time.

I went back to work.

CHAPTER 6

I FELL asleep in my sliver of a room as the midday sun beat down oppressively on the roofs and the parched, dusty camp and the people filling buckets from the slow, muddy tributary of the White Nile.

Time must have passed, because I awoke to dark skies and the lovely, lilting sound of children singing in the little L-shaped enclosure between the women's house and the maternity ward.

Nurse Berna had gathered a dozen girls and boys together. They sat in a line on a split log balanced on two rocks, and Berna stood in front of them, leading them in a song about the *gbodi*, or bushbuck, a kind of antelope that lives in sub-Saharan Africa.

Berna sang, *"Gbodi mangi were."*

And the kids answered, *"Gbodi mangi were, gbodi o!"*

I'd learned from Berna that this means, "See what the bushbuck does, the bushbuck, oh!"

It was Berna's turn again. This time she sang, *"Gbodi wo ti turn."* The children stuck up their forefingers along the sides of their heads and waggled them, singing, *"Gbodi wo ti turn, gbodi o!"*

Translated: "The bushbuck turns her ears. The bushbuck, oh!"

The children laughed and clapped their hands as they sang. Even the donkeys braying outside the enclosure seemed to join in.

I was struck by the resilience of the orphaned, displaced children, and of Berna, too. She had loved so many, tended to their wounds, buried the dead, and repeated it day after day for four years running. While God had not forsaken this place, He was clearly expecting us to hold up our end, as it appeared He was needed elsewhere.

I left the singing children to do rounds and went first to Nuru and his family, lying in a bed together in Recovery. I clasped Nuru's mother's hand and bent over the little boy, who was sleeping under a scrap of cloth.

"How's little brave-hearted Nuru today?" I asked. He opened his eyes, looked right into mine—and wailed.

I laughed, and so did his mom.

"Better, yes?" she asked.

"Way better. He's *mad*."

After checking Nuru's vitals and changing his dressings, I struck out for the O.R. and dove back into the bloody work. I set bones, cleaned infected wounds, stitched together the ragged edges of injuries, until late into the night. I was grateful that there was no shooting and that our brave contingent of volunteers was armed and at the perimeter.

By the time all surgical patients were in the recovery ward and the operating tables were empty, my back was stooped like that of a little old lady, and my joints ached, too. Jup yelled, "Bar the door!" and we were all too tired to laugh.

I was seeing double, and I was starting to talk to myself.

"That's it, Brigid. Put down the knife. Take off your mask. Day is over. You've done good."

I sang out to Jup and Colin—well, croaked out, to be accurate: "I'm leaving now. Don't anyone try to stop me. I can't do anything else. I'm used up, worn out, past dead on my feet."

"Good night, Brigid," Jup called.

"Go," said Colin. "You don't need to explain."

I went. I walked along the dusty track to the ladies' dorm. I waved to the people who called my name, and minutes later, I was in my little room. I wolfed down the crackers and tinned, porklike meat and slurped up the delicious bowl of canned peaches that Toni had left on the table by my bed.

After stripping off my scrubs and kicking off my shoes, I showered in cold water, and it was good. I wrapped myself in a wet sheet and got into the creaking, sagging cot, which was the best and most welcome spot in all of South Sudan.

I had a few words with God, asking Him to please try a little harder to protect the people whose lives were entwined with mine, and dropped into a dead sleep.

I awoke to someone calling me. It was Colin.

"No, no, no," I said, rolling over, facing the wall. "Leave me alone. I have to sleep. I have to . . ."

But he didn't go. He pulled a chair over to my bedside and told me that it had been a good day. "We saved more than we lost. New tally. Fifty-one percent to the good."

Why was Colin in my room, talking to me in the dark? I rolled over and asked him, "What's going on, Colin? You okay?"

He reached out and put his hand behind my neck and gently brought my face to his. And he kissed me.

He *kissed* me. I opened my eyes, and in that moment, he was gone—but I was wide-awake.

What had come over Colin? What a strange, strange man he was, but I had to admit to the only person I could talk to about this—me—that I liked the kiss.

I liked Colin, too. Seriously liked him. It was stupid to have a crush on this abrasive and combative and often thoughtless man. But there I was—instead of sleeping, I was staring up at the ridges in the corrugated tin roof, dreamily replaying a brief, whiskery kiss from Dr. Colin Whitehead.

CHAPTER 7

AZIZA AND Jemilla were waiting for me in the staff dining hall when I got there for my morning cup of tea.

It was a real stretch to call this room a hall, but it was a pleasant space, with a hand-hewn slab table and two benches, three windows, and a ceiling fan. An old Philips radio rested on top of the fridge, and when there was no one eating here, the medical staff had been known to dance.

But there would be no dancing this morning. The girls had come for their math class, along with a whole-grainy cereal with goat's milk and bananas, their paycheck for running errands around the hospital compound.

I hugged them both at once, and the giggling cracked me up. I braided Aziza's hair while Jemilla braided mine, and after breakfast and tidying up, class began.

Math is far from my strongest subject, but I manage basic arithmetic with dried beans. This morning, math devolved from bean counting to bean *jumping* on a *kalah* board, a game something like checkers, which Aziza took seriously but which made Jemilla literally fall off the bench laughing.

Breakfast and beans over, the girls and I hurried to the O.R. I was gowning up in the scrub room when young Rafi flew through the door and grabbed me around the waist, screaming, "They killed them! It's Zuberi's work, Doctor. It's a massacre!"

I'd seen pictures of Zuberi's work. It was beyond hellish. In another realm altogether. I felt faint, but I fought it off, dug in my feet, and grabbed Rafi's shoulders. I yelled down into his terrified, upturned face.

"What happened, Rafi?"

"They killed so many."

I disengaged from the little boy and shouted to my colleagues in the O.R., who were up to their wrists in blood.

"There's been—I don't know. Something bad. I'll go."

Sabeena came with me. We climbed into the donkey cart we use as an ambulance, Sabeena taking the reins. We caught up with Rafi as he ran down the road, and slowed to let him into the cart. I put my arm around him and held him tightly as the donkey pulled us to the front gate.

I didn't say this out loud, but in my mind, I was asking God, *What now? What bloody horror now?*

The gate is made of hinged chain-link fencing anchored to concrete posts and walls that are topped with barbed wire. There were more than a hundred people bunched up at the gate, and I couldn't see around them. Someone helped me down from the cart, I don't know who. The crowd parted to let me through, and I remember the terrible wailing.

I stepped outside the settlement walls alone and saw something so gruesome, so inhuman, that at first, I couldn't make myself believe what I saw. The hacked and shot-up bodies, stacked like firewood and covered with a moving blanket of flies, were real.

CHAPTER 8

THAT NIGHT, Jemilla and Aziza came to my open door and crowded into my room. They'd slept with me before, but I didn't want this to become a habit. The room was hardly bigger than the narrow bed, and tonight, I was so done, I had nothing left, even for the two girls.

"Not tonight, kids, okay? I need the whole bed. I have to sleep. I'm on call, you know?"

Jemilla was persistent, and Aziza looked terrified, and I relented, of course. When Aziza was lying on my left side, tight up against the wall, and Jemilla, with her gun clutched in both hands, had pinned me in on my right side, Rafi came in and shut the door.

A great cloud of suffocating heat had collected under the tin roof and went all the way down to the dirt floor. We needed any small movement of air in this windowless room. Needed it. Rafi leaned hard against the door with his shoulder to make sure that the latch was closed, then he said, "I'll be right here."

I couldn't see him in the dark, but I heard him settle down on the floor between the bed and the door. I had thought that the children wanted me to keep them company. Now I understood. They were there protecting *me*.

We sweated together in the dark, and I tried to think. After the bodies of the twelve soldiers had been buried, and while I was doing an appendectomy, there had been meetings. Senior staff, meaning not me, had gotten together in the dining hall. Then the staff had called the home office in Cleveland.

As Colin explained it to me, the two-thousand-person contingent of Black Like Me soldiers hadn't planned to stay at Kind Hands. That had been a wishful interpretation of what was meant to be a stop on their way to help in a larger battle against the Grays in the ongoing, unofficial civil war.

Colin had told me, "They're leaving within a few days. All we can do is wish them luck."

Lying in this oven with the children, I began to shake. The attacks were increasing. We had limited means to hold off the militia, and now we were losing our last hope.

I had come here without a clue. Now I had one hell of a clue. We could all die. I could die.

Aziza squeezed my hand.

I knew a lot about Jemilla, but Aziza had kept the horrors she'd lived through to herself. She looked to be about thirteen, but even *she* didn't know her age. I loved these orphans. I was pretty much an orphan myself.

Aziza asked now, "Do you believe in God, Dr. Brigid?"

"Yes. I do."

"What is His idea for us? Why must we suffer so?"

"I don't know, sweetheart. But I know He has a reason."

She sighed deeply, truly breaking my heart, and got a tighter grip on me. She held on, fiercely.

I didn't want to cry, but the tears were coming anyway, and I couldn't get my hands free to wipe them away. I wished I could answer Aziza's question to my own satisfaction, but sometimes, while failing to save yet another wounded or starving or disease-ridden child, I had the same doubts.

Jemilla whispered, "Try to sleep, Dr. Brigid."

"You too."

"I love you, Doctor."

"Shhhh. Shhhhh. I love you, too."

What would happen to the people in this place if we were sent home? What would God do?

CHAPTER 9

THAT MORNING, patients lined the benches outside the operating room. Our beds, our operating tables, and the spaces between them were fully occupied.

The medical staff were working like machines—maximum efficiency, no time for rethinking or consulting—and *none* of us had been trained for *this*.

I was assisting Colin, whose patient, a twenty-three-year-old BLM soldier named Neil Farley, had refused anesthesia for the infected bullet wound in his thigh. He was gripping the table, thrashing his head from side to side, and groaning, trying not to move his leg but not really managing it.

Farley's C.O., Captain Bernard Odom, stood at the table, his arms crossed behind his back, feet shoulders' length apart, at ease as he watched Colin dig for the bullet that had made a roadway for the infection that had traveled far and deep.

"What are you trying to prove, Neil?" Colin asked his writhing patient.

"Just keeping you on your toes, sir," said the young vet through clenched teeth. Clearly, this show of bravery was to impress his C.O. and was completely counterproductive.

"Neil, you're wheezing," I said. "I'm going to give you a shot of Benadryl. It won't affect your reflexes or anything."

"You're sure?"

"Uh-huh. If I learned one thing in my six years in med school, this was it."

The soldier laughed through his pain. I shot him up with Benadryl, which is not just an antihistamine but also a mild anesthetic. Colin poked around in the wound and finally extracted the bullet. I mopped up.

"When will Farley be good to walk with his backpack?" the captain asked.

"In a few days," said Colin.

I injected Farley with antibiotics, then gripped his forearm and helped him up into a sitting position.

The captain asked Colin again, "He can walk tomorrow, right?"

"What's the rush?" Colin asked, peering over his mask at the young officer.

"The rush is that we're leaving tomorrow at oh six hundred. If he can't carry his gear, he stays behind."

"What do you mean, 'leaving'?" Colin asked.

"Leaving, like, we're pulling out."

For the past week, the Black Like Me volunteers had camped inside the settlement walls and patrolled the perimeter in shifts. Now, four days after the massacre of twelve of their troops, their plans to withdraw had firmed up.

Odom had Colin's full, highly disturbed attention.

"You *can't* leave us here," Colin said stiffly. "Do you know what that would *mean*? You're leaving us to *die*."

Odom replied, just as stiffly, "I have my orders, Doctor."

Farley eased his legs off the table and said to Odom, "I'll be ready, Captain, just need a good sleep tonight—"

Colin ripped off his mask and said, "Captain. You didn't hear me. You can't leave us right now. Zuberi's goons will come in and kill *everyone*. We're relying on *you*."

"You didn't hear *me*, Doctor. It's not my call—"

Colin went around the table and grabbed Odom, pulled him up to his toes, then violently shoved him backward. Odom fell against Berna, who stepped away, and a very surprised-looking Odom went down. Colin leapt at the opportunity to straddle Odom and press a length of PVC pipe across his throat. He then shouted into his face, "*Get your orders changed. Buy us some* time."

By then, Jimmy Wuster was yelling at Colin, "Hey, hey, Colin, disengage, buddy!" and he tried to pull him off Odom's body. Farley had also joined the fray, and I screamed, "*Stop, everyone, just stop!*"

Colin got up with a disgusted look on his face and threw the pipe down hard. Farley helped his captain to his feet, limped over to Colin, and extended a hand. As Colin was about to extend his arm, Odom punched Colin in the face.

Colin staggered back, sputtering "Bloody hell," and clapped a hand over his eye. He was gathering himself to get in a good return punch when Rafi and Ahmed got between Odom and Colin with a stretcher, then swung a new patient onto the table. The patient was old, barely clinging to consciousness.

I bent over him and ripped open his bloody shirt, and Berna tried to take his blood pressure.

I said, "Mister, I'm Dr. Fitzgerald. What's your name? Tell me what happened."

The patient couldn't speak. While I assessed his injuries, Colin paced and vented behind me. He cursed about our situation: the fighting a quarter mile from this room, the lack of even basic supplies, the inability to fix what could be fixed easily anywhere but here.

He was in a crazed state, but he wasn't crazy.

We were treading water in the center of a full-blown tsunami. I admired Colin for taking a stand, for speaking up, and because he was right.

If BLM left, we were all doomed.

CHAPTER 10

HELL ON earth continued to dominate the O.R. all day, as the sick and injured flew from vicious attacks on their villages and found their way to Kind Hands.

I was verging on heat exhaustion and physical collapse when Dr. Victoria Khalil took the scalpel out of my shaking hand, put her hand on my back, and just kept it there until I looked into her eyes.

"I've got it," she said. "Get out of here."

I went outside with a bottle of water and a chocolate bar and sat down with my back against a tree.

I was blinking into the setting sun when Colin came outside and sat down with me.

"I would buy you a steak if I could."

"With fries?"

"Fries and bourbon."

"Sounds good." I looked at him. "I should buy you a steak for your eye."

"That guy," he said, not laughing. "He sucker punched me."

"You got your licks in, in your way," I said.

Colin patted the puffiness around his eye, then said, "Let's take a walk."

"Where to?" I asked him.

"Big city. Dancing. Pretty people in nice clothes. All kinds of excitement."

I laughed, gave him my hand, and he helped me up.

Surprise.

We strolled past our prepubescent guards, holding long guns, and stepped through the gates and outside, into the flat, monochromatic landscape.

To the right of the gates was a thin copse of dead trees that had been stripped of bark, which had been used as firewood. Beyond the trees was the sluggish tributary with steep banks during the drought, a trap for the women and girls who went for water and were cornered there, raped, and sometimes killed, more often than we could track or remember.

Colin and I turned left and walked parallel to the bullet-pocked concrete wall. There was a road out there, which flooded during the rainy season. Now it was a dusty, rutted track that connected the next-closest village, a hundred miles away, with the gates to our settlement.

Colin put his hand lightly to the small of my back. He said, "I must apologize, Brigid."

I turned to look at him. He looked beat-up and out of gas. Still, I loved looking at his handsome face. I loved the way he was looking at me.

"Apologize for what?"

"For being such a rude bastard. For losing my temper today. For being inconsiderate to you."

"Colin, you're not that bad."

"Nice of you to say, but I'm trying to apologize, for Christ's sake. I need to."

"Well, all right, then. I accept. You bastard."

He laughed. I did, too. I forgot how achy and hungry and fatigued I was. Laughing with Colin was a new experience, and I liked it. A lot. I stepped in a little closer, and Colin put his arm around me, rested his hand at my waist. My arm went around him too.

And Colin kept talking.

"I want you to know something about me, Brigid. About ten years ago, when my daughter, Rebecca, was nine, something went wrong. We took her to our family doctor and then to the best neurologist around. And then to another neurologist in London. That was where we got an explanation for her headaches and seizures.

"Rebecca had a brain tumor in a very bad place. We were told it was inoperable, but I didn't accept that. Well, why would I? I loved her, dearly. And I had this genius brain and my very talented hands."

I nodded, and we kept walking north, our own path between the wall and the road. The streaked sky was like sundown over an ocean, or so I imagined it. The waning sun mirrored the sadness in Colin's voice.

"I looked at her films," he said. "I consulted with the cowards who refused to do the operation, then I signed the disclaimers and did the operation myself."

He said, "Rebecca died on the table. It was horrible. I couldn't bring her back, and, trust me, I did everything imaginable. After that, my wife divorced me. And from that point on, I divorced myself—from feeling anything."

And then he stepped away from me, shook his head, wiped his eyes with the backs of his hands.

"No excuse for bad manners, Brigid. But there's the backstory," he said.

I was looking for the right words to thank him for trusting me, to tell him that I was sorry for what he'd been through. I was forming some questions, too, but I never got the chance to ask them.

CHAPTER 11

ONE MINUTE, Colin and I were walking along the wall, toward the village. A moment later, trouble sped out of the dark. Tires squealed, and high beams bounced and flashed over the ground. The sound of whooping male voices and bursts of gunfire got louder as the all-terrain vehicle headed directly toward the gate to our settlement.

Which meant that it would drive right past us.

My feet wouldn't move. I was utterly frozen in the headlights, but Colin, thank God, had wits enough for us both. He pushed me down and fell on top of me so that we were against the wall, faces to the ground. The deadly chattering of gunfire, the war whoops, and the roar of the motor were too close, and too real.

I didn't think to pray. I was remembering the stacked bodies outside our gates, and then, while bullets pinged into the wall right above my head, my mind was flooded with vivid images of people I would never see again.

The gunfire amped up and seemed to come from all directions. Shouts turned into screams, and then the racing motor struggled, as though the vehicle was trying to get traction in the dirt. Wheels spun furiously, and then, finally, the wheels grabbed the ground, and the vehicle sped back the way it had come.

There was total silence. My eyes were still covered. I was still pinned by Colin's body, and now I was aware of his breath on my cheek, his elbows in my back, the whole weight of him.

And then he rolled off me.

"*Brigid*. Say something. Are you okay?"

"I think so."

He helped me up, and boys from our camp flowed around us, all of them bright eyed and exhilarated.

The one grabbing at my arms was Andrew.

"Did you see? We stopped them. I shot one of them. I shot out the tires, too."

"Thank you, young men," Colin said. "You saved us. You saved our arses."

I was still panting from adrenaline overload, and blood was hammering against my eardrums. Colin was talking to me, but I couldn't quite make out what he was saying.

I looked into his eyes, and he said it again.

"I'm sorry, Brigid. I'm a damned fool for taking you out here. You should get the hell away from me."

And then he put his arms around me and held me against him from hip to toe and back up to where my cheek rested against his collarbone.

He said, "I've wanted to do this from the moment I first saw you."

I didn't say it, but I'd had the same thought since the moment I first saw *him*.

CHAPTER 12

THE YOUNG men and boys circled back, jumped up and down around us, laughing, one of them, Nadir, shouting out, "*Ba-bam. Ba-bam-bam.* I got you. I killed you, dead."

Nadir was about fourteen, spunky and irrepressible, even in a place as hopeless as this. He had befriended the doctors and often went on supply runs to the village with Colin and Jimmy. Now he volunteered to escort us back to the gates.

"Doctors. Stay close to me. Please pick up your feet and keep up."

"Right behind you, Nadir," Colin said. "Lead the way."

Nadir said, "Dr. Whitehead. Next time we go for a run, I sit in the front seat. Shotgun, right?"

"Okay."

"You fixed my arm. You remember?"

"I've fixed a lot of broken arms," said Colin.

"Look at it again."

Nadir pulled up his sleeve to show off a shiny scar. Then he made the scar jump when he flexed his muscle.

"Nice," said Colin. "I did a pretty good job."

By the time we had walked through the gates, my heart rate had slowed. Nadir waved good-bye and drifted into a pack of other young men. Colin took my hand, which caused my heart to pick up speed again.

We walked the dirt track toward our compound, acknowledging the waves and hellos from people crouched outside the *tukul*s at the edge of the track. But I couldn't think of anything to say to Colin that wouldn't sound forced or lame.

When we got to the women's dorm, Colin took both my hands and looked at me as though he was looking *into* me. I thought maybe he would kiss me again. Maybe he'd come up with an awkward excuse to come inside my toaster oven of a room.

But, no.

He released my hands and said, "See you in the morning, Brigid. Sleep well."

"You too, Colin."

I watched the target on his back recede, and when Colin had rounded the corner of the building, I went inside. I washed and prepared for sleep, and I pushed thoughts of Colin Whitehead out of my mind. I prayed.

Thank you, Lord, for giving me another day, for saving Colin and me and all of those brave little boys. Please bless this camp and give us the strength to care for these good people. And please speak a little more plainly. I'm not sure what I'm meant to do.

I had just said amen when there was an urgent knock on my door.

Was it Colin?

I cracked the door. It was a little girl in a thin dress, her hair in braids, a very worried look on her face. Jemilla.

"Honey, I've told you. I need to sleep, and I really can't rest when you are in bed with me."

"It's not that," she said. "The BLM soldiers have pulled up their tents and left, Dr. Brigid. I found this stuck between the links in the fence. I don't know who to give it to."

On a sheet of plain paper was written the letter Z. This was the signature of Colonel Dage Zuberi, the leader of the Grays, the man who had directed massacres across sub-Saharan Africa and the one who was be-hind the recent slaughter of our BLM soldiers.

The note was stark and unambiguous. We were marked for death. I opened the door wider, grabbed Jemilla by the arm, pulled her into my room, and shut the door.

CHAPTER 13

IN THE morning, Jemilla was standing by the door frame, and Sabeena was shaking me awake. There was an expression on her face that I'd never seen before.

It was horror.

"What's wrong?" I asked her.

"They killed him," she said. "They shot Nadir and hung him over the barbed wire."

"No," I said.

Sabeena handed me a bit of paper, telling me that it was in the chain-link fence under Nadir's body. On the paper was the zigzag mark of the devil himself, Colonel Zuberi.

What was it that we were supposed to do?

How could eighty thousand people move out of what Zuberi considered his territory? There was no place to run or hide. Would he really shoot us all?

I told Jemilla, "Stay here."

"I've seen this before," she told me. "I've seen worse."

Sabeena, Jemilla, and I walked to the gates, and there, horribly, the boy who had been so happy last night had been thrown across the top of the wall. His eyes were open, but he was gone.

"Please," I said to a few of the taller boys. "Get him down. Right now."

Nadir had no family, and so Sabeena, Berna, and I washed and wrapped his body for burial in the spot we used as a rough cemetery, not far from the hospital.

I was raging at the brutal death of this sweet, funny boy. I silently raged at God as I handled Nadir's body with my shaking hands. I think a kind God, a loving God, would forgive me for being furious. Why had this boy been killed? Had Nadir been too brave? Taken too much of a risk? Or was his death as senseless as it would have been if he had died of starvation or disease?

Later, as we were dressing in our surgical gowns, I spoke to Berna, a clever and kind and tremendously competent nurse who was twenty years older than me.

"*My God*, Berna. How can you endure this day after day?"

"What choice do I have, Brigid? You will leave, and I will stay. These are my people. This is my home."

Inside the dining hall, outside of my hearing, calls went back and forth to Cleveland, and discussions were held. I did my job, but I was jumpy. I pulled a chest line out of a young man without inverting his bed. Sabeena heard the air sucking and, thank God, sealed the wound with Vaseline before harm was done.

Colin was back in the O.R. by then. He saw what I had done. I expected him to shout at me, to call me an imbecile.

He said, "Get some water, Brigid. Take a little break and come back."

I walked toward the dining hall, passing so many starving people, now under threat of being murdered for no reason by a primitive despot with nothing but time, money, and raging young men to do his dirty work.

It was a sin. It was all sinful.

And there was no end to it.

CHAPTER 14

THROUGHOUT THE day of Nadir's death, thousands of displaced people arrived at the gates to the settlement. I could see them coming to us by way of the long road, with bundles on their heads, children in their arms. When they reached the gate, they spread out along the base of the wall where a strip of shade provided some relief from the hundred-and-fifteen-degree heat.

These people had walked for weeks, even months, to get to us, and, tragically, we had no room. The *tukuls* were crammed. Tarps had been strung between them as tents, and the refugees who lived there camped and slept outdoors.

We had no room, we didn't have enough food, and we had to turn people away.

At day's end, Colin, Jimmy, Jup, Victoria, Sabeena, and I walked the line outside the gates. We looked at the kids in particular, trying to pick out the ones who had any chance of survival at all.

Mothers quickly saw what we were doing and pushed their children toward us. Dear God, could anything be sadder than this?

I said to one of them, "Mother, please, I can take the little boy. Keep your baby with you."

I put a dot of clay on the back of the little boy's hand and led him through the gates and lifted him into the donkey cart. Half his face was swollen and inflamed. If he had an abscessed tooth, I could pull it. And that was all I could offer, some relief from some pain.

But there was no relief from the hunger and thirst and hopelessness.

When the cart was full, we drove our patients to the compound. But we couldn't keep them longer than overnight.

I remember this day in particular because when it couldn't have been bleaker, a caravan of military personnel arrived in open trucks. We could see their shiny, blue helmets from far away. Cheers went up and flowed through the camp like a wave.

For as long as the UN soldiers stayed, Kind Hands and the settlement would have protection.

"Thanks," I whispered to God. "Thanks very much. And now, if you don't mind, could you make it rain?"

CHAPTER 15

WHEN SABEENA and I went out of the gates the next morning, I was surprised to see a portly white man among the hundreds of starving African people massed around the foot of the wall.

He was wearing black pants, a short-sleeved black shirt with a white collar, and a panama hat.

"You're one of the doctors?" he asked me.

"Yes. I'm Brigid Fitzgerald. You're joining us?"

"I hope to. I'm Father Delahanty. William. Nice to meet you, Brigid."

I asked Father Delahanty to wait for me as Sabeena and I selected a handful of people we might be able to help. Once the donkey cart was fully loaded and Father Delahanty was on board, we trotted back to the hospital.

"I heard what you folks are doing, and I hitched a ride with the UN," Delahanty said. "Do you have a chapel here?"

"Actually, that's just one of a thousand things we don't have. You could do outdoor services, maybe."

"That would do quite well, Brigid."

"I speak to God whenever I get a chance," I said. "But it's been a long time since my last confession."

"We can address that."

We had just pulled up to the hospital when Colin walked over to the cart with Rafi and Ahmed and began to help people down.

Colin said to Father Delahanty, "You must be the priest from Chicago. Here to save some souls, perhaps?"

"I may try."

"Father, we need less talking to God and more helping the sick and dying. Do you have the stomach for that?"

Colin lifted out the boy with the bad tooth and headed with him toward the operating room.

I said to the priest, "Sorry, Father. Dr. Whitehead is very angry about how little we have to work with and how many people we lose. But he is a good doctor. A good man."

"I'm sure he is. I can understand why he might lash out. I'm not afraid to get my hands dirty."

"Come with me to the operating room."

Father Delahanty was willing to do everything, and that included changing beds, sweeping floors, and boiling sheets. He worked alongside our volunteer aides, doing laundry, rolling bandages, scouring the sink, and doing it all over again.

At the end of the day, I found Father Delahanty sitting on the floor in a corner of the maternity ward, consoling a woman whose baby had just died. He was telling her, "We don't know why God does what He does. But we have faith that He loves us. Right now, your child is with Him."

I slipped out before he saw me, and a few minutes later, Colin and I were taking turns washing up at the scrub sink.

"I'm inviting him to join us at dinner, Colin. Please find him a bunk in the men's quarters."

"He should go back to Chicago before he gets hurt."

I scowled. "Stop it. Be nice. You might like it."

Colin handed me a towel. And he smiled.

It was out of my mouth before I knew what I was saying.

"I can't imagine what will happen to us after we leave Africa."

"I can," Colin said. "You'll have an extraordinary, exemplary life, and I'll drink myself to death."

"You're not going to do that."

He gave me a dazzling smile.

No doubt about it. As bad as Colin Whitehead was or tried to be, I was falling for him.

CHAPTER 16

A DRIVER from the village stopped in the dining hall to drop off mail and medical supplies. I was worried about the BLM forces and asked Mosi if he'd heard any news of them since they left Kind Hands.

Mosi shrugged and said, "I haven't heard anything. I think you should say to yourself that they went back to America."

After a guilty breakfast of cereal and fruit, Jemilla, Aziza, Sabeena, and I took the donkey cart to the gates. Another large group of refugees had arrived at the settlement, and soon, Sabeena and I would pick through them, looking for people we could save for a day before turning them out to be slaughtered.

Father Delahanty had gotten a head start on us this morning, and I saw him at the gates, praying quietly, looking about as sad as anyone could be.

When he opened his eyes, I said, "How can God allow this?"

He said, "We do what we can and leave the big picture to Him."

That afternoon, I had a young girl on the table. She had a bacterial infection that had run through her body like wildfire and had begun to shut her organs down. In order to save her, limbs would have to be amputated. Several limbs. And then what would happen to her?

Colin said, "Brigid, you're wanted in Recovery."

"What do you mean?"

"Your patient with the head wound. If I were you, I'd go take a look."

I went. The boy with the wound was alive. I knew that when I went back to the O.R., the girl who was dying on the table would be lying in a bed, intact and dead.

I dropped to my knees outside the hospital, and once again, I prayed. "Please, help me understand. Am I helping? Is this good for anyone? Are you testing me? And if so, why, dear God, why?"

I finished by asking Him to bless everyone, and then I went back to work. I spoke to all my patients. I held their hands, told them that they would be okay, and I closed the eyes of the ones that died.

That afternoon, I walked over to the radio and shut off the Red Sox game. I had no idea if my team was winning or losing, and for the first time in my memory, I didn't care.

CHAPTER 17

THE LOUDSPEAKER crackled and squealed, and then Jup's amplified voice boomed, "Wounded at the gates. We've got incoming wounded."

Sabeena and I had been making beds, but we dropped everything and ran for the donkey cart where Jemilla and Aziza had already grabbed places in the back.

I knew this donkey. Colin had named him Bollocks, and he was wicked stubborn. Sabeena took the reins, clucked her tongue, slapped the reins against his back, saying, "Come on, Bollocks, you old goat. Let's go."

But, while he brayed, twitched his tail, and stomped his feet, he wouldn't move forward, not an inch. And we didn't have time to waste.

I got out of the cart and went around to his head, where I scratched his forehead, wiped some dirt out of his eyes, palmed his muzzle. And I said, "Bollocks, please, no funny business. Be good. I'll make it up to you. Do we have a deal?"

When I got back to the cart, I saw that Father Delahanty was sitting in back with the girls. Colin started up his Land Rover, and Victoria and two boys got in.

We followed Colin, choking on his dust, and when we reached the gates, they were wide open.

Gunshot victims had been dropped right there, where they waited for help outside our gates. Some were alive; all of them were a warning. The moans and cries of the wounded were horrific and almost unbelievable. It was as if a Breughel painting, *The Triumph of Death*, had come to life between the gateposts of our settlement.

I scrambled out of the cart and ran with my bag, passing wounded UN workers as well as our own downed people. Father Delahanty was right behind me, and Sabeena was bringing up the rear. My eyes were on the wounded, lying in the dust, many of them writhing in agony. I never noticed the Grays, boiling up over the riverbank on foot, until they were spraying bullets at us with their AKs.

Nothing about my life in Boston could have prepared me for an attack like this. Father Delahanty grabbed me by the arm, and we ran back through our useless chain-link gates. Everyone who could flee was doing so, and I saw the young men, our self-appointed volunteer militia, along with UN workers, staging a defense.

Sabeena had been racing ahead of me and was now standing at the cart. I ran toward her. And then I felt a sudden weight on my arm, Father Delahanty pulling me down. I knew he had stumbled, and I whipped around to help him to his feet. But he hadn't simply fallen. He'd been hit. I dropped to the ground beside him.

"William. *Father.* Hang on. Help is coming. We've got you."

He rolled to his side and coughed up blood. I looked around for help. Colin was leaning across the hood of his Land Rover, firing on the Grays, who were now coming through the gates.

I yelled, *"Sabeena! Help me!"*

She had her hands full. The girls were with her. Bullets were flying. I wasn't sure that she had even heard me.

I said to Father Delahanty, "I'm going to help you up. You have to help *me* get you to your feet. Grip my forearm."

But he didn't do it.

He was losing so much blood. He was going into shock.

And then he said in a whisper, "It's been two weeks since my last confession."

"You have to get up," I said. I was *frantic*.

"I must confess."

I sat back down beside him and held his hand. I wanted to fall on his chest and cry, but I contained my sobs and tried to keep my voice even.

"Tell me," I said.

CHAPTER 18

COLIN SWORE all the way back to the hospital. Victoria sat in the back-seat with me, held me while I sobbed. Behind us, in the rear section, was the dead body of my new, late friend, Father William Delahanty.

I knew so little about him, but enough to know how good he was, enough to be able to speak over his grave, enough to be able to tell his parishioners and friends in Chicago how kind he was and how bravely he had died.

If only I could.

I stared out the window at the dust flying up from our tires, turning everything outside the car an opaque ocher-brown.

I was picturing the devastation we had just left at the gates. I didn't know how many people had just died, but I thought all of our attackers had been shot or had run away. Still, I was sure that this skirmish was not the full force of Zuberi's army.

The young Gray murderers were scouts or recent recruits, wearing the rebel group's colors and leaving bodies and the letter Z before the real on-slaught began.

We parked outside the hospital. Eyes followed me from the waiting benches to the O.R., but I was single-mindedly looking for Ahmed and Rafi. I found them stoking the fire for boiling water and asked them to take Father Delahanty's body out of Colin's car and put him in the O.R. until I could tend to him.

I went back through the O.R., and I got a bottle of water from the shelf over the sink. Half the water was for me. I went out to the cart and poured the other half into Bollocks's mouth. I patted his shoulder. I talked to him about what a horrible day this had been.

"It's not over yet, Mr. B."

Sabeena came outside and stood next to me.

"I can't find Jemilla."

"But . . . she was with you. I saw her in the cart."

"I turned my back to help a woman into the cart, and she disappeared. I shouted, I looked, but we had to go. And now I can't find her anywhere."

"And Aziza?"

"She doesn't know where Jemilla is."

Jemilla didn't come back to the hospital, and I was pulled into so many pieces, I couldn't look for her. No one could. I worked with Victoria. I assisted Jup. Jimmy assisted me. By the time Colin came back on duty, we had a collection of extracted shells in a quart-sized pickle jar, and patients sleeping against the outer walls of the building, all the way around.

I went to bed knowing that I had to find a beloved child and bury a friend in the morning.

CHAPTER 19

WHEN I woke up in the heat of my room, I was immediately flooded with dread. Where was Jemilla?

I dressed quickly and jogged to the O.R. Father Delahanty's body had been wrapped in a sheet marked with a cross and was lying in the back of the donkey cart. More bodies were being carried into the cart, all to be buried in a single, large grave, as there was no other way to do it.

But I would be there for Father Delahanty.

Or so I planned.

Colin came over to the wagon and said, "Brigid. We found Jemilla. She was shot—no. No. She's alive. But she's asking for you. She won't let anyone else examine her."

"I'm coming. I'll be there in a minute."

Colin turned his back to me, but he didn't leave.

I sat beside the priest who had spoken his last words to me. I prayed, "Dear Lord, please look after this good man, Your servant, whom I came to love so quickly. I promised him I would tell his friends what happened to him. And that he was in Your care when he died. Thank You, God. Amen."

I wiped my cheeks, and when Colin turned back to me, he helped me down from the cart.

Jemilla was lying on top of the bedding in one of the iron-frame beds in the O.R. She pulled her shirt away and showed me the bullet wound in her right arm, just above the elbow.

"Oh, darling," I said. "This really hurts, doesn't it?"

"I wrapped a piece of cloth around it tightly until the wound stopped bleeding," she said.

I grinned at her. "That was exactly the right thing to do."

I examined the wound. The bullet had gone through the back of her skinny biceps and had exited in the front. I asked her, "Where were you? Why didn't you come to me or anyone here?"

"I passed out," she said, shrugging. "How bad is it?"

"I'm going to look at this with an X-ray. But I think that shot missed the bone. That's pretty amazing."

"I can still shoot with my right hand?"

"Hold out your arm. Make a fist."

She did it.

"You're good," I said.

"Okay," Jemilla said. "I'd like to go to sleep now."

I cleaned and closed the wound, and when I was finished, I asked Colin to carry Jemilla to my room.

After we'd tucked Jemilla into my bed, Colin said, "I need to talk to you, Brigid. And I don't want you to fight me. Please. Just do what I say."

"What, Colin? What are you talking about?"

"You must go home. There's nowhere to hide. This hospital, this camp, is going to be overrun by Zuberi, and you know it."

I switched my eyes to the girl in my bed, but Colin kept speaking. "It's inevitable, Brigid. This place, what we're doing here. It's turned into a bloody suicide mission. You have to get out. And better a few days early than one minute too late."

I took in a ragged breath and tried to absorb what he was telling me.

I asked him, "And you?"

"I'm going back to England as soon as I can arrange it. I've made calls. I'll make calls for you."

The breath went out of me. I looked down at the dirt floor of my room, feeling bereft. My heart was broken in more ways than I knew a heart could break.

Colin reached out and gripped my shoulders. I looked up, of course, and he pulled me close. And he kissed me. I kissed him, too. I never wanted the kiss to end, but for those few moments, I felt that nothing else was real.

And then the kiss did end. Colin dropped his arms and said to me, "I've tried so desperately hard to just be your friend, Brigid. I just couldn't bear to care about you and to lose you.

"Please do what I say, dear. Please go home."

CHAPTER 20

I WAS having a very vivid dream.

In it, Father Delahanty was alive. He was seated inside the confessional, and I was on the other side of the screen. I couldn't see his face, but it was definitely him, and he was earnestly explaining something, possibly arguing with me, but whatever he was saying, it was important.

And then his words were flushed out of my head by someone shaking my shoulder.

"*Brigid,*" said Sabeena. "They found the BLM soldiers." I had been sleeping in the buff. I grabbed the sheet up around me and said, "What? Where?"

"There was a massacre about fifty miles north of here. There may be survivors."

I blinked at her, open mouthed.

"Snap out of it, Doctor," she said. She tousled my hair. "We have to go."

"We're leaving?"

"Correct. Please clothe yourself and hurry to the O.R."

She put a bottle of water and an energy bar on the stump of wood next to my bed and fled.

A massacre? *Please, God, let that be a gross exaggeration.* I talked to myself as I dressed, swore like mad until I found my left shoe. Then I pocketed the energy bar, grabbed my kit, and headed out.

Sabeena was waiting for me on a bench outside the operating room. She had her kit, and a canteen was strapped across her chest. I ducked into the O.R., filled a canteen, and snatched up the mini X-ray machine. After that, we climbed aboard the donkey cart, and Sabeena took the helm.

Sabeena had well-developed intuition and was right more often than anyone I knew. She had been known to anticipate incoming wounded before trucks, carts, or helicopters arrived, and—more than I could do—predict whether a patient was going to survive or die. She was superb at reading moods, too.

Now she said, "I had a very bad feeling when those soldiers left the settlement. Sometimes I hate to be right."

Our cart rolled out down the dirt track that passed between our compound and the *tukuls*. We passed families clustered around cooking fires and children playing in the dirt, and by the time we reached the gates, the *whacka-whacka* din of a descending helicopter made me cover my ears.

Colin was already there, waiting for the chopper to land. He and Bailey got out of the Land Rover, followed by Jimmy and Vander. Colin walked toward me, scowling as he said, "Brigid, Sabeena, no. You can't come with us. Don't even think of arguing with me."

Sabeena jumped down from our cart, pulled her satchel after her, and said, "I don't work for you, Dr. Whitehead. I go where I'm needed. And if you don't like it, you can go to hell."

I grabbed my kit and got out of the cart after Sabeena.

I yelled over the racket, "I don't work for you, either, Doctor!"

Colin was exasperated, but he was clearly trying to control his temper. He stepped in front of me, blocking my way.

"Brigid," he said at full volume, a foot from my face, "the intelligence on this so-called military action is sketchy. We don't know what we're going to find. The four of us," he said, sweeping his hand to take in the three other male doctors, "will assess the damage and transport survivors back to hospital. The best thing you can do is be ready for us, get it?"

I shouted back, "Colin, we're coming! We'll make ourselves useful, I promise."

"Why are you so stubborn?"

I glared at him. "Are *you* stubborn?"

The helicopter landed. It was a large Mi-8, a Russian-made aircraft, common in South Sudan. This one had the blue UN logo on its tail section. The rotors sent up a blinding dust storm.

Sabeena and I ran toward the chopper, her incongruous pink Skechers slapping the dirt.

I wondered what her intuition was telling her now.

CHAPTER 21

SABEENA AND I sat next to each other in the cargo bay of the huge helicopter. We took turns peering through a scratched Plexiglas window as the helicopter flew over the battlefield, the engine and the rotors providing the sound track to the hellish sight below.

I saw hundreds of bodies. Some were in heaps, and others lay like far-flung sticks as far as I could see.

As the helicopter descended, I identified the uniforms of the dead. Many wore the camouflage and red scarves of the Gray Army, but the BLM, in gray-and-green fatigues, outnumbered the Grays two to one.

I didn't know many of the BLM soldiers personally, but I felt that I knew them *all*. Most were Americans my age, from small-town USA and from cities like Boston. They had come here to help these savagely victimized and disadvantaged people whose roots they shared.

Because of their selflessness, these brave kids had died not only terribly but anonymously. Not even their bodies would go home. There were no refrigerated trucks in South Sudan. The BLM dead might be photographed for later identification, or not. But for certain, the corpses of both armies would be bulldozed into mass graves.

Our helicopter touched down, rocking on its struts. The engine whined, and the pilot shut it down. Colin helped me out of the cargo bay, and for a moment, he held me above him and looked into my eyes.

I wanted to say something meaningful, but I was still annoyed with him. I couldn't find the right words—and then, the moment was gone. My feet pounded the ground as I ran across the flat and stinking field, sending up flights of vultures as my colleagues and I looked among the bloated bodies for signs of life.

The immense number of bodies finally stopped me cold.

I stood on the flat, brown field that stretched from nowhere to nowhere else and took in a panoramic view. My first estimate had been wrong. There weren't hundreds of corpses. There were *thousands.* The BLM soldiers had been shot, and many had also been hacked with machetes and decapitated.

A hot wind blew the stench of decomposition across the field. Tears sheeted down my face. No healing would be done today.

And then I heard Sabeena shout, *"Over here!"*

She was hunched over a body that seemed to be twitching. I ran with my kit in hand, sliding the last few yards on my knees to where the wounded soldier lay. His breathing was ragged, and I counted six bullet holes punched into his bloody uniform. Somehow, he still held on to his life.

"We need a stretcher!" Sabeena shouted out through cupped hands. "Stay here," she said to me, and then she ran toward our chopper.

I lifted the young man's head into my lap and gave him a sip of water from my canteen. He coughed and asked for more.

I gave him another sip, and I pinched his thigh.

"Did you feel that?"

"Feel what?"

"Can you move your feet?"

His expression told me he thought that he *had* moved them, but I was sure he was paralyzed from the waist down.

"What's your name?" I asked him.

"Nick," he said. "Givens. My parents live in Biloxi." He gasped. He grabbed at the chain around his neck, pulled it over his head, and pushed it and his dog tags into my hands.

"Givens. Melba and Roy. They work. At the high school."

I said, "Nick, you have to keep your ID with you," but he shook his head and looked at me with huge, pleading eyes. He knew that he had very little time left.

I said, "I'll find them."

I was holding the young man's hand when automatic gunfire sounded behind me.

I jerked around and saw one of the Gray soldiers weaving around the obstacle course of bodies, running erratically toward us. He had been injured. Blood soaked his uniform, but he wasn't down and clearly had more killing in mind. He saw me staring at him, and he lifted his gun and screamed, "Zu-ber-i!"

Givens strong-armed me out of his way and raised his weapon, but before he could squeeze the trigger, he grunted and rolled onto his side.

I had no choice.

I seized the gun from Givens's hand, sat with my back to him, and used my folded knees as a gun brace. I pointed the AK at the Gray soldier, who was closing in. I was looking him squarely in the eyes when I fired.

The burst of bullets was shockingly loud, and the kick of the gun threw me back onto Givens. I caught my balance even as the soldier staggered backward and dropped.

I didn't need to check his pulse to know what I'd done.

Dear God. This is me. Brigid Fitzgerald.

I've just killed a man.

CHAPTER 22

THE ENTIRE field was in chaos. The helicopter chopped shouted words into strings of nonsense, and the whirling dust storms colored everyone and everything a dull yellow-brown.

Colin had been standing between the helicopter and where I sat with Givens. Now he was heading toward me, waving his hands wildly, frantically calling out to me, something like, "*Brigid.* Come to the helicopter. Come *now.*"

"*I need help!*" I shouted back.

Nick Givens was still *alive,* and as long as he was breathing, I was determined to save him.

I leaned close to the young man's ear and said, "Nick, you hang on, okay? I'm getting help for you. You're going home."

A new sound washed over the field.

There was another helicopter high overhead. I felt a flash of hope. More help was coming in, and surely there were other people on this field who might be alive and, with medical assistance, could be saved.

I prayed for that.

And then another shock blasted the hope right out of me. As the helicopter descended we were sprayed with gunfire. We were *under fire*.

Our own helicopter was rocking and beginning to lift off, and now Colin was running toward me.

"Leave him," he shouted over the roar of the engines. "Brigid, come with me, or I'm going to throw you over my shoulder and carry you."

I still didn't understand—and then I did.

The logo on the tail section of the second aircraft was not the blue UN letters with the image of the globe.

The logo was the letter Z in black.

Other helicopters appeared overhead, joining this one. *We were being attacked by Zuberi's army.*

Colin was only yards away. I shouted, "Colin, he can't *walk*. But we're taking him back with us. We *must*."

Colin's face contorted as bullets flew and the enemy helicopter landed a hundred feet away, sending up thick, stinging waves of dust.

I could hardly see, but I grabbed hold of Givens's feet, and Colin, following my lead, lifted up the young man from under his arms. He was heavy, but I was damned well going to keep a grip on him. More bullets pinged into the dirt. We were making progress toward the UN airship— it was so close, I could see the pilot's face—when Colin let go of Givens.

I screamed, "Colin! Pick him *up!*" when I saw the look of shock come over his face. He clutched at the bull's-eye on the front of his T-shirt. I yelled his name, but he looked confused as he stared at his bloody palm.

He started to speak, but he couldn't get air. His knees buckled, and he collapsed, falling onto his side.

I released Givens's feet and ran over to Colin. A bullet had gone through the center of the target on his back and out the front. *Maybe it missed his heart.*

I rolled Colin onto his back, put an arm under his neck, and grabbed his dear face with my hand. His eyes were open, but he seemed to be looking past my shoulder.

"Colin, I'll get you out of here. Please, don't leave me."

I pressed my lips to his and kissed him. I felt him respond, and for a moment I was filled with relief. But then he went slack. I needed help desperately, but I couldn't leave Colin alone, even for a second.

I stood up to look for Sabeena as fusillades of gunfire sprayed around me. I felt a hard thump to my rib cage. My vision blurred and slid sideways. I was screaming inside my head when all that I'd known went black.

NO. PLEASE, GOD. NO.

PART TWO

CHAPTER 23

I WAS seated comfortably, speeding through total darkness toward a soft light far away. I smelled nothing, heard nothing, and I was not afraid. I wiggled my fingers, and I flexed my toes, but I had no desire to stand or stretch my arms or look in any direction but straight ahead.

I became suddenly aware of a warm place inside my chest that was not part of me. It was an unknown presence, knowing and alive, and it conveyed an idea to me. A big one. That what was happening to me now was meant to be.

I formed words inside my mind.

I asked, *What is this?*

I wasn't answered in words, but I had an understanding, something like, *You know. You called out to Me.*

The warmth expanded out from my chest to the ends of my fingers and toes. What was happening? Was I with God? Was His spirit inside me? Was He protecting me?

Why now?

Am I dead? I asked.

There was no answer.

I had another question, equally pressing.

What happened?

The silence was accompanied by a warm breeze, and then the void was filled. I was far above the killing field in South Sudan, above the birds that cast circling shadows over the ground, and I heard blades chopping at the air. Thousands of bodies stretched out to the horizon. It hurt me to see them, but I could not look away.

Why has this happened? What purpose has it served?

I was sitting on the ground that radiated dry, baking heat. My eyes were half-closed to keep out the dust, and my mouth was dry. At my feet was the wounded soldier, Nick Givens.

But Givens became Nadir, the brave and hilarious boy who'd been shot and had his body hung on the wall. His arms were stretched out, and he looked up at me with light in his eyes.

Nadir is dead. Givens is dead. Why? What is the point of this?

A voice came to me, loud and echoing. "Brigid. Hang on." It was Sabeena. I watched as my dear friend ran toward a helicopter. Men jumped down from the aircraft and headed toward where I sat in the bloodied dirt with Colin's head in my lap.

Colin is dead. He's gone. This can't be.

A sound inside my mind seemed to say, *Be with Colin.*

I was with Colin entirely. I felt his terrible guilt and emotional pain. I understood his shame and how hard he had tried to redeem himself in the company of Kind Hands. But now, his expression was gentle, as though he had found peace at last. His voice, but not his voice, entered my mind.

I truly love you, Brigid. Do you know that?

My thoughts went out to him,

I love you, Colin. And I'm so very sorry. It was my fault that you were shot. Forgive me, please. You shouldn't have died.

His silent words came to me again. *Please listen to me, Brigid. Live a good life. Live.*

Hands came from above and lifted me roughly onto a stretcher. I heard running feet, felt my weightless body being hoisted up, passed to other hands inside the helicopter.

"Brigid. Can you hear me? *Brigid.*" That was Sabeena.

I was inside a confessional booth. I saw Father Delahanty's silhouette through the curtain. I had been holding his hand when he died.

He had wanted to confess, but he had said, "God has a plan for you."

The last words of a dying man made no sense. I had only hoped to give him comfort.

Father. Why did you have to die?

A reply seemed to come from a presence warming my body and filling my mind, a presence that felt other than mine.

He lived the full extent of his life.

No. I reject that. A black rage filled me, and I thought, *This is all wrong. What kind of god are you? Answer me.*

No answer.

I thought, *And me? Have I lived the full extent of my life?*

I was in the back of the donkey cart with the remains of the dead. Father Delahanty's body was wrapped securely in a sheet. I crossed his forehead with my thumb, and a thought bloomed in my mind fully formed. Father Delahanty wanted me to know that *God* had a plan for me. That He had more for me to do.

A plan? What plan is this? Speak, damn you.

A soft light was all around me. I could see it through closed eyelids, and I could almost touch it.

What is the plan?

Someone shook my shoulder.

Sabeena? Is it you? Was this all a dream?

CHAPTER 24

I OPENED my eyes. I was leaning against a man in the seat beside me. He was wearing a dark coat, a brimmed hat, and leather gloves. He looked to be in his sixties, and his wrinkled face was very kind.

"Oh," I said, pulling back. "*Mi dispiace tanto.* I'm so sorry."

We were on a train, and it was decelerating. Lights flashed in the windows, and the flip sign at the front of the car read CIVITAVECCHIA.

The man spoke to me in Italian.

"I hated to wake you, miss. But we are coming into Roma Termini. I'll get your bag down. We're here."

People got up from their seats and gathered their possessions. The man with the hat reached up to the rack and took down my satchel.

"Watch out," he said. "Be aware of your surroundings. Rome is a big city."

I thanked him.

He touched his hat and was absorbed into the crush of people moving to the exit doors as the train squealed to a stop. I followed the crowd to the terminal, and from there to the street, where I joined a long taxi queue outside.

The city scene was loud and jarring, a mixed-up puzzle of sights and sounds that did not fit together in my mind. In the place of donkey carts and old Land Rovers were sports cars speeding, shifting gears, braking suddenly, accompanied by the constant blaring of horns.

Pedestrian traffic was also loud and clashing. Fashionable people carried shopping bags and computer bags. They laughed and shouted into cell phones as they strode purposefully down the sidewalk, hardly looking up at all.

Where were they going? To what end? It had been two long years since I had lived in a city.

I moved along with the queue until I was at the front of the line, and the driver of a white Fiat opened the door for me. He saw the way I held my arm and took my battered leather bag and put it in the trunk.

I got into the taxi and gripped the armrest as the driver shot away from the curb. He knew the address I had given him, and he sped through the streets of Rome. Centrifugal force pinned me painfully to the side of the cab, then threw me toward the far side of the seat as we drove around the traffic circles.

The driver had a picture of his wife and children in a frame stuck to the dashboard, and he had hung a rosary from the rearview mirror. The cross swung hypnotically as we took the many high-speed turns. That swinging rosary made me physically sick. I looked away.

I was wearing the same jeans, blue cotton shirt, and crocheted cardigan that I'd worn when I first went to South Sudan. And now I was also wearing Sabeena's secondhand pink Skechers that, evidently, she had passed down to me.

Sabeena's shoes were all I had of her, and they were the most precious things I owned. They reminded me that it had all really happened.

I had died with Colin on the killing field.

It was Sabeena who had gotten me off the ground and into the helicopter. Jimmy Wuster told me that she had decompressed my lungs with a needle while we were in the air and literally brought me back to life.

She had assisted Dr. Wuster and Dr. Bailey in the O.R. at Kind Hands, where they did emergency meatball surgery. Then she had gone with me to the airport in Entebbe and had handed me off to an in-flight nurse for my trip to a hospital in Amsterdam.

I imagine survival odds were small.

That was six weeks ago. I hadn't seen or heard from Sabeena. Was she alive or dead? Had she been able to rescue Jemilla and Aziza when our hospital had been shut down?

And what was I to do now? I could not imagine ever working as a doctor again. And I no longer believed that if there was a god, he was good.

CHAPTER 25

MY DRIVER looked at me in the rearview mirror.

He said, *"La signorina, dovrei prendere da un medico?"*

He was asking if he should take me to a doctor. I felt more lost and more vulnerable than I had in my life. I could only tell this stranger the truth.

"Sono un medico. I am a doctor," I told him. "I've been in a war zone in Africa. A lot of people died. I lost a man I loved to this war, and I had to leave people I loved behind."

The man's face reflected my pain.

Horns blared. He swerved the car, got us back on track. We were on a broad avenue, Piazza del Colosseo. The Colosseum was on my right, ancient, crumbling, and at the same time still standing after thousands of years. I barely glanced at it.

We turned onto Ponte Testaccio and were crossing the bridge over the Tiber when a gang of motor scooters came up from behind. As they passed us, their loud, popping motors shot me back to the slaughter in South Sudan.

The driver was looking into the glass, watching me hunch down and cling to the corner of the backseat.

"Were you hurt?" he asked in Italian.

I nodded.

"I'm sorry," he said. "Rome will be good to you."

The cab slowed as we entered the section of Rome called Trastevere, which means "beyond the Tiber." He turned onto a narrow street that was laid with cobblestones and lined with low, pastel-colored buildings. It was sweet and beautiful, like an old, hand-tinted picture postcard.

He stopped the cab in front of a three-story building the color of peaches, with ivy clinging to the walls and a tile with the number 23 painted in cobalt blue.

I pulled a wad of euros from my handbag, but my driver refused the fare.

"Be well," he said. He unhooked the rosary from the mirror and bunched it into my hand exactly the way Nick Givens had with his dog tags. I couldn't say no, so I said, "*Grazie*. I'll keep it with me."

He nodded and smiled and took my luggage from the trunk and set it down at the feet of a row of potted plants.

"Go with God," he said.

"And you."

A voice called out to me from above.

"Brigid. Brigid, up here. Oh, my God. I'm so glad to see your face."

CHAPTER 26

TORI HEWITT was calling down to me from a window on the third floor. The open shutters perfectly framed the sunny face of my dear friend from medical school, who was leaning out over the street. I hadn't seen Tori in two years, and she looked fresh and healthy and beautiful.

"I'm coming down!" she shouted.

A moment later she burst through the door with her arms open wide and pulled me into a hug that I needed more than she could possibly have known.

She asked me a million questions as she grabbed my battered bag and led me through an archway to the main entrance and the interior stairs to the apartment where she lived with her husband, Marty.

"How are you feeling, Brigid? Are you famished? I'll bet you are. Did you have trouble finding us?"

The apartment was extraordinary. The high ceilings were made of beamed antique wood. The floors were made of terra cotta tiles, and the enormous windows let in brilliant light.

I stared at the fruit-colored upholstered furniture and the kitchen that was made for cooking as though I had never been inside a home before.

"What can I get you, Brigid, my dear friend?"

"A hot shower?"

"Done," said Tori. "And if you don't mind, I want to take a look at you."

We were inside a shining, white-tiled bathroom. Tori turned on the shower, and as I undressed, she took away my clothes, clucking her tongue as I gave her a bit of a guided tour.

"One bullet went in here," I said, pointing to the scar in my belly. "It went through my spleen and left lung and exited in my back."

"It was the splenic trauma you had to worry about," said my friend the doctor.

"Yeah. It's good, though. They got to me quick in the O.R."

"And the lung?"

"Collapsed. My friend decompressed it in the chopper. I lost a lobe, but no big deal. I lost blood flow to my brain for a while. But I'm good now."

"You had neurological workups, right?" Tori asked me.

I nodded. "Yep."

"How many fingers am I holding up?"

"What are fingers?" I asked.

Tori burst out laughing, and I had a laugh, too; it felt like the first time in my life. I showed off the scars over the plates in my right arm, which had been shattered in three places, and then I said, "That's all I've got."

"That's plenty," said Tori.

I hadn't seen a mirror in a long time, and now I stared at myself in the prettily etched mirror over the sink. My red hair looked like a dead shrub. My skin was brown, and my cheekbones were sharp. My eyes had lost their innocence. I wouldn't be getting that back.

Tori put a fluffy white bath sheet on the toilet seat and said, "I'm going to help you in."

She gave me her arm to grasp as I stepped over the side of the tub and into the hot spray.

"Good?" she asked.

"Good" couldn't begin to describe it. "Blissful."

"Try this lavender shampoo, Brigid. It's my favorite. And use the conditioner. I'm going to sit here, okay?"

She was making sure that I wouldn't slip on the porcelain and reinjure myself. Her tenderness made tears well up. I couldn't take it.

"You know what, Tori?" I said as the hot water streamed down my body.

"What, Brigid? What do you need?"

"I would love a very milky coffee with sugar."

"Sit down in the tub. Here."

She unhooked the showerhead on its long, snaky cord and put it in my good hand. "Sit down. That's right. I'll be back to help you out of there. Coffee's coming right up."

CHAPTER 27

TORI AND Marty Hewitt were more of a family to me than my own.

Still, I felt alone.

I stayed in their apartment for a full week without going outside. I craved the quiet and the solitude and the security of the large, old rooms. Some days went by as if I were gently riffling through the pages of a book. But the nights were bad. I had violent dreams, physical pain, and regret that I had lost my way.

Tori and Marty worked long days at the Rome American Hospital, and while they worked, I made notes in a journal. I brushed up on my Italian, cleaned up around the house, and read. Falling asleep on a velvet-covered sofa with a peach in my hand and an open book across my chest was a delight beyond anything I could have imagined a few months ago.

On this particular day, I was having a nap on the sofa before dinner when I woke up to footsteps on the stairs and the sound of masculine laughter.

The front door opened, and Marty Hewitt came in carrying a case of wine. He was followed by a tall, dark-haired man, also in his twenties. I wasn't so burned out that I didn't notice how good looking he was.

Marty said, "Brigid, get over here and meet my friend Zachary Graham.

Zach, this is Brigid Fitzgerald. I told him already that we're all outta Johns Hopkins. Have a seat, you guys. Let's sample this wine."

I walked over to the big farm table and shook Zach's hand. Glasses appeared, a bottle was opened, and wine was poured. Following Marty's lead, we made an outrageous fuss over the *vino da tavola,* and when we were all comfortable, Zachary Graham said, "I was telling Marty about this story I'm writing for the *Times.*"

Zach had just come back to Rome from the French Open and told a few anecdotes about Djokovic and Serena, using terms like "wide-open slams" and "long rallies." I know nothing about tennis, but I loved the animated way he told a story. It was great to hear these two big men laughing and to be able to join in without thinking about enemy artillery and dirt storms and an O.R. full of mortally wounded children.

Marty was refilling my glass when his phone rang. He spoke with Tori briefly, hung up, and said, "She's on her way. We can meet her at Leonardo's in half an hour. You guys up for dinner?"

I was already shaking my head no when Marty said, "Brigid? You're in Rome. Time to see some of it. Doctor's orders."

"In that case, absolutely," I said.

Tori had opened her closet to me. She's a generous size twelve, and I'm an emaciated size six. Her black dress floated around me, but I belted and bloused it, and it looked as if it were made for me. I was ready to go to an actual restaurant.

By the time the sun had set, the four of us were seated under the big, yellow awning outside a trattoria on a busy street less than a block from the Hewitts' apartment.

We were still drinking, eating bread dipped in olive oil, while our dinners were being prepared, when Marty's phone rang. Seconds later, Tori's phone vibrated on the tabletop.

"Sorry, everyone," said Marty. "The emergency room just filled up. It's the full freakin' moon. We have to go in."

"Always happens," Tori said. "Just when you can smell the lasagna, but before you get a fork in."

I jumped to my feet out of pure reflex.

Tori said softly, "Where ya going, Brigid? You're off duty."

Oh.

"We've got a running tab here," said Marty. "So enjoy. By the way, Brigid, Zach here is an avid baseball fan."

"Really?" I said.

"Yankees all the way," said Zach.

"Red Sox," I said, setting my jaw.

"Oh, man," Marty said, grinning widely. "I'd like to be a fly on the wall."

And then the Hewitts were gone, and Zach and I were looking at each other over a steaming-hot dinner for four.

CHAPTER 28

THE WAITER had put the four enormous platters of everything in tomato sauce on the table. Zach unfolded his napkin and said, "So, you're a Sox fan, huh?"

The waiter snapped my napkin open and laid it across my lap as I said to Zach, "Since as long as I can remember."

Zach grinned, said, "My condolences." And stabbed one of his shrimp scampi.

I kept my hands folded.

I said, "For what? Two thousand four, 2007, and 2013?"

"No. For the almost one hundred years it took after Babe Ruth left to win those World Series."

I shot back, "Which would be Yankees time, correct?"

He took a gulp of vino and said, "As they say, do the math. Twenty-seven wins for the Yankees, three for the Sox."

"Yeah, well that's the old math. This is the new math, and we've won three World Series to your two since Y2K."

"Don't worry, we're just warming up."

"Well, I wish you the best getting loose."

And suddenly, we both cracked up. It really was too funny to be sitting outdoors on a balmy night in Rome, talking about American baseball.

Zach said, "You should try this, Red. It really is the specialty of the house."

Without waiting for me to say okay, he swapped out my untouched rigatoni *alfredo* for Marty's steak *pizzaiola*.

"I'll try it on your recommendation, *Yank*. Tell me about yourself," I said, sawing into the steak.

Zach said, "Reporters don't really like to talk about themselves, you know. We like to ask the questions."

"Oh, try something new," I said.

Then I tried the steak. It was, as advertised, very good.

Zach said, "Okay. Here I go. Born in Minnesota, degree in journalism from where else, Northwestern. Live in New York, and, as a single guy with no baggage, I've been assigned to the international sports desk and odds and ends, which is a dream come true. Mind if I have a bite of that?" he said, eyeing the steak. "You want to try the eggplant?"

"I'm not so big on eggplant."

I put the plate of steak in the middle of the table, and we worked on it together.

And then Zach said, "Your turn, Red."

I just shook my head no and kept going with the steak. I didn't want to talk about myself. Not now, and maybe not ever. But Zach was one of those reporters who wouldn't be brushed off.

"I hope you don't mind that I grilled Marty about you."

I glanced at him through my lashes, then dropped my eyes back to the table.

"He told me about the settlement being knocked down. Your injuries."

"I can't talk about that," I said.

"Okay. I'm sorry, though. That you had to go through that."

I put down my fork and knife.

I said, "Zach, the war was awful. Indescribable. But my life in South Sudan was about the displaced people who had less than nothing, the mothers with babies had no milk to feed them."

I don't know what came over me, but I *sang* right there at the table overflowing with food.

Baby boy, baby boy
Hello, baby, please be quiet
When your hunger is very painful
Just lie down and sleep
Better to just lie down and sleep.

I said, "In South Sudan, that's a lullaby."

The sadness on Zach's face showed me a lot about him. He stopped eating, and so did I. And then, without our realizing that the full moon had been eclipsed by clouds, the sky opened up, dropping heavy rain on the awning.

Waiters poured out of the restaurant and began moving the tables and customers away from the loud and slashing rain. Zach said, "What do you say we get outta here?"

I stood up, and we ducked into the trattoria. And I remembered when I was in the camp, the heat radiating in waves off everything, and there wasn't enough clean water for drinking. And I had asked God to make it rain.

He does things in His own time.

CHAPTER 29

WE WERE on Zach's shiny red Vespa, tearing up the ancient roads and boulevards of modern-day Rome. My arms were around his waist, I was pressing hard against his back, and the hot air was just about blowing my eyelashes off.

Zach turned his head to look at me, and I shouted at him, "Eyes on the road!"

I had been in Rome for two weeks, and after my self-enforced week of lockdown in the Hewitts' apartment, I now had a very engaging play pal who had wheels and a lot of free time.

As it turned out, Zach knew Rome but didn't speak much Italian. I knew Italian well but didn't know Rome at all.

Perfect combo.

Every day at about ten, after Zach had checked in with the *Times*, he picked me up at the Hewitts', and we went for a ride. Since our first self-guided tour, I'd seen a lot of Rome at sixty miles an hour: the Pantheon and Trevi Fountain, the Colosseum and the remains of the Circus Maximus. But I'd avoided Vatican City. I just wasn't ready to confront the hub of the Roman Catholic Church.

Not yet. Maybe not ever.

Right now, we had the wind in our faces. The river rolled on to our left, and we were weaving through crazy traffic on Lungotevere Raffaello Sanzio. A couple of turns later, we were on Via del Moro, and we followed it along cute cobblestoned streets flanked by Italian-ice-colored buildings. We made our way to the center of Trastevere, the picture-perfect Piazza di Santa Maria.

Zach parked the scooter at the northwest side of the enclosed plaza, shut down the engine, and removed his helmet. He looked wild. His hair was matted down, his goggles had left white circles around his eyes, and his grin was almost maniacal.

Call me crazy, but he looked pretty hot.

I saw that he wanted to kiss me, but I smiled and handed him my helmet. Then I stretched out my hand, and he helped me off the Vespa.

The Caffè di Marzio was further perfection. We were shown seats at a small table under the awning with a full-on view of the fountain and the clock tower across the square. We ordered lunch from Giovanni, a young man with a mustache and *Amo Angelina* tattooed on his biceps, and he returned to our table with a bottle of Sangiovese.

We were sitting shoulder to shoulder, knee to knee, and by the time the pasta arrived, we had each put down a glass of wine and were working on a second. Heat lightning flashed back and forth between us—which was both fun and unnerving.

He said, "You know you have a two-part laugh?"

"I have what?"

"Yeah. You start way up here with a giggle, and then it drops to a belly laugh. That just kills me, Red."

I became self-conscious. I didn't know what to say.

But Zach wasn't going to let my silence drag on. He was a reporter, after all, and he could handle a little glitch in the repartee. He topped up my wineglass and said, "You know, you haven't told me your plans. Like, where are you headed from here?"

I pictured the interior of the O.R. at Kind Hands. I knew every windowless inch of it. There was no view of the future.

Zach said into the lengthening silence, "Let me put that another way. Are you planning to stay in Rome?"

I said, "I honestly don't know what I'm going to do next. I might take myself on a world tour."

Why leave Rome? Why leave Zach?

He was smart and funny, and he was honestly trying to get to know me even as I pushed him away.

He said, "Oh. That sounds like fun."

Clearly, that wasn't what he wanted to hear. He leaned in and reached for his glass. His knee touched mine, and the electricity just shot through me.

I was this close to leaning against his shoulder and tucking my head under his chin. But I didn't want to start what I knew damn well I couldn't finish.

Zach said, "You're a funny girl, Brigid. You won't tell me where you're going or where you've been."

I wanted to give him *something*.

I said, "I really should tell you what it was like in South Sudan."

CHAPTER 30

I DIDN'T know how to tell Zach about hell on earth without feeling it all over again. But I had decided to try.

I dropped my hands into my lap and said, "Imagine a dirt-poor town of eighty thousand people who've been driven from their homes and are now living under tarps, Zach. A lot of these people have been brutalized, their families killed, and now they have no possessions, no work, just decimated lives and nothing to live for.

"The food is bare subsistence. The water is contaminated, and you can add to all of that drought and hundred-and-fifteen-degree heat and infectious disease and an armed militia looking for opportunities to murder anyone who steps outside the gates."

Zach kept his eyes on me, encouraging me to go on.

"There were six doctors and a few volunteer nurses to care for every kind of medical condition you can imagine and about a thousand you can't. We did surgeries with dull knives and drills and with watered-down anesthesia, if we happened to have anesthetics at all.

"A lot of people died, Zach. Every stinking day. They died when you slept or when you went outside to take a breath of air. You came back, and your patient was dead. For us, working in that hospital was like trying to carry water in a bucket full of holes."

Zach said, "You should write about this, Brigid. People don't know anything about the conditions in these settlements. They *should* know."

I was lost in thoughts of Kind Hands. I heard Zach say, "Please. Go on."

Amid music from car speakers and the *put-put* of scooters in the square, the clamor of customers and the clashing of silverware and dishes in the trattoria around us, I described the routine at the hospital to Zach.

I told him about Sabeena and the orphan girls whom I loved. I told him about my colleagues from all over, about Wuster and Bailey, Khalil and Vander; about our twenty-hour days operating by the light of flashlights in our mouths. The patients' terrified families standing at our elbows.

"You said six doctors," Zach said.

I hadn't mentioned Colin. I couldn't do it. I actually had a sense that Colin was sitting with us. That he was listening and about to make a rude comment. Or tell me that he loved me.

I said, "A lot of doctors were on the field the day I was shot. They're scattered. Or buried."

Zach put his hand on mine and said, "Your bravery.... It's inspirational, Brigid."

I shrugged and kept my eyes on his big hand, covering mine. It looked strange there, but it felt good.

Zach blurted, "I want to know everything about you."

And right then, with the impeccable timing of waiters all around the world, Giovanni appeared between us to ask if we would like coffee and dessert.

"Brigid?" Zach asked me.

"No, thanks. Not for me."

Zach removed his hand from mine, and as the waiter presented the bill, I was struck with a weird impulse I didn't see coming. I tossed my napkin to the table, jumped to my feet, and said, "Time to go."

CHAPTER 31

AT 9:27 the next morning, I was in a window seat on a plane flying out of Fiumicino to Charles de Gaulle in Paris.

I was wearing new jeans, a nubby cotton sweater, a lightweight denim jacket, Sabeena's pink shoes, a crucifix on a heavy gold chain that Tori had fastened around my neck before we kissed good-bye on both cheeks, and I had the taxi driver's rosary in my pocket.

I rolled up my jacket and wedged it between the armrest and the window and laid my head against the glass. I'd never been to Paris. It was as good a destination as any. I needed to get out of town, and there were flights to Paris nearly every hour.

I watched Rome recede until it looked like a sepia drawing in an old history book. Then a layer of clouds filled in between the plane and the noble city many thousands of feet below.

I missed Zach already and felt guilty for bolting without telling him that I was going and why. I couldn't imagine explaining to him that I was still in love with Colin, a man I'd been inextricably bound to by tenuous life and violent death.

No holiday romance could compare, not when I was still suffering such a profound loss of love in my heart and soul.

And yet, I was vulnerable. I could still get hurt. I thought Zach could get hurt, too.

The flight attendant offered food and drink, but I shook my head no and watched sunlight limn the clouds as we sailed across the morning sky.

I closed my eyes, and as soon as I did, an image of our IDP settlement came to me in minute detail. I saw the hundreds of rows of *tukuls*, the individual faces of men and women and children whose names I hadn't known—I knew those people now. Their eyes turned to me as I passed them on the dusty track.

How many of these innocent people had been slaughtered since I left Africa?

Two weeks ago, when I'd taken the train from Amsterdam to Rome, a warm feeling filled my chest, and I had a sense of something "not me." I'd found myself asking why. And I was doing it now.

Just as it had happened then, I heard or sensed something like a voice that I didn't feel was coming from me.

Brigid. You want to know why.

I opened my eyes. I wasn't asleep. The flight attendant was still walking up the aisle. A mother and two children were in the seat ahead of me, and the children were throwing candies at one another and laughing.

I had a shocking revelation.

I was *on* the plane, and at the same time, I was *outside* it. A pretty village came into focus just below me, as if I were flying over the treetops on my own power. I saw people tending a community garden, children playing in a park. I felt wind in my hair, the warmth of the sun on my back, and a sense of incredible peace.

The voice—if that was what it was—cut into my thoughts. *This is happening.*

Air hissed through the vent overhead.

I said, out loud, "Tell me. Are you God?"

A little boy with big, blue eyes threw a fistful of candy over the seat back at me. His mother turned and apologized—"*Scusa, signora*"—and scolded the child.

And, still, while I was seated in row 11, seat D, on an Air France flight to Paris, I was "flying" freely over adorable shops on a lane in the heart of the village. As I watched, a baby carriage rolled into the street, where it was struck by a car, full on, crushing the carriage under the wheels.

I clapped my hands over my mouth and clamped down on a scream.

I heard the words inside my head.

This is yours. Take care of it.

There was a sparrow in my now-outstretched hand. It was brown and black, with white streaks on its wings. It looked at me and blinked its sharp, knowing eyes. Then it flew away.

I said, *Come back.*

More birds joined the one that was mine. Hundreds of little birds, thousands, millions, all rising up from the trees and power lines, filling the air to the horizon and beyond, shutting out the sunlight until all I could see was a shimmering blackness.

The vibration, like a voice inside my head, said, *Can you care for your bird? Does it obey? Or does it have its own will?*

I spoke out loud, "Stop. No metaphors. Please."

An African village appeared in my mind. It might be Magwi, the closest town to our settlement. I had been there only once, when the driver who had taken me from Juba to Kind Hands had skirted the village center on the way to the camp.

Now, I saw the whole town from my flight path overhead. I saw the individual *tukuls* and a church and low buildings built within the curl of an estuary. I saw umbrellas over the street market. I saw barefoot children herding thin cattle with sticks.

I said, "Why are You showing me this?"

You know.

"I only know that I've lost my faith in You."

The "voice" resonated in my mind.

I haven't lost mine in you.

103

CHAPTER 32

A METALLIC squeal and warble called my attention to the public address system. A flight attendant announced the start of a movie and requested that passengers lower their shades.

I lowered mine and tried to call up the now-broken connection to the presence in my mind. But the line was down. Had I imagined the voice, the birds, the close-up view of Magwi from above? Had I been dreaming?

Or was I crazy?

It was possible. Two months ago my brain had been deprived of oxygen for however long it had taken Sabeena to get me into that helicopter, find the appropriate needle, and shove it with surgical precision into my chest. I was technically dead for four minutes, maybe five.

Oxygen deprivation can cause brain damage, but recovery is possible, even common. Top neurologists in Amsterdam had checked me out and declared my brain perfectly fine.

Still, residual injury might cause hallucinations.

Or possibly, because of this injury, a part of my brain that was normally closed off had become a two-way channel for communication with God.

Was that possible?

Was I delusional? Or was I hearing the Word of God?

Either way, this "voice," these visions, scared me a lot.

I stared at the seat back in front of me. Lights flickered as a movie played on a couple hundred little screens throughout the cabin. Eventually, I got up from my seat and retrieved my bag from the overhead rack. I dug around until I found my iPad, and then I created a new page in my journal.

I wrote, *If I could ask God only one question, it would be the same question Aziza asked me not long ago. "Why must we suffer so?" This question has been addressed in biblical verses and theological writings and notably in the book of Job.*

But the answers seem hazy and theoretical on the page.

In real life, I see suffering. And I see faith. And the second doesn't cancel out the first. When I ask why, the answer comes back, "You can't see from God's point of view."

If today God was putting thoughts and words and images in my mind, He conveyed that He has faith in me. And He showed me a path.

If I have no faith, how can I follow Him?

If I follow Him, does it mean that I have faith?

I thought about what I had written, and then I went to my email in-box and I typed:

Dear Zach, You did nothing wrong. I'm a coward, and I'm sorry to have left without saying good-bye. I was afraid that if I saw you, I wouldn't be able to go, and I must.

I care about you very much, but I am a broken woman.

All I can do is run.

I won't ever forget the wonderful times we spent together.

Yours, with a sad heart,

Brigid

When the plane landed, I reread my email to Zach, and then I launched it.

I got off the airplane with purpose. I stood in front of the arrivals-and-departures board and got my bearings. Then I crossed the airport and booked a flight to Juba, the capital of South Sudan.

God called. I answered.

CHAPTER 33

BUT I couldn't leave France just yet.

There would be a two-hour wait in Charles de Gaulle Airport before my plane departed for Juba. And then there would be a change of planes and the next leg of my journey, for a total of twenty-six hours en route.

I ate a croque monsieur at a fast-food brasserie. I had a beer. Then I had another one.

I bought three new T-shirts in an airport shop, along with a pair of socks and a green rubber slicker. I washed much of my body in the sink in the ladies' room and put on a new shirt, a pink one with the Eiffel Tower outlined in sequins. I purchased bags and bags of hard candies and some American newsmagazines. I found a seat at the gate and read for hours.

The big stories were startling. There was a severe drought in California that threatened wildlife and agriculture. Sea level and pollution were up. Ice was cracking off the poles. Planes had crashed. There were terrorist attacks in several countries and a plague in Saudi Arabia. Nine people had been shot to death during Bible study in a church in South Carolina. There was another mass killing in South Sudan that tested my belief, not in God but in the human race.

At two in the afternoon, I boarded the plane, and this flight was full. Again I had a window seat, and I didn't wait for takeoff to fall asleep.

I awoke to change planes in Dubai, and once we were aloft, I took a pill and slept again. I wasn't in communication with God or anyone else, but while I slept, I was making plans.

I arrived in Juba, the capital of South Sudan, at sundown. The sky was heavy with clouds, and there was a line of red at the horizon. I walked a half mile past the far end of the airport, to the bus stop, and I waited inside the shelter for the coach to Magwi.

I was going there on faith, according to some kind of voice in my head that had suggested rather strongly that this was what I was meant to do.

And I had my own reasons.

I had to find out what had happened after I left the continent wrapped in bandages, going in and out of consciousness and having almost no awareness until I'd passed a month in a hospital in Amsterdam.

What news I had, had come to me from Kind Hands. A paycheck had been wired, my health insurance had paid the tab, and in a brief email from Human Resources, I learned that my former colleagues, Drs. Wuster, Bailey, and Khalil, had each returned home, but KH wasn't permitted to give out contact information.

I was told that Jup Vander was missing and presumed dead. And there was no information on the whereabouts of a volunteer nurse by the name of Sabeena Gaol.

As the rim of the earth burned red, five people and I waited for a bus in a lean-to shelter alongside Route A43. There was a tree across the road, two hobbled goats standing beneath it. The bus shed with the corrugated tin roof, the bone-thin animals, the nearly bare trees, and the brown dirt beneath them were more familiar to me now than Fenway Park.

Out on the highway, two cones of light bore down on us. The man sitting next to me stood up and pointed down the road, saying, "Miss. The bus. She comes."

CHAPTER 34

THE BUS that rumbled and creaked and squealed to a stop looked as though it had been a veteran of many crashes. The side panels and hood were different colors. Windows were broken. The grille was gone. The tailpipe dragged. But there was a sign in the windshield that read *God Is Good*.

Riding in one of these coaches was a test of faith all by itself. Juba Line was a serial killer. Buses collided with cars and carts, ran over pedestrians, lost control and flipped over in the rainy season, when the dirt roads turned into slippery clay and tires could no more get traction on mud than they could if the roads had been paved with ice.

It was raining as I boarded the bus with my bags and went to the long bench seat in the rear. I shared my sweets with everyone but the chickens. I thought of the experience that had brought me back to Africa: the warmth of a presence inside my chest, the reverberation that was something like a voice in my head, and the images I had seen that I knew I hadn't created by myself.

I wondered again if I had slipped over the edge into psychosis, or if I was truly following a vision from God.

Meanwhile, the rain poured down, and the bus slid along the road. After three hours of nauseating twists and sloppy turns, it eventually stopped at the side of Magwi's main drag.

As we passengers exited the bus, a hard, slanting rain beat on the rusted, multicolored chassis and the people who were running toward the bus shelter. The nearly toothless fellow in his twenties who had ridden next to me since the start approached me when I was out of the rain. He had told me that his name was Kwame, and now asked, "May I give you a ride, lady?"

I thanked him very much, and, even though he was a stranger, I liked him. I got into the passenger side of his 1970s Dodge Charger, parked just beyond the shed.

"Where are you going?" asked Kwame.

"Is there a clinic here?" I asked him.

"Yes, lady."

He gave me a towel from the backseat, and I thanked him again and dried my face.

Kwame released the brake and revved his engine. We shot off the mark as the rain came down harder.

CHAPTER 35

THE RAIN sheeted down the wiperless car windows. I peered through the watery curtain and took in the shapes of the buildings along the darkened main street.

The strip of road, the spindly trees, the silhouettes of the squat buildings, and the tall spike of the radio tower all felt as familiar to me as if I'd lived in Magwi for years. That both creeped me out and made me feel that I was supposed to be here.

We cleared the small town and continued on down the road that was barely recognizable as a road. And I said to Kwame, "It's right up there."

Kwame gave me a sidelong glance, and I read his expression. *He* knew quite well where the clinic was, but how did I know? Then something like recognition lit up in his eyes.

That, I didn't understand at all.

He turned the car off the main road, onto a ribbon of muddy track. A few minutes later, he braked his junker outside a long wooden building with a sign reading MAGWI CLINIC under the peak of the roof. Tents were set up under the red acacia trees—a small village, I thought, of patients under care.

A porch ran the length of the building and was furnished with white plastic chairs, some of them occupied by patients. Light glowed behind the glass, and I could hear the soft roar of a generator over the rain pattering on tarps, the car's rusted body, and a peaked tin roof.

I thanked Kwame for the ride, and I paid him in dollars and a packet of M&M's. He was happy.

"When are you going back to the airport?"

I told him that I didn't know, but for sure it wouldn't be tonight.

"I work at the post office, lady, if you need me."

I wanted to hug him, but that wasn't the right thing to do. So I shook his hand, gathered my bags, pulled up the hood of my raincoat, and got out of the car. I waved as the old Dodge went slip-sliding away down the track to the road that divided the town.

When the taillights were out of view, I felt a flash of panic. What the hell was I doing here when I could be in Paris, or Brugge, or Panama City, or Malibu—anywhere but this place? Oh, right. I'd had a vision of Magwi, and now I was here.

I reached inside my raincoat pocket and felt for the rosary the cabdriver in Rome had given to me. It wasn't in any of my pockets, and after a hasty search of my leather bag, I found that it wasn't there, either. I'd lost the rosary somewhere.

I turned back to face the clinic and saw that the people on the porch were staring at the dazed and dripping woman standing calf deep in the muddy water.

A moment passed. And then a young woman got up from her chair and leaned over the porch railing.

"Doctor?" she said.

"Yes. I'm a doctor."

She clapped her hands together, smiled broadly, and said, "Welcome to this place. Come this way, Doctor."

She ran down the steps to meet me, led me up to the porch, and opened the door for me.

I was in a corridor paneled with plywood and lined with people. A light

113

flickered on the wall, and I saw a painted door at the far end. A teenage boy who was in the line pointed.

"Doctor is there."

I said thank you and kept walking. If Sabeena had passed through Magwi, she might have stopped at this clinic. A doctor here might know where I could find her.

If Sabeena was still alive.

I knocked on the door, and the sound of my knuckles on wood suddenly brought reality home.

I had been rash and probably crazy to travel for a day and a half to get to Magwi without any contacts or confirmation that I was on the right track.

I had gone on faith, and I knew what would happen now.

The door would open, and a doctor would say that he had never heard of Sabeena Gaol. Right after that, he would close the door in my face.

I realized in that instant that I didn't have a backup plan, and once that door opened, I had no plan at all.

The door swung open, and inside the wedge of light, I saw a scowling face, a face I loved.

She said to me, "Brigid? This can't be *you*."

I reached out to embrace Sabeena, the woman who had saved my life. But I didn't make it.

I felt weightless and at the same time as heavy as rocks.

My knees buckled, and I dropped to the floor.

CHAPTER 36

I WOKE up between clean sheets, looking over the footboard of a metal-frame bed.

A candle burned on the bedside table, casting a dancing yellow light on the plywood walls and on the woman who was watching me from a chair by the window. She was wearing a white lab coat, and her braided hair was wrapped around her head like a halo.

I remembered—or had I dreamed it? Sabeena caught me as I fainted and put me to bed. Had I actually found Sabeena exactly where I had looked for her? Was it really her? How else could this have happened except by some kind of miracle?

I was nearly overwhelmed. I spoke in a whisper.

"Sa-bee-na."

Ten feet away, Sabeena clasped her hands together and said, "Thank you, Jesus."

She came over and sat on the bed, and she stretched her arms out to me. I went into her hug and held her so tight. I no longer felt faint. I was jubilant. Oh, my God, Sabeena was here and alive. And I still hadn't thanked her.

"Thank you, Sabeena. Thank you for saving my life."

"My dear, of course, and you would have done exactly the same. My God, Brigid. I've missed you like crazy."

I prayed right there in her arms.

"Dear Lord. Thank you for showing me the way to my dearest friend. Thank you for this amazing gift. Amen."

Sabeena said, "Amen," and we rocked and cried for good long time, and then she rubbed my back and let me go, saying, "I had a feeling I was going to see you when I least expected it. But this, Brigid? I never thought you'd come right to my door."

"You just never know what I'm going to do next."

We had a good laugh, and then I said, "Lie down, Sabeena. Tell me what happened at Kind Hands."

She wiped her eyes with the heels of her palms, sighed deeply, and flipped around, and we shared the pillow.

She said, "It's an ugly story, Brigid. The day after you were shot, Zuberi came into the settlement with troops, big vehicles, and explosives. A lot of everything. They shot up the settlement. Burned down what would burn. I heard that Jup died."

"I heard the same."

"Most of the IDPs got out, but not all. I heard terrible stories, Brigid. Children and people who couldn't run were just gunned down. The South Sudanese arrived at the last minute and fought a good fight. Zuberi re-treated. Some of the survivors are here in Magwi. Some are in Yida or Jamam. Some are in camps in Uganda. So I've been told."

"How did you escape?"

"On my two feet. When I came back from taking you to the airport, the action was just starting. My ride took off without me. I wanted to hide, but Wuster said, 'Get out while you can.' I started walking out. Many people did. I saw the smoke rising where the settlement had been and kept going for maybe two weeks. Then I got a ride to Magwi. I was needed. I stayed."

I wanted to ask about Jemilla and Aziza, but I thought she would tell me that she didn't know where they were. Or that they were dead. I wasn't ready to hear that.

And then Sabeena rolled toward me so that we were lying face to face. She was excited.

"Guess what, Brigid?"

I said, "Give me a hint."

"I got *married*."

"*No.* You *did not*."

She smiled and nodded. Showed me her ring. I squealed. She squealed, too.

I'm sure we woke up some of the patients sleeping in the wards around us, but joyful screaming was on the program.

"Tell me more," I managed to say. "Tell me everything."

"His name is Albert. You'll meet him tomorrow, and he will tell you a lot in great detail. But now, I must ask, what have you been up to, my darling girl? Last time I saw you, you weren't saying anything at all."

I squeezed her hand. She squeezed back.

I told her, "After I was released from the hospital in Amsterdam, I stayed with friends in Rome. And then God showed me a picture of Magwi."

"Did He?"

"How else could I have found you?"

"Then of course He did," said Sabeena. "I'm going to thank Him for this big blessing. But right now, I have rounds. You sleep well, and I'll see you in the morning, Brigid. Sweet dreams."

"I love you, Sabeena."

"Me too, Brigid, dear."

She put a bottle of water on my night table, blew out the candle, and kissed my forehead good night.

CHAPTER 37

MAGWI WASN'T paradise, but it also wasn't hell on earth. There were cattle raids, but so far, there had been no massacres. Nonstop rain made conditions ripe for infectious disease, but fortunately we had antibiotics. The buildings didn't have electricity, but we had fuel for the generator.

People got sick from diseases no longer seen in most of the world, but families stayed on in the tent village outside the clinic and helped care for their loved ones. Often, they sang and danced. I was able to follow up with my patients, and helping them get well helped me, too.

One day during my first weeks in Magwi, I was injecting babies in the midst of a scene of controlled chaos. Kala-azar is a horrific insect-borne disease. Left untreated, it's often fatal. We had enough amphotericin and miltefosine for now, and we had patients' families filling the tents in front of the clinic, helping with patient care. But the shots hurt.

The serum was thick. We had to use big needles, and injections had to be continued every day for a month. Toddlers screamed when they saw me coming, and they fought back. It took two people to keep an angry child still.

That morning, Obit, a boy of twelve, sat down next to me on the blanket as I worked. We had been treating him for an infected foot, and he liked hanging out at the clinic. He was good with the younger children, and now he assisted me and the mothers by holding their infants and distracting them with toys he made out of brush and twigs.

During a rare peaceful moment, he said to me, "Your hair. I have never seen hair like this."

"Red, you mean?"

He asked to touch my hair, and I said, "Sure." I told Obit that I had Irish roots, that my mother had had red hair. Obit became quiet.

"What are you thinking, Obit?"

He teared up and told me that he had no family left, that Zuberi had come to his village and killed everyone.

"They even took down my old grandmother," he told me. "With knives. I saw this. She love everyone. She die hard."

"I'm so sorry, Obit. What was her name?"

"Joya. Grandmother Joya."

There is a radio station in Magwi, and that day I heard that Zuberi's people had attacked the city of Juba. They had captured a hundred and twenty-nine children. They castrated the boys and left them to bleed to death. They had gang-raped the little girls before killing them. Little boys who had been unable to run were roped together, and their throats had been slit.

I couldn't stop thinking about this horror.

God, why? Why didn't You stop this?

That night, I wrote in my journal about the attack on Juba, and then I created a new section and a new page. I called the first entry "This Was Joya." I wrote down what Obit had told me about what his grandmother had taught him, and anecdotes about his parents and siblings, who had been brutally slaughtered.

Since "Joya," I've written sixty memorial stories in my journal. As I recorded Zuberi's crimes against humanity, one real person at a time, I became a historian of bloody murder in South Sudan. I prayed every day that soon, the eyes of the world would be fixed on Colonel Zuberi. And that he would pay on this earth for what he had done to these poor people.

CHAPTER 38

MY FIRST three months in Magwi passed like a med school dream. I worked with Sabeena, and since we could just about read each other's minds, we made an excellent team.

Medical supplies were delivered to the Magwi post office directly from Juba. We received virgin bandages, saline solution, and an autoclave for sterilizing equipment. Most important, we got cases of medicine for kala-azar.

A new doctor joined us from Connecticut. Dr. Susan Gregan was an emergency doctor and as committed as we were. She brought her bubbly personality, a trunk full of paperback thrillers, and a soothing way with the most fearful of patients. Susan liked working the night shift, leaving Sabeena and Albert to their newly wedded bliss in their room at the end of the clinic. I spent my long, lovely nights writing in my room under the eaves.

On this particular day, about three months after my arrival, I noticed that doors closed and conversation stopped at my approach. What was happening?

I found Albert repairing a motor behind the clinic.

Albert was Egyptian, with a degree in electrical engineering. He loved Sabeena madly, and she was wildly in love with him. Albert was in charge of the clinic's mechanicals, especially the critically important generator and water pump. He made up stories for his own amusement and had a truly great laugh. He also cooked.

That morning, a delicious aroma came from the clay oven in the patch of ground beyond the back porch. When I asked Albert what he was baking, he said, "The queen of England is coming. It's special for her."

"Really, Albert? Come on."

He let out a deep, rolling laugh, and when he finally took a breath, I said, "Al, people are acting weird. What's up?"

He smiled up at me. "How old are you, Brigid?"

The scurrying and whispering suddenly made sense. Sabeena trotted down the steps and into the yard. She looked at Albert's face, then mine.

"I guess my big-mouth husband has already ruined the surprise. So, Brigid, close your eyes."

Albert said in a spooky voice, "Nooo peek-ing."

I covered my eyes, and Sabeena spun me around until I was dizzy. I heard a commotion on the steps, and then Sabeena said, "You can open them now."

Two grinning girls stood before me, smiling and plump, their hair braided, and dressed in pretty clothes. They were almost unrecognizable. And then, I *screamed*.

Aziza threw herself at me, and Jemilla did the same. Albert broke into "Happy Birthday," giving it tremendous importance with his baritone voice. Sabeena served the banana cake that Albert had baked in the clay oven, and Dr. Susan somehow produced a bunch of flowers.

I don't remember many of my birthdays, but I'll never forget this one. I was twenty-eight. I was happy. I wanted for nothing. Just before we sliced the cake, I prayed.

"Dear Lord, thank You for leading me to this place, for the good health and safety of these wonderful people, and for this incomparable day. Amen."

That night, the young ladies pushed a bed up to mine so that we could sleep together as we had at Kind Hands. They were living now in Juba, going to school, and no one was suffering that night. We had a window with a screen, clean beds, and full stomachs, and we were surrounded by people we loved.

While Colonel Dage Zuberi was still roaming free and planning genocide, Aziza, Jemilla, and I were snug in the attic room under the eaves.

We were giggling as we floated off to sleep.

CHAPTER 39

I STEELED myself for my trip to the village center of Magwi, which was an hour from the clinic, over a winding and rutted mud road. I had the use of a cart, and I was on good terms with the donkey, an old soldier called Carrot. But this wouldn't be a ride in the park.

Kwame, the nearly toothless young man who had driven me from the airport bus stop to the clinic four months ago, worked at the post office in Magwi. He had called me over the radio channel the previous night and told me that a shipment of antibiotics had arrived for Zuberi's Gray Army.

We had been waiting for this.

I said, "I'll come for the drugs tomorrow. You understand, Kwame? I'm coming."

"Lady, the *Kill on Sight* posters of the doctors at Kind Hands are still on the door. Your face is still up there. Maybe you should stay home."

"Make the calls for me, please, Kwame. Make them now."

On any day, going into town was very dangerous. I was scared but not suicidal. I had a good and very important reason for going to Magwi by myself.

I was going alone, but I wouldn't *be* alone.

I held the crucifix hanging from a chain around my neck, and I prayed. After getting off my knees, I made notes in my journal, then tucked it under my pillow. I got a carrot from the kitchen for the donkey and left a note for Sabeena.

I had to make an emergency call. I'll be back by dinner.

Then, at midday, when everyone was busy inside the clinic, I pulled on my rain slicker over my scrubs, borrowed Albert's waterproof boots without asking, and took off in the cart.

I clucked to Carrot and told him he was a good fellow. He lowered his head and forged through hock-deep water, his hooves sucking at the mud as he pulled me without complaint toward Magwi's small town center.

After about three miles, the dirt track merged with an unpaved two-lane road that morphed into Magwi's main street. I stopped just outside the town and tied Carrot's reins to the branch of a tree. I said, "Best to keep you out of traffic, buddy." I gave him his treat and patted his shoulder.

The post office was located at the far end of the town, on the corner of an intersection of the main street and the road toward Torit. My heart was beating way too fast as I wondered if I would sleep tonight in my bed under the eaves.

Only God knew.

Was He busy with other people or things? Or did He hold this particular sparrow in His hand? Just before I entered the village proper, I spoke out loud, and I put everything I had into it.

"*God?* It's me, Brigid. I really need you. *Now.*"

CHAPTER 40

MAGWI'S MAIN street was only three hundred yards long, lined with decrepit mud-and-wood-frame shacks and shopkeepers selling sleeping mats, cooking oil, and sacks of dried maize. I walked past the open-doored shops, the one-pump gas station, a brick-faced municipal building, and farther along I came to the market where men and women sat under umbrellas and sold produce out of suitcases.

Music and dancing broke out under the steel-gray sky. Beat-up cars, motorcycles, and pedestrians in bright clothing mingled in the street, and men on bikes with bundles on their backs wove through light traffic.

Several cars and trucks, including Kwame's old Dodge junker, were parked at the end of the street, bounding the one-room post office building on two sides. A bare flagpole angled out from the peak of the metal roof, which had been half torn off by a storm. A line of people stood out front, and when I joined the line, they stared.

I smiled, but I was trembling.

As the line crept toward the open front door, I silently rehearsed what I would say when I got to the window inside.

I'm Dr. Fitzgerald, from Magwi Clinic. I'm expecting a package from Juba.

I was focused on the length of the line and the distance to the open doorway ahead. So when I was seized from behind and thrown violently facedown in the mud, I was stunned, and for a long second, my mind scrambled—then I screamed.

I tried to get to my hands and knees, but a voice behind me barked, *"Be still,"* and a heavy boot pressed hard on my back and kept me down. The people who had been in the line and those who had been walking in the street didn't try to help me. They fled. They simply *ran*.

I gagged on mud and my stomach heaved, and that was when I became aware of a blade biting into the skin of my throat. I started to black out, but if I lost consciousness, I would surely die. So, by sheer will, I stayed in the horrifying present.

Then, just as suddenly as I had been thrown down, I was hauled to my feet. I was so weak my knees wouldn't lock, but two men behind me had that covered. One still held his knife to my jugular, and the other gripped my arms so that I couldn't slip to the ground.

A male voice with a trace of an English accent came at me from the street.

"Could this be Dr. Fitzgerald? What a fortunate surprise."

Standing ten feet away, dressed in fatigues, with an AK strapped across his chest, was an average-sized man in his forties, going bald, with black-framed glasses and a beard giving cover to a double chin. He was backed by a half dozen Gray soldiers with clay-smeared faces, all of them heavily armed, and he radiated a powerful presence.

I'd never seen his picture, but I knew I was face-to-face with Colonel Dage Zuberi, a diabolic monster and one of the most terrifying people in the world.

CHAPTER 41

ZUBERI'S SMILE was way too familiar, and he spoke to me as if we were friends.

"Oh. I have wanted to meet you, Dr. Fitz-ger-ald. Brigid, correct? How interesting that we both had business here today."

Zuberi didn't know that I had set up this showdown. Or did he? My pulse boomed in my ears. I couldn't swallow or blink or speak. I couldn't even think. I just stared until he said, "You're afraid? Why, Brigid? Did you do something wrong?"

I was twenty-eight years old, a city girl, a doctor with three years of work under my belt. I wasn't a soldier or a spy. And yet, I had brought this upon myself.

Of course I was afraid. As Christ is the Word made flesh, Zuberi was evil in the flesh. And the reality of that was overwhelming.

I wanted to shout for help, but I didn't dare. Instead I said, "Please ask your man to put down the knife."

"Kofi is his own man," said Zuberi. "Kofi, do you wish to walk away from Dr. Brigid?"

The man behind me scoffed.

I felt the edge of that blade cutting me, and my arms were pinned. I wasn't going anywhere on my own power. I forced myself to say what I'd come here to say.

"Colonel Zuberi—yes, I know who you are. You have killed so many people. Your soldiers have killed mothers and their babies. You've slit the throats of little children and hacked old people to death. Doctors and missionaries who came here to help with food and medicine—you've murdered them, too.

"These terrible acts are an affront to humanity and to God. We are all God's creatures, and He loves us all. How can you dare to take away what God has given?"

Zuberi flicked his eyes up and down, from my eyes to my boots, and when his inventory of my features and baggy clothing was complete, he said, "How do you know what God wants? He speaks to people differently. It's too bad that you can't hold conflicting thoughts in your tiny mind. I expected you to be—I don't know. Smarter. More impressive."

Sighing with disappointment, he pulled a long knife from a scabbard on his hip and walked toward me. It was only a few paces, and he took his time.

My reaction was born of pure, impotent fear.

"Stay where you are!" I shrieked. "I'm an American. Don't you dare screw with me."

The monster was very amused.

"Don't screw with you? I'll decide that. Let me see you first, Doctor. Don't be shy."

I imagined my face on the kill poster tacked inside the post office door. I envisioned my picture and a fresh red stamp across my forehead. *DEAD*.

Blackness swallowed me up, and I just let go.

CHAPTER 42

I HEARD that voice as if from a long way away.

"Wake her."

I was slapped hard across the face, and then the blade was back at my throat. Blood seeped down my neck and mingled with the icy sweat rolling down my body.

Where is the damned cavalry?

I tried to pull away, but, as before, the men behind painfully gripped my arms as Zuberi slipped his blade into the flap of my coat and sliced through the fasteners as though they were made of cheese.

My arms were released long enough for one of the men behind me to yank my opened coat down my back, further pinning my arms to my body. When my upper arms were restrained again, he held his knife to my neck.

I saw deep pleasure on Zuberi's face as he placed his blade precisely at the V-neck of my scrub shirt and cut straight down. Fabric parted with a whisper as the sharp steel divided my shirt, the center of my bra, the elastic of my pants, along with a layer of my skin from my clavicle to my belly.

I screamed with all the air in my lungs and struggled to get my arms free, but I might as well have been nailed to a wall. I knew what was going to happen to me. People were routinely beheaded in South Sudan. I'd seen the decapitated bodies outside the gates. I'd seen detached heads on the killing field.

I tried to send my mind to God, but I was distracted as the monster sheathed his knife and mumbled, "Now, let me see."

He grabbed a fistful of my clothing in each hand and tore my scrubs apart in one movement.

The entire front of my body was naked and exposed.

The Gray soldiers laughed and hooted and gathered around. Instinctively, I tried to cover myself, but it was futile. The man behind me pressed his blade to my throat. I couldn't move.

Zuberi laughed.

"You look better *with* clothes," he said. "No. I don't want to screw with you. I want whatever your stinking government will pay to get you back alive. A million dollars U.S., at least. Thank you, Brigid Fitzgerald, for coming to Magwi."

"They'll pay *nothing!*" I shouted into Zuberi's mocking face. I was helpless. Humiliated. He had won. All I had was the spit in my mouth, a very poor weapon, but I let it fly.

My saliva hit Zuberi between the eyes.

It was a feeble gesture, but Zuberi went crazy, wiping frantically with his sleeve as though I'd flung acid in his face. He cursed me in a language I didn't know.

And as I expected, the man standing directly behind me grabbed my hair and pulled my head back, baring my throat to the leaden, drizzling sky.

He growled, "Do you love life? Apologize to Colonel Zuberi or die."

I had written to Sabeena, *I'll be back by dinner.* That had been a wish, a prayer, and, although I had been bluffing, I had visualized my triumphal return.

I had thought too highly of myself. I had thought I could do the impossible. I saw that now. No more than three minutes had passed since Zuberi's men had grabbed me from the line outside the post office. I'd accomplished nothing. I never had a chance.

Dear God. Forgive me my trespasses. I'm ready.

CHAPTER 43

I FLUNG the doors of my mind wide open to God and braced for death. But He didn't speak to me. Rather, I heard pops of gunfire, and in a pause, a distinctly American voice shouted, *"Drop the knife!"*

The blade bit into my neck and I fully expected to feel it slide across my throat. Instead, there was more gunfire. The man with the knife grunted and fell to the mud at my feet. The one holding my arms also dropped, moaning and coughing out his last breath.

I didn't hesitate.

I dove for the ground and covered the back of my neck with my hands.

There were more shots, and then a heavy-duty vehicle tore around the corner from the main street and braked within yards of me. I stayed down as bullets strafed the street. A third man, part of Zuberi's armed guard, ran, and he too was cut down.

I lifted my face and saw Zuberi, along with several of his men, zigzagging around the bodies and running toward the odd assortment of vehicles parked across the street.

Another salvo of bullets chattered, and someone grabbed my arm. I wrenched it away.

I heard, "Lady, it's *me*."

It was *Kwame*. It was *Kwame*.

He helped me to my feet, and we ran to the side of the post office. From there, I saw a truck swerve to avoid a pedestrian and collide with a car, which in turn skidded into another car. In the midst of the chaos, Zuberi had reached his Land Rover and had gotten in beside a driver.

Kwame yelled, *"He's going now!"*

Zuberi's Land Rover rammed into a parked car in front, then backed into a truck behind it. The driver was trying to make an opening, an avenue of escape, and, in fact, the nose of the vehicle now had a clear shot at the road to Torit.

But as the Land Rover lurched ahead, two U.S. Army Humvees roared up and blocked it.

American soldiers poured out of their Humvees. Bullets sprayed Zuberi's ride, killing his driver. Zuberi stuck his hands up and shouted, "Stop shooting! I give up!"

Soldiers pulled open the doors and dragged Zuberi out of the Land Rover, then slammed him across the hood and stripped him of his weapons.

I heard Kwame saying, "Lady. Look here."

He had taken off his long, boxy shirt, and after peeling off my raincoat, he stuck my numb arms through his shirtsleeves. I couldn't manage buttonholes, so Kwame closed the shirt for me, picked up my raincoat, and draped it over my shoulders.

Someone called my name.

I looked up as a gray-haired U.S. Army officer bolted out of a junker parked on the same side of the street as the post office. Holstering his gun, he hurried over to where Kwame and I stood. I blinked stupidly as the officer said, "Dr. Fitzgerald? I'm Captain Jeff Gurney. We spoke last night. Are you hurt?"

I shook my head no, but my hand went to where the knife had sliced into my throat. I was bleeding, but the chain around my neck, the one Tori had given me with a crucifix, had stopped the blade from cutting into my artery.

I closed my hand around the crucifix.

Thank you, God.

Captain Gurney said, "I'm sorry for what those men did to you, Dr. Fitzgerald. We were watching you the whole time, but I'm no sniper. I was waiting for support, but this situation went critical so fast. Finally, I had to risk it."

I got it now. It was Gurney who had shouted, *"Drop the knife!"* Then he had taken his shots. If his aim had been slightly off in any direction, he could have shot me.

I thanked him for saving my life, and he thanked me in turn. "Your courage is amazing, Dr. Fitzgerald. Because of you, Zuberi is out of the game."

The captain introduced himself to Kwame, saying, "Good work connecting the dots, sir. First-class job."

Kwame was smiling now, shaking the captain's hand with both of his. He had been the perfect go-between. He had conspired with me. He had let Zuberi know that a package had arrived. He had contacted the army and made arrangements with Gurney. As Gurney had said, Kwame had done a first-class job.

My voice quavered when I said to Kwame, "I know what you risked for me. Thank you. I'm your friend for life."

"You are the brave one, lady. You did this. You stood up to Zuberi. Only you."

We hugged hard, both of us crying.

Is it over? Am I going to live?

And then, the noise on the street got even louder.

CHAPTER 44

A SOFT flutter overhead turned into a loud, choppy roar as helicopters settled down on the street. Tarps and umbrellas took flight, and people shrieked as they ran from the whirling blades.

While our soldiers looked on with guns in their hands, the onlookers who had fled the shooting returned, and now they circled Zuberi. They shouted into his face. They used stout sticks like baseball bats, swinging and connecting solidly with Zuberi's back and thighs.

When I looked again, Zuberi was naked, lying facedown in the mud. He cried for help. He ordered people to leave him alone. He covered his head with his arms. But the blows kept coming.

Gurney shouted to me over the racket of helicopter engines, "Dr. Fitzgerald! We have to get you out of here. Stay with me!"

"You'll take me to Magwi Clinic?" I shouted.

He looked at me with stark disbelief.

"You're kidding, right? Doctor. You just baited the trap. If you don't leave now, Zuberi's troops will kill you, *today*. Tell me you understand."

"Captain, I can't just *go*. I have patients. I have people depending on me. Thank you, though. Be safe."

I turned away and headed up the street to where I had tied the donkey. Gurney stopped me by grabbing my arm, and, you know, I'd had enough of being manhandled today.

"Let go of me."

I pulled my arm free and began to run in my oversized boots. I was desperate. I had to get to Sabeena and tell her what had happened. I had to warn her to leave the clinic. Because of me, she might be the next target.

But Gurney wouldn't take no from me. He chased me down, grabbed me by the shoulders, spun me around, and held on until I stopped fighting him.

He shouted, "You're being crazy!"

"My *friends* could be in *danger.* Don't you *understand? I have to tell them to get out."*

Gurney held on to my shoulders and shook his head.

"You're a kid, Brigid. Listen up, as if I were your father. If you don't leave here now, you are going to die today."

I glared at him and could almost hear Colin telling me to get into the helicopter, saying that it was time to go. If I had listened to Colin, he might still be alive. His death was on me.

I said to Gurney, "I'm *not* a kid. And you're *not* my father. Don't you understand that I'm responsible?"

"I have responsibility, *too.* Say I let you go. You walk about three hours or so to the clinic. You warn your friends. And then what? You have no backup, no escape plan. Picture it, okay? Really picture that."

I got it. I saw a massacre. White coats spattered with blood. Bodies in heaps.

I said, "You have to evacuate the clinic. Promise me you'll get the doctors out."

"I promise."

"You'll do it *now?"*

"Yes. Now."

Would he do it? Would he get to the clinic in time?

After Gurney released me, he walked me back to the helicopter and helped me into a seat. He buckled me in, then spoke to the pilot.

He shouted to me, "Good luck, Brigid!" Then he climbed back down.

The blades whirled, and the helicopter vibrated. In the moment before we left the ground, I looked down at the mob surrounding Zuberi. He was bloodied, and the crowd was still beating him, shouting and throwing rocks at him.

Just when I thought they had killed him, a man in a blue shirt turned Zuberi over so that he was lying faceup, then used the stock of Zuberi's own gun to break his knees.

Zuberi was rolling from side to side in agony when two American soldiers jerked him up off the ground and dragged him toward another helicopter.

The chopper I was in lifted.

We were peeling off when a flickering movement on the side of the street caught my attention. It was Kwame.

He was waving good-bye.

CHAPTER 45

ONCE WE were airborne, I slipped into a kind of shock.

Within a ridiculously short period of time, I'd been terrified, humiliated, and bloodied, and now I had been officially kidnapped. I didn't know where I was going or even if our military had the right to take me out of Magwi.

What now?

I shivered in Kwame's shirt and the remains of my raincoat as the helicopter delivered me to the Juba airport. A jeep was waiting, and the chopper pilot handed me off to the driver, a U.S. Air Force lieutenant named Karen Triebel. She gave me a temporary American passport and a knapsack, and as she drove to the terminal, she told me that the knapsack contained a tracksuit, a bottle of Advil, bandages, and a tube of triple-antibiotic ointment.

"Let's get you cleaned up," she said.

"I've got this," I told her.

Still, she accompanied me to a ladies' room inside the terminal, where I washed my wounds and tossed my ripped clothing into the trash, an unceremonious conclusion to my last four months in South Sudan.

Within the hour, Lieutenant Triebel and I were streaking toward Entebbe, Uganda. There, we boarded another flight, this one bound for the U.S. Air Force base in Ramstein, Germany.

I slept hard on the plane and had violent dreams that I couldn't remember whenever I was awoken to eat. I had no appetite for food. Instead, I looked out at the clouds and formed the thought, *Lord? Was this Your plan?*

Even if I had been delusional when I'd last "spoken" with God, I wanted to feel His presence again. But all I heard was my own anxious chatter visiting every front: past, present, and unknowable future. *Where am I going? What will happen next?*

Lieutenant Triebel had shaken out her hair and was putting on a sleep mask when I touched her arm.

"Brigid. You okay?"

I asked, "What will happen to Zuberi?"

She said, "I don't know. Maybe he'll fall out of a helicopter. Or maybe that just wouldn't be bad enough for that bastard."

Twelve hours after we left Uganda, we landed at Ramstein. Lieutenant Triebel accompanied me to the base hospital, where I was kept overnight for observation. In the morning, the doctor said, "Surprisingly, you're good to go."

Triebel and I were driven to a square, stucco-faced house within rows of identical houses close to the base. I was given a key to the upstairs apartment, and Triebel had the apartment below.

"Right now, my job is all about you," she said, turning the key in the lock. "Whatever you need, I'll do my best to make it happen. Tomorrow, you need to brief some government men on whatever you know about Zuberi. After that, just do what makes you happy. Here's a tablet and a phone, Brigid. Call someone you love."

CHAPTER 46

I CALLED Tori, my dear school friend, living with her husband in Rome.

As soon as I heard her sweet voice, I broke down.

I burbled into the mouthpiece about the crucifix she had given me, how the chain had stopped the blade at my neck. She got the gist of what had gone down and comforted me. Her husband, Marty, got on the phone after that and said, "You should get a medal. Or a town named after you. Brigidsville."

Finally, I laughed.

Then Marty said, "Zachary is in New York. You want his number? Or should I give him yours?"

I called and got Zach's outgoing voice mail.

"I'm on assignment in New York. Leave a message, and I'll call back."

I spoke into my phone: "Yank. It's Red. I'm in Ramstein, Germany, calling to say hello."

I was both disappointed and relieved that Zach hadn't answered, but he called back at three in the morning his time.

"What's wrong?" he asked.

"I was kicked out of Africa for my own good," I told him.

"I'll come to Ramstein," he said.

"Funny, Zach, but, seriously, that makes no sense."

Zach said, "You keep fending me off, Brigid. Why? You know you want to see me. I've grown a beard."

I told him that I was the guest of the U.S. Air Force at present, and I sketched in some of what had gone down in Magwi. After answering a couple of questions, I changed the subject by asking Zach to tell me about his New York assignment.

"I'm tailing the Yankees. It's that time of year."

"Sounds like fun."

"Keep my phone number handy," he said. "I return calls at night. Brigid. Please take care."

After we hung up, I went to the beautiful, white-tiled bathroom, turned on the shower, and got inside. I sat in the corner of the tub, soaking my wounds while doing my rounds of Magwi Clinic in my mind. I said good-bye to all the patients and volunteers and especially to Obit. I hugged Sabeena, and then I sobbed for a long time under the hot water.

When I got out of the shower, I felt, at the very least, clean. The apartment had a stocked fridge, a television, a bookcase, an excellent shower, and a soft bed. I wanted for nothing.

I went to my knees at the side of my bed. I folded my hands and closed my eyes.

Dear God, if You can hear me, I humbly thank You for saving my life. Please protect Sabeena, Albert, Dr. Susan, and everyone at Magwi Clinic. And put Your arms around Kwame, who was so brave. I hope he found Carrot and took him home. Amen.

CHAPTER 47

I WAS still dazed by all that had happened when, the next morning, I was taken to Ramstein for a series of debriefings. I told various officials from several American agencies all that I knew about Zuberi. And I was briefed in return.

Fantastic news.

Sabeena, Albert, and Dr. Susan had all been evacuated from Magwi. I was given a box of my things from my room at the clinic. My hands shook as I opened the box and found my well-traveled leather hobo bag with my actual credentials inside, along with my nubby sweater. Under the sweater, wrapped in my jeans, was my journal, with a note just inside the cover.

Mission accomplished. Best regards, J. Gurney, Captain, U.S. Army

I was overjoyed for the news of my friends' safety. And I was ecstatic to have my journal back in my hands. This euphoria lasted until I was back inside my temporary apartment.

Then my new reality set in.

After the few meetings at the base, I had nothing but time to myself. I was invited out, but going from the takedown in Magwi to restaurants with strangers was just a bridge too far.

I copied my old journal onto my new tablet, added new entries, and wrote for long hours at a time, and I drank. Quite a bit.

I was safe and I was comfortable and it was a luxury to drink as much as it took to dull the pain in my heart. But after drinking and moping for far longer than was good for me, something finally snapped. I was sick of myself. Really. What a joke to indulge myself in self-pity. Me. This thought led to the next.

I had had purpose in Africa.

Whether I'd returned to Africa because of the voice of God or my own need to do something worthwhile, I had gone. I had helped people. My life had had meaning. I'd stood up to Zuberi and helped to bring him down.

Who was I now?

That night, I was drinking my dinner and watching TV.

Most of it was stupid, but while watching the news, I learned about MERS, an infectious disease that, after killing thousands in Saudi Arabia, had spread to Europe.

MERS was a freaking stealthy virus. No one knew how it spread—was it airborne? food borne? It was entirely inconsistent. One person could be struck with severe pneumonia, and another would be asymptomatic until just before death.

The World Health Organization had issued a report on MERS saying that this disease had a mortality rate of almost 40 percent, that there was no known effective cure, and that there were reasonable concerns that MERS would become a pandemic.

A *pandemic*?

I ran downstairs and banged on Karen Triebel's door.

She had cream on her face. Her hair was wrapped in a towel. She tied the sash of her robe.

"Brigid?"

"You know about MERS, Karen? I'm actually an expert on infectious diseases," I told her. "Please hook me up with a hospital or, better yet, a clinic."

"Let me see what I can do," she said.

CHAPTER 48

BECAUSE OF my new military connection, an apartment was waiting for me when I arrived in Berlin. It was a wonderfully crazy little place, with bright colors and patterns, big windows, and a spun-glass chandelier over the dining table. The bedroom was huge, with a bed so large, it could have slept four, and, best of all, it had a balcony off the living room with a fifth-floor view of the park.

First thing the next morning, I put on an actual skirt, a smart blouse, and low heels and went for a job interview at the Berlin Center for Torture Victims.

BZFO, as the clinic was called, specialized in treating refugee patients from forty countries, mainly Middle Eastern, but there were African patients as well.

The clinic was new and looked immaculate. My interviewer, Dr. Mary Maillet, wore a severe black suit, red combs in her wavy, gray hair, and lime-green-framed glasses, making her look simultaneously warm and tough.

She told me that the staff at BZFO was made up of multidisciplinary doctors and therapists of all kinds. Then she sat back in her swivel chair and grilled me about my training and my experience in South Sudan.

I was describing our 24-7 surgery at Kind Hands when she interrupted me to say, "When can you start?"

"I have the job?"

"We'll be lucky to have you, Brigid. Welcome to BZFO."

I started at the clinic the next morning, and I stayed late into the night. My new patients had terrible physical injuries and profound emotional ones. They were all refugees with horrific stories like the ones I'd heard in South Sudan.

A young woman named Amena, just twenty-three, had escaped from war-shredded Syria. Her town had been shelled either by ISIS or Assad, from which side of the conflict, she didn't know. Her beloved husband and two young boys had been killed in the blast. She had lost an eye, and her neck and hands had been burned. But, still, she had escaped, making a long and arduous journey by foot and boat and train to Berlin.

Amena said to me, "God is great, Dr. Fitzgerald."

Her faith in the face of appalling tragedy simply brought me to tears.

"You are great, *too,* Amena. Now, please, cough for me."

Within the week, I was seeing patients with flu-like symptoms. I had worked with Ebola, HIV, and kala-azar, and now I was tackling MERS in a new infectious-disease quarantine wing at the torture clinic. I was helping desperately sick people, and they needed me. I needed them, too.

And then I got sick myself.

CHAPTER 49

ONE MINUTE I was tending to a patient.

The next, I had collapsed in her room.

I was helped to a bed, where I hacked and threw up and wheezed for days I couldn't remember, and I was so weak, I couldn't sit up. I had feverish sleep in which I felt as though I were drowning. I dreamed of Africa during the flood season and that I was sinking to the muddy floor of the White Nile. I heard my own underwater screams.

I wanted to die.

In conscious moments, I grabbed my chart from the end of the bed, and I read the stark truth. My white blood cells were losing the battle against the disease.

I was going to get my dying wish.

I'd always heard that God works in mysterious ways. Now I was right there at the heart of the mystery. I had survived the plagues of Africa, bullets and near death on the killing field. I'd survived the blade at my neck, only to lose my life to a virus inside a clean German clinic.

I used some of those lucid moments to reflect on what I had done with God's gift of life, now that I had lived out the extent of it.

Images of my childhood, my school years, the people I'd loved and ones I hadn't loved well enough, flashed through my mind in random order and vivid color. Although I prayed, I didn't look for a connection to God.

I just wanted to leave.

I dropped off into a haze of watery memories, and sometime later, I came out of this sweaty dream state with a normal temperature and a great thirst. I knew that I was past the worst of it. I had survived.

I thanked God humbly, passionately, and then I asked Dr. Maillet for a report on the patients in the MERS wing. My wing.

She dragged a chair up to the side of my bed.

"I don't have great news, Brigid. Half our patients were transferred to Charité."

She was talking about the largest, most advanced hospital in Berlin. That was good, wasn't it?

"Why only half our patients?" I asked.

"Fourteen people died. I'm sorry to have to tell you this, Brigid. That sweet girl from Syria. Amena. She asked about you before she passed away last night."

Amena's death was devastating. I hadn't known her well, but she was like so many people I had known who had come through Job-like adversity with shining optimism and glowing faith.

It wasn't *fair*. It wasn't *right*. *Why did it happen?*

I broke down in deep sobs, and when Dr. Maillet failed to comfort me, she injected me with a sedative, and I fell into a deep, drug-induced sleep.

I didn't want to wake up.

It felt to me that God had forsaken me and everyone on earth.

CHAPTER 50

THE THIRTY of us from the BZFO clinic had gathered at the edge of the pond in Volkspark to say a few words about our patients who had died from MERS.

We all looked how we felt: heartsick, exhausted, and breaking down from frustration because the disease was still taking lives, and nothing had been found that could stop it.

At the same time, other epic tragedies were erupting around the planet: earthquakes where none had been before, and opportunistic disease that swept into ruined cities and killed tens of thousands. Financial collapses had bankrupted countries, induced even more poverty, and swept corporations, along with potential technological and medical advances, off the table. Crazed shooters got away with mass murders in malls and schools, and the genocide in sub-Saharan Africa not only continued but intensified.

Why was all of this happening?

Was God testing humanity? Or was He unwilling to intervene?

When it was my turn to speak at the service, I thought of Amena, that sweet, young widowed mother of two dead children. I pictured her scarred face and empty eye socket, and how she glowed like a neon sign in the dark with her love of God.

I said to my friends and coworkers, "You know that Amena survived what for most would have been soul-crushing tragedy—the loss of her home and entire family. But she rallied, and she was brimming with life and faith.

"I wished I had gotten to know Amena better. I would have loved to have been her friend. She told me that she had spoken with her dead boys since their deaths, and she said, 'Don't be sad for me, Dr. Fitzgerald. I will be with them again.'"

I teared up as I searched inside myself for an authentic, hopeful note that would represent Amena's undiluted faith. Just then, a small bird flew across my line of sight and skimmed the glittering surface of the pond before disappearing into the tree shadows.

I snapped back into the present.

I said, "I am thinking of Amena now. Her husband sits with his arms around her, and her children are in her lap. I see her safely reunited with God."

Was she with God? Really? Was God real? If so, did He care?

The sun was still high when the service ended.

I was still weak and depressed and thought I would simply walk home to my quirky apartment, write a journal entry about today's service, and then drop into a dead sleep in the huge bed. I was heading toward Friedenstrasse when a gentleman coming up behind me on the same path called out, "Dr. Fitzgerald, may I give you a ride?"

I recognized Karl Lenz, one of BZFO's benefactors. I'd seen him at the clinic but was surprised that he seemed to know me. Still, I wasn't feeling chatty.

"Thanks anyway, Mr. Lenz. It's a short walk."

"Please. Call me Karl. Would you mind if I might walk with you?" he said. "I feel pretty awful, and I'm not ready to be alone."

"Of course not," I said.

We skipped the small talk and jumped right into the horrific week at the clinic. Karl said that he was relieved our MERS caseload had been moved to Charité. "We just weren't equipped for it," he said.

We had reached the edge of the park by then, and Karl asked me to lunch. I found that I wasn't ready to be alone, either.

CHAPTER 51

A TAXICAB took us to Patio Restaurantschiff, a glass-enclosed restaurant on a boat moored on the Spree River.

I'd been complaining about life; then, in pretty much the next moment, a chair was pulled out for me, and a napkin dropped into my lap in one of the prettiest little restaurants in all of Berlin.

I do have restaurant German but was happy to turn the ordering of lunch over to Karl. He chose a fish soup, venison goulash with chanterelles, and a Künstler Riesling. I couldn't help but look him over as he spoke with the waiter.

Karl looked to be in his mid to late fifties. He had good-uncle features—glasses and longish, gray-streaked dark hair. He also looked fit, and I loved that he had such expressive hands.

When the wine had been poured and the waiter was gone, Karl let me know that he was aware of my life-over-death battle with MERS. That I had almost died.

"How are you feeling now?" he asked me.

I said, "I'm not running laps around the Tiergarten, but I can tie my shoes without falling over. With my eyes closed. Pretty good, right?"

"I have to say this, Brigid. Doctors like you are why I support BZFO. Dr. Maillet told me a little about your background. I don't want to embarrass you, but for a young woman with so many opportunities to make money and live well, to risk your life in South Sudan—well, it's pretty impressive. Ach. I've embarrassed you now."

"It's fine," I said. "But tell me about yourself. You're a writer?"

"A playwright, yes," he told me. "For me, writing plays is about the most perfect work imaginable."

Karl told me about his play in progress, a political satire, and from there, we talked about geopolitics along the world's worst fault lines. He was fully aware of the bloody civil war in South Sudan, and even after the dishes had been cleared away, we were still discussing the senseless conflict that was destroying the country.

"Greed and corruption are the root cause of this," he said.

I saw it in his face: he actually *felt* the pain of the war. And after two and a half glasses of wine, I found myself telling Karl about my epic clash with Dage Zuberi.

It was a hard story to tell, but I felt as if I'd known Karl well and for a long time. And as I talked about that day in Magwi, I could see that Karl felt my pain, too.

We were politely thrown out of the restaurant so that it could be set up for dinner, and Karl did give me a ride the few blocks to my apartment.

Once home, I kicked off my shoes and emailed Sabeena. She was living in Mumbai with Albert, and they had adopted Jemilla and Aziza.

I wrote, *Sabeena, guess what? I've made a new friend in Berlin.*

CHAPTER 52

I HAD hardly hung my bag up behind the exam-room door when Dr. Maillet waved me into her office.

She pushed her green-framed glasses back into her hair and said, "Brigid, as much as you like the overnight shift, I'm putting you on days only. Get your strength back. Eat. Sleep. We need you to be in top form so we can exploit your youth and stamina later on."

"Done," I said.

She laughed. She had been expecting a fight. "Good," she said. "Now take the night off."

Since we'd closed our infectious-disease wing, I was attached to BZFO's day clinic, and it was almost a vacation.

I didn't miss the violence of South Sudan. I didn't miss the upside-down days of breakfast at midnight, tinned ham at dawn. I practiced everyday medicine on refugee patients who had never had a routine doctor's appointment before coming to Berlin.

I cleaned wounds. I set bones. I prescribed medication, and I sat in sunlit rooms with patients who, over paper cups of sugary tea, told me stories of savagery that I both understood and would never understand. I made friends with my coworkers, and I went on dates—nothing serious, but I was happy and enjoying every day, and in this way, two years passed.

Sometimes Karl stopped by the clinic at day's end, gathered up everyone who was heading out, and took us to dinner in a local tavern, a *wirtschaft,* up the street.

He was the best kind of patron: supportive and a great listener, and he was a hilarious storyteller, too. One evening as I was leaving work, Karl invited me to see the rehearsal of his play *Der Zug.*

He had told me that the one-act play took place entirely on a train platform. Characters representing people from all over Europe waited for a train that does not come, a send-up of the unmet expectations of the eurozone.

Karl met me at the stage door to the Kleines Theater, on the Südwestkorso. He showed me around backstage and introduced me to the actors and the crew.

Clearly, Karl had told them about me.

They hugged me. Told me how they admired the work I was doing. And Karl stood by nervously, looking as if he was pacing inside his head as he waited for the curtain to go up on the train that would not come.

We sat together in the front row, and when the rehearsal began, I was completely drawn in. The set was so *real*—with the rumbles coming over the sound system, the intermittent dimming of overhead lights—that I felt that I was sitting on the platform right across the track.

The characters were a Greek leftist, an Italian economist, a Spanish millionaire, a Belgian bureaucrat, and a Polish plumber. They were first shown at ease, and then under increasing pressure, reacting in idiosyncratic ways.

There was a beautifully comic moment when the expectation of the coming train peaked. The actors leaned forward, air whooshed up from under their feet, and they turned their heads to see *der zug* rush by. Their quizzical expressions as they stared at one another were priceless.

I laughed out loud, that two-part giggle followed by a belly laugh that Zach had pinned on me, and Karl, sitting next to me, wrapped me in a spontaneous hug. Then he kissed me.

Karl Lenz *kissed* me.

CHAPTER 53

KARL'S KISS surprised the hell out of me.

First, there was the fact of that kiss, and even more unsettling was the electricity that came along with it that kind of lit me up.

Karl was my friend. And now?

He took my hand, and as the play went on in front of us, I stared at *him*. I was not cool. Karl smiled, squeezed my hand, and when the action on the stage broke for a discussion with the lighting man, Karl leaned toward me and whispered, "Don't be shocked. I love you, Brigid."

"What? No, you don't."

"I do. I fell for you the moment I saw Mary congratulate you on getting the job. It was just that instantaneous. And now that I know you, I want to be with you. I want to make you happy. I want to give to you. I want to marry you."

"Karl," I whispered fiercely back. "That's *crazy*. We've only known each other..."

"As friends?"

I nodded.

"I had to tell you or explode," he said. "Okay, Brigid. Maybe I see us as more than friends, eh? Or maybe this gives us an opportunity to see what we might have. No rush. We can spend as much time together as we want. Why not?"

I thought of several reasons why not, and all of them surfaced in my mind as the rehearsal commenced and I stared ahead at the stage.

Karl *was* crazy. He didn't know me or my moods and habits or what had made me the person I am. And I knew only one side of his story.

Another thing—I'd never dreamed of getting married, didn't know the first thing about being a wife, or if that was anything I should ever do. And, by the way, Karl was almost old enough to be my *father.*

I flashed on my heady feelings for Colin and even Zach, which were tumultuous, a little wild, a little dangerous. Karl didn't ride a scooter at sixty miles an hour in crazy traffic. He didn't risk his life in a medical battlefield. He wrote plays. He drove an old Daimler.

But—I liked that. Karl made me feel safe and cared about. I had come to treasure his friendship. I liked his complexity and his kindness. I liked him as a human being. As a man.

Were those reasons to marry him? He had said, *No rush.*

"Say something, Brigid, will you? I feel a little lost right now," Karl said.

"I'm sorry. I forgot something."

I stumbled across his knees as he stood up to let me out to the aisle. "Stay," I told him. "I have to go. I'll call you."

I marched up the dark aisle and out the lobby door, onto the Südwestkorso. I was running again. I knew that running was old stuff, but my feet took me through and around clumps of pedestrians and all the way around the block.

What's with you? I asked the air. *What's your problem, Brigid?* And I wondered. If not now, when? If not Karl, who?

Was that a reason to get married?

I stood again in front of the theater and looked up at the sign reading DAS THEATER IST GESCHLOSSEN. "The theater is closed."

I, too, was closed. The last time I had loved a man, he had died.

I knocked on the lobby door, and a young woman let me inside. I entered the dark lobby and went down the carpeted aisle, at last slipping into the seat next to Karl, in the front row. He whispered, "Are you all right?"

"Yes," I said to Karl. "Yes, I'm okay. Yes, I would love to be your wife."

"Really?"

"Really."

Karl kissed me again. I took his face in my hands and kissed him back. The lights came on. The assemblage applauded the performance, and they turned to give Karl an enthusiastic hand. It was a standing ovation.

We both started to laugh. It was as if everyone had known except for me. I was going to marry Karl Lenz. He was going to be my husband.

CHAPTER 54

AT SEVEN A.M., I was sitting in a pew in Herz Jesu Kirche, the Church of the Sacred Heart, only two blocks from where I lived with my husband, Karl.

I still found it hard to believe that I had gotten married in a Lutheran church, wearing a long, white, and completely perfect wedding dress, surrounded by Karl's family and good and shared friends from BZFO and *Der Zug*.

I'm pretty sure God had been there, too.

These past months were so unlike my previous life, it was almost comical. *Who are you now, Brigid? Is this you?*

As soon as we were settled into "our" three-room, top-floor apartment in the arty neighborhood of Prenzlauer Berg, Karl showed me Berlin. We walked miles, saw monuments and parks and stunning architecture. We went to the theater, of course, and I bought a new wardrobe because we were invited to so many dinner parties and benefits.

I'm a plain-looking woman, but when Karl looked at me, I felt like a cover girl. When we weren't having nights out in the city, we nestled down in the study, where both of us did our writing.

I would read lines for Karl's new play in progress, and sometimes my reading was so hilarious that Karl would say, "Terrible, Brigid. Terrible. Now I have to write that again. It will never sound good to me after that reading."

I laughed so hard, and so did he.

While Karl struggled with his play, I wrote in my journal of human tragedy, one person at a time. When I put my writing into his hands, he read each word, never skimming, never patronizing. Once he said to me, "I tell you this, Brigid. Your writing is unflinching truth. You're a better writer than I am."

"Oh, shut up."

"Trust me."

Having never lived with a man before, I had to learn my way around Karl. He could get cranky when he was writing, either in his head or on his laptop. If I clashed pots in the kitchen or asked questions while he was "in the zone," our happy flow could get interrupted. I was slow to apologize, but Karl was apologizer in chief and the best at hugging it out.

Sometimes, in bed late at night, I would awake with a start, thinking that I was back at Kind Hands, that Jemilla and Aziza had crawled into bed with me and that Sabeena was waking me up because someone was dying in the O.R.

But, no, thank God.

I was lying with my arms around the big, snoring man I trusted and loved with my whole heart.

Now, inside this lovely neighborhood church with the stained glass behind the altar throwing brilliant light on the stone floor, I had some things to say to God.

I thanked Him for the baby I was carrying inside me and for the happiness that filled me up from the bottom of my soles to the ends of my incorrigible red hair, and every part of me in between.

Pretty good joke on me, Lord. This is what I get for doubting You. I get everything good in the world. I am pretty sure You knew all of this, but I am more surprised than even You can imagine. How is it that I sit here, when six years ago I was full of bullet holes, stuck in a subterranean depression, barely alive at all?

I sometimes can't be sure if this life is real. Is this a peek at my future? Am I dreaming? Or, dear God, is this my actual life? Am I allowed to have all of this?

I waited for an answer, and I heard nothing.

But I didn't need the voice of God to tell me what was self-evident. The pews were solid cherry. The altarpiece was bejeweled gold supported by columns of marble. And a stained-glass Jesus Christ spread his arms wide open to me.

I am thankful, Lord. I will be the best wife, doctor, mother, friend, that I can possibly be. With Your help.

Amen.

I felt woozy when I got to my feet. I steadied myself with a hand on the back of the pew, thinking for a moment how nice it would be to go back to bed. If only. I flashed on my full day at BZFO, which would unfurl from the moment I stepped through the doorway.

I had just promised God that I would be the best possible doctor, despite the risks to myself and the little one curled up inside me.

I whispered out loud, "God, please watch over us."

I crossed myself. And then I went to work.

CHAPTER 55

I HAD brought hundreds of babies into the world, during floods and droughts and in the black of night, holding a flashlight between my jaws.

However, because I might not be able to deliver my own child so easily, I was under the care of a superb ob-gyn at Charité, a world-class hospital.

Karl had purchased an apartment next to ours and opened a doorway between the two units, and, using our combined talents, we made the sweetest of nests for the baby we were expecting.

I continued to work the easy shift at BZFO, wearing loose clothing and shoes with good rubber soles.

Karl cooked delicious dinners and doted on me. We spent long evenings in his study writing in matching lounge chairs under the windows. This was really the best of times. I began to read more, and my writing improved in the sanctuary of a writers' room for two as I turned sketches written in the trenches of Magwi Clinic into tight prose.

I wasn't prepared for my water to break while I was on duty at BZFO, but, of course, that was how it happened. I said, "I can handle this."

But I was suddenly afraid to cross this threshold.

Would my baby be all right? Would he or she be healthy and strong? What was I supposed to do now?

Dr. Maillet had Karl on speed dial.

He drove me to Charité himself, and he stayed with me while I labored and gave birth. Giving myself over to the greater wisdom of my doctor was one kind of miracle. Holding this child Karl and I had made was like a supernova of love that both humbled and expanded me.

I hugged our baby daughter to my breast, the two of us enclosed in Karl's embrace, and I thanked God for the beautiful gift of this precious new life.

And Karl did take videos, priceless little movies of me flushed and worn out but giddy, nursing my bitty baby girl, who had red hair like mine.

We named her after St. Teresa, and we called her Tre. We both stayed at home for a month with Tre, and then, while Karl worked in his at-home studio and I went back to BZFO, a visiting nurse took care of our daughter.

I came home every night to my job as Tre's personal stand-up come-dienne, hoping to get our baby to smile. And then, at six weeks, while I wore a toy elephant on my head and made funny noises, she gave me a genuine non-gassy grin. My little girl laughed.

That laugh triggered me to send a note and photo "home" to Cam-bridge. I felt obligated, and I wasn't disappointed when I didn't hear back.

I started a new journal for Tre, Karl, and me.

This book was devoid of horror stories, completely personal, and with-out any commercial merit at all. In other words, it was perfect. I noted the firsts. I pressed a fine, red curl between pages. I stuck in cards from friends and took photos of gifts and opened a Facebook page for Tre.

I was having a perfect life.

God was great. What could possibly go wrong?

CHAPTER 56

I WAS working in the peach-colored exam room at BZFO, giving an injection to someone else's darling baby, when Dr. Maillet appeared at the doorway. Her expression was frozen, as if she was in shock.

I excused myself and went to Dr. Maillet, who pulled me through the doorway and closed the door behind us.

I said, "What's wrong?"

"I'm sorry to tell you, Brigid. There's been an accident," she said. "It's Karl. It's Tre, too."

I stared at her for a long second; then my fear caught up with her words and exploded inside me like a bomb.

I shouted, "NO! *What happened? Both* of them? *That's crazy.*" Her mouth moved, but she didn't speak.

I pictured a car accident and immediately thought, *Karl and Tre will be all right.* The car was *big.* It had seat belts and air bags and a kiddie seat in back. I ducked into the exam room, grabbed my bag, and ran toward the exit, with Mary Maillet following me.

"Wait. *Brigid.*"

I stopped running and half-turned to face her.

She had clasped her hands under her chin and looked absolutely stricken when she said, "Karl is dead. It may have been cardiac arrest. I'm so sorry. He had Tre with him in a Baby Björn when he fell down the stairs."

"*What* stairs? What are you *talking* about? *Where are they?*"

"I'll drive you to the hospital," Maillet said.

During that frantic, frustrating, stop-and-go drive to Charité, Maillet told me that Karl had been found at the foot of a long flight of stone stairs in Volkspark. The baby had been strapped across his chest and had hit her head on the treads when he fell on top of her.

"She's in the ICU," Maillet told me.

That, I remember.

I was screaming inside my head, seeing ahead to the hospital, to the ICU, to shoving people aside to get to my child. I begged God, *Please, please, let her be all right.*

I got out of the car before it stopped. I bulled my way through reception and onto the ICU floor, crashing into orderlies and gurneys, knocking chairs over. I entered the glass-enclosed ward, medical personnel staring at me as I shouted, "Lenz! Her name is Theresa Lenz! Where is she?"

By the time I found her small pod, the vital-signs monitor was flatlining.

I screamed out loud to God, "*No, no, take me! Damn You, take me instead!*"

The only answer was the high-pitched squeal of the machine.

God's gift was gone.

CHAPTER 57

I FORCED my eyes open, hoping that Karl was still asleep. I would wake him and tell him that I'd had the most horrible dream. I would say, "Karl. See a cardiologist, *today*."

Tori was sitting by the side of my hospital bed.

"I'm here, darling," she said. "I'm here."

"How?"

"Dr. Maillet called me. My number was in your wallet."

I saw it all in her face. I hadn't been dreaming. My husband. My child. They were dead. And the future I'd imagined, of seeing Tre grow up, of becoming even closer to Karl—all of that was dead, too. Tori reached for me, and I let my hysteria have its way. When I pulled away, after I had dried my face on the sleeve of my gown, I said, "Tori. I want to see them."

Tori grabbed my hands. "Are you sure?"

I nodded and sobbed again.

"I'll be right back."

I swung my legs over the side of the bed, and soon, Tori returned with a nurse. The nurse put slippers on my feet, then brought us to the morgue, where a pathologist was waiting for us in the stainless-steel, ice-cold storage room.

I stood in my cotton gown and leaned on Tori as the assistant slid out a drawer and folded the sheet down from my dear husband's face.

The tears streamed down my cheeks as I saw Karl lying there, gray faced and inanimate. The bridge of his nose had been sliced through where his glasses had cut into his flesh in the fall. His forehead and chin were abraded, but not the palms of his hands. He hadn't tried to break his fall, which told me that he'd been dead before he dropped, crushing our three-month-old between his body and the hard stone treads of the staircase.

Had he had heart problems before this attack?

I thought not. He would have told me.

Was his consciousness still alive somewhere, perhaps in the corner of the ceiling? I did not feel his presence at all.

Where was God? I didn't feel His presence, either.

But I called to Him, silently speaking to Him through our private conduit in my mind.

You're a monster, I said to the Almighty God of Moses and Solomon, the Father of Christ and all of humanity.

I'm taking this personally. You gave to me, only to take it all away, and You've done this to me before. I don't care why. You've lost me. You can never make this up to me, and You can never get me back. You're diabolical. Go to hell. Or go back to hell. And don't give me any shit about millions of birds.

A stool appeared beside me. I sat beside Karl's body and told him that I didn't hold Tre's death against him.

"I love you. I will always love you. You and Tre are part of me, now and forever."

I kissed his forehead. I straightened his hair.

I apologized to the pathologist for any outbursts or rudeness and asked to see my baby. He didn't want to show her to me, but, reluctantly, he opened her drawer.

I folded down Tre's thin cotton blanket, and I saw what had been done to her while surgeons had tried to save her life. I counted four incisions where tubes and drains had been inserted through her pale skin and into her organs. I saw the horrible violation of her skull, where it had been opened and bone plates removed.

My poor, tiny girl. My little Tre.

I took her out of the drawer and held her against my chest. I rocked my baby's cold corpse, and I pictured every minute that I could remember of her three months of life.

I tried, but I couldn't envision her in a safe, warm place with her father, or anywhere with God.

CHAPTER 58

TORI WRAPPED her arms around me as Tre was taken away, and she walked me with me down the labyrinthine corridors and through glass doors to the street.

A black car was waiting, and once we were inside the apartment, I stripped naked and got into the vast, empty bed where I had awoken this morning with my husband.

I thought of our little one, who had been sleeping safely in her crib, just next door. My broken heart seized up again.

I have known so many mothers who have wept over the bodies of their dead children. I had sympathized with them. I had tried to console them. I had prayed with them, and I had held them while they cried out from the depths of their souls.

But there was no preparing for this.

I awoke sometime later to hear Tori speaking in the outer room, on the phone with her husband, Marty. I heard her crying. Then she was in the doorway saying that Zach was on the line.

Zach's voice was in my ear, saying, "I'm so sorry, Brigid. I'm just so sorry."

I managed to thank him and say good-bye. There was nothing more I could say. Nothing.

I went into the master bathroom that I had shared with Karl and cut off all my hair. I used his razor and shaved my head, after which I gulped down Valium and went back to bed.

The next day, Tori brought me coffee and told me that she'd been in touch with Karl's lawyer. She made arrangements with a funeral home, and I'll never be able to thank her enough for keeping me safe in a dark room during the most terrible days of my life.

Three days after Karl and Tre died, I got out of bed. I dressed in black. I covered my head with a scarf, and I buried my husband and my child in the Lenz family plot, in a Lutheran cemetery in Zehlendorf, just outside the city. I shook hands and hugged Karl's weeping friends and family. I had depleted my reservoir of tears, and I had nothing to say to God.

Back in our apartment, Karl's lawyer let me know that Karl had left everything to me. I didn't care about the money, and I couldn't live in our place anymore. It would be unbearable to walk through the rooms where I had been happier than at any time in my life.

I told the lawyer to sell our apartment and everything in it, to provide for the actors in *Der Zug,* and to put the rest into BZFO and other charities of Karl's.

He said, "Karl wanted you to have money, and, like it or not, you have a bank account and a credit card. The bills will come to me. I'll make suitable donations to his charities, and I'll make arrangements as you wish for the bulk of his estate."

I signed documents, and I booked a flight. I changed into pants and a sweater. I packed a bag and tucked in my journal, my laptop, and a framed photo of myself with my husband and child. Then I buttoned myself into a hooded black alpaca coat.

Tori and I went to the airport together, and when her flight to Rome was open to board, I hugged her for a long time. We both wept at the gate. And as soon as her plane was rolling down the tarmac, I called Sabeena.

"I wish you had let me be there for you," she said.

"I was happy to think of you at home with Albert and the girls. You can't imagine, Sabeena, how much that meant to me. Kiss everyone for me."

My voice broke, and Sabeena murmured soothing words that couldn't soothe.

"You deserve happiness," she said, her voice flooded with tears. "Have faith."

"I'm out of faith," I said. "I need *proof* of His love, of His *existence,* or I'll turn my back on Him as He has turned His back on me."

What could anyone say to *that?*

After I said good-bye to Sabeena, I went to the flight lounge and pulled up the hood of my coat so that no one would dare talk to me.

The last time I had worn this coat, I had dropped one of Tre's rattles in the pocket. It was pink plastic, shaped like a little barbell, hand-painted with blue forget-me-nots.

I clasped the rattle in my fist and shook it incessantly, as if she might hear it and cry out for me. I shook the rattle and jiggled my feet and waited for my flight to board.

CHAPTER 59

I ARRIVED in Cairo at night and hired a car to take me to Mt. Sinai. My destination was the Orthodox Chapel of the Holy Trinity, built in the 1930s over the ruins of a fourth-century Byzantine church.

Legend has it that beneath the church is the very rock from which God had taken the stone tablets that He inscribed with the Ten Commandments and handed off to Moses. You could say that the tablets were the bedrock of Judeo-Christian teachings.

It was a good place to look for God.

As the car cut through Sinai in the dark, I thought about the beginning of my own beliefs.

I hadn't been captivated by the power and the love of God from the first time I stepped into St. Paul's Church in Cambridge. But the barrel-vaulted ceilings, the biblical stories told in stained glass, the large crucifix behind the altar, and the homilies of our kind priest, Father Callahan, moved me. The more I learned, the more I trusted in God.

I acted on that belief in the real world, but, having lived through the ungodly horrors in South Sudan, having entertained death in my own house, my trust in God was gone.

Was God real?

Or was He all gilded myth tricked out in ceremony, illuminated by fear and stories and blind faith?

I had to know.

When my driver parked at the foot of the mountain, the sun was just rising. He said, "This is the best time to make the climb, miss. You'll see."

I felt very light as I began my slow journey up the 3,750 Steps of Penitence through the morning mist. I'd lost weight. I'd lost love. I'd lost faith. I was hardly there at all. Other, more substantial pilgrims mounted the steps with love for God shining on their faces and cameras in their hands.

Except for a water bottle and Tre's rattle, I was empty handed. I had no expectations, but I was willing to be moved if God sent me a sign.

The climb up the staggered steps opened an increasingly higher and wider view of the mountainous landscape, lit with pale, slanting rays of sun and defined by deep shadows. And this magnificent view stretched as far as I could see.

I walked around the imposing stone walls of the church with my hands in my pockets, my thoughts on Father Delahanty, the priest who'd come to Kind Hands only to be murdered within his first week. He had asked God for forgiveness, but his final words were some kind of confession to me.

I'm here for you, Brigid. God has a plan for you.

How did he know? Was he speaking *to* God and *for* Him?

Or was he just crazy and deluded?

God. Are You here? Got anything for me?

I walked to the edge of the stone staircase and looked down the mountainside to where St. Catherine's Monastery nestled between the clefts and crags, on a flat patch of stone far below.

St. Catherine's is a working monastery and a holy place. St. Catherine's remains are entombed there, miraculously intact after her beheading in the fourth century. It is also the site of the burning bush from which, according to the Old Testament, God called Moses to lead His people out of Egypt.

I joined the throng of backpackers on the downward climb from Mt. Sinai to St. Catherine's Monastery. I placed one foot in front of the other, making my way down the thousands of hand-chiseled stone steps, every single one of them reminding me of the steps that had been the death of my baby girl.

A college-age boy with a backpack tapped my shoulder and asked me to take his picture with Mt. Sinai in the background. After I did it, he asked me where I was from. Had I come to Sinai alone?

He couldn't have made a worse choice for a pickup.

I said, "Sorry. No English," and pulled the edge of my hood down so that it didn't just cover my bald head, it deeply shaded my eyes.

I was a tourist in a place where I didn't belong. There was nothing for me here.

My driver was waiting for me at St. Catherine's.

I had a plane to catch.

CHAPTER 60

MY LONG day had started with a sunrise climb up and then down 3,750 steps carved into Mt. Sinai by penitent monks from St. Catherine's Monastery in the seventh century. I hadn't found peace or resolution or revelation, but I hadn't quite given up.

Now, as the sun set on the Middle East, my plane landed at Ben Gurion Airport in Tel Aviv. I was met by Nissim, a driver in a polished Lincoln sedan, who took me to my hotel in the modern section of Jerusalem.

My plan was to steep myself in Jerusalem's Old City and the holiest sites of its three major religions. I'd been told that God's divine presence never left the Western Wall and that this site, as well as the Dome of the Rock and the Church of the Holy Sepulchre, had been visited by millions of pilgrims over the last two thousand years.

If I couldn't revive my faith in God in Jerusalem, it was truly lost.

At seven the next morning, Nissim picked me up at my hotel, and we set out for the Old City. Nissim had been a tank driver in the Six-Day War, back in 1967. He was a grandfather, a soldier, and a tour guide who claimed to know every niche in every wall of the Holy City.

We spent the day at the Church of the Holy Sepulchre, which had been built over the sites of Christ's Crucifixion, burial, and resurrection and enclosed five stations of the cross.

While standing in the church's atrium under the open sky, Nissim told me about the succession of kings, pharaohs, emperors, caliphs, and sultans who had conquered the Holy City, and about the religious wars, the Crusades; stories of saints and pilgrims; the destruction of this church in AD 1009; and the disputes over reconstruction up to the present day.

It was a glorious story, rich in detail, woven with passion for the Father, the Son, and the Holy Ghost. I appreciated Nissim's animated telling of it and the history I walked through within the walls and under the domes and across the stones walked by multitudes.

But I didn't feel anything shift inside me: not my skepticism, nor my raging fury at God.

At day's end, Nissim drove me back to my hotel, on Yafo Street, a four-lane, traffic-choked thoroughfare that cut through the business district. There was no parking in front of the hotel, and in the spaces beyond the no-parking zone was a bus stop, and a municipal bus had pulled in to let on passengers.

Nissim pulled around the bus and the half dozen cars in front of it and parked the Lincoln at the far end of the block. He opened the back door for me, and I told him I'd see him in the morning.

I walked back down Yafo and was mounting the steps to the hotel entrance when a concussive *boom* cracked through the air, lifting me off my feet and hurling me against the wall of the hotel. Glass shattered and fell on and around me like icicles in a winter hurricane. I was stunned from the impact. I couldn't breathe.

What had happened? What the *hell* had happened?

As if a switch had been thrown, cars drove up onto the sidewalk, crashed into streetlights and buildings, collided with other cars. Pedestrians ran through the street, a monochromatic scene of chaos drawn in the charcoal gray of dusk, cut by headlights shining at crazed angles.

I smelled bitter smoke.

But I couldn't *hear* a thing.

CHAPTER 61

SMOKE ROILED through the air, and crowds of terrified people stampeded down Yafo Street.

I was deaf and nearly blind from the smoke, and I realized that a bomb had gone off. *A bomb.*

Nissim had parked his car a block north of the hotel. Was he alive? Did he need help?

My legs were weak, but I pushed back against the wall and inched up until I was standing. I kept one hand on the wall and stepped down into the pandemonium on Yafo. I peered through the dense smoke, hoping to see to the end of the block, but my eyes were immediately drawn to the remains of the bus we had pulled around only minutes ago.

The explosion had gone off inside it and had surely been deadly. The warped metal crackled with fire as smoke poured up through the void where the roof had been.

And then the bus exploded again.

I saw the back of the bus erupt in flames. I turned my face to the hotel wall, flattened myself against the granite as the silent, roaring heat blew across my back and neck and hands.

When the blast subsided, I turned toward it and ran.

I skirted the flaming bus and kept going through the body-strewn street, which felt much like the killing fields in South Sudan. I was choking on smoke and tears when I reached the car at the corner of the block. Was it Nissim's Lincoln? I hoped not. I hoped that he had pulled back into traffic before the explosion.

Please.

I walked to the street side of the car and saw Nissim wedged between the car door and the frame. It was him. I knew his white curls, now soaked with blood. His left arm, with his wedding ring on his hand, protruded from the door frame, and he was motionless.

Still, I called his name.

I reached through the shattered window and put two fingers to his jugular. He had no pulse.

"I'm so sorry, Nissim," I said.

I stepped away from the car and saw a man half under the car behind Nissim's sedan, lying in blood, his arms covering his head.

I went to his side, but he was gone. When I looked up, I saw a small body in the intersection that could only be that of a child. His legs had been blown off, and his blood was still running into the gutter.

God? What is this? What do You want me to see?

Ten yards away from the man and the child, a young woman struggled to sit up. Her right forearm was gone, and her blood was spouting onto the pavement.

"Please lie down," I said. "I'm a doctor."

The woman's breathing was shallow, and her heartbeat was quickly pumping her life away.

I grabbed at my waist for my handbag, thinking I could use the shoulder strap as a tourniquet. Then I remembered that I had locked up my bag in my room this morning. I wasn't wearing a belt, and neither was the woman in the street.

A strip of tire was lying nearby, and I needed it. I went back to the woman whose arm had been crudely amputated by the explosion and tied off the ragged wound with the rubber strip. I spoke to her in words I couldn't hear as red and blue flashers lit up Yafo Street. Firemen, police, medics, and bomb squads were coming into the devastated area.

An ambulance braked next to me, and two medics jumped out of the back. One spoke to me. I pointed to my ears and said, "I can't hear."

Would I ever hear again?

The medic's partner stooped over the woman I had just tried to save. He shook his head no and made a thumbs-down motion.

The woman with the tire tourniquet was dead.

CHAPTER 62

COLORED LIGHTS spun and flashed in the bomb-riven night. Three of Yafo's four lanes were closed, and the bus and surrounding sidewalk had been cordoned off. The walking wounded, even those desperately seeking loved ones, were ushered beyond the tape.

I shouted to a medic, "I'm a doctor!" but I was walked firmly to the cordon and sent away. I made my way around the obstacles and down the street to the hotel, where I found the lobby crowded with injured and panicked people. I took the stairs to my room, and first thing, I downed a minibottle of scotch from the honor bar. Then I stripped off my clothes and got under the sheet.

I lay on my back, absolutely still, and as I stared up at the ceiling, I thought about dead people.

Karl's cold, dead face leapt into my mind, and so did the lifeless body of my precious baby, dressed in her christening, then burial, gown, wearing my cross and chain around her neck.

I flashed on the hundreds of dead at Kind Hands, or maybe it had been thousands—the babies, the BLM soldiers, Father Delahanty, and Colin—

and the bulldozer pushing dirt over mass graves. I thought of Nissim, who had survived wars only to die on the street today.

Then something like a gust of wind rushed over me, clearing the thoughts from my mind.

My view of the past was gone, the dead people were gone, and I was seeing in two dimensions at once, as I had when I was both inside the airplane from Rome and flying outside it.

I was not insane. This was not delusionary. I was aware of the bed beneath me, the sheet draped over me. My arms were outstretched to the sides of the mattress, and my ankles were crossed. At the same time, my mattress and I were floating on a clear, sunlit, glass-colored sea.

It was simply amazing and completely real. As my raft and I bobbed on this blue-green water, I had a thought. *If only I could stay here forever.*

If only.

Just then, the air changed, becoming thick and oily with the stink of gasoline. There was a concussive *ka-rump* of an explosion, followed by a loud *whoosh*. The water had transformed into a dancing wall of flames surrounding me on all sides.

I think I screamed. I sat up and tried to get away from the inferno lapping at the sides of my raft of a mattress, singeing my skin and my bristly hair, but there was no escape. Fire was all around me, everywhere.

I collapsed back down onto the mattress.

I accepted this death. I wanted this consummation.

And then a new breeze brought another sea change.

The smoke thinned, and the dense blackness of it coalesced into marbled gray. Thunderheads formed at the height of the ceiling. Lightning sizzled and snapped.

I watched, transfixed by the swirling storm. A drop of water fell on my forehead, then on each of my eyes, like the softest of kisses. Another drop fell on my left hand, and my right, and then the drops came down in the thousands, the millions, merging into freezing-cold torrents.

I heard the hiss of doused flames. A mist rolled across my body, and, just as suddenly as it had risen from the sea, the fire was gone. Just gone.

The air brightened, and a warm breeze dried my face and the sheet still covering me. I remained motionless, suspended in place on my raft, which rose and fell, rocking gently on the waves.

Overhead, the gray sky diffused into a luminous blue veil, which became a pure-white ball of light enclosing me at its center.

I was overcome with awe, and I sensed His presence.

There was a feeling of warmth in my chest and a wordless voice in my mind. It was as if I was in a waking dream.

Brigid. This is your life. It belongs to you.

CHAPTER 63

I HEARD, with my deaf ears, those nine resonant words.

And then they were gone. The ceiling was plaster, not divine light. I was dry, and my skin was not burned.

I had not been sleeping or dreaming or hallucinating. The vision had come to me from outside my own mind, and I had been shocked and amazed at every turn.

I replayed the words in my mind.

Brigid. This is your life. It belongs to you.

I lay almost paralyzed on the bed.

I recalled the vision I'd had when I'd flown from Rome and had seen the beautiful Italian town beneath me. A baby carriage had rolled out into the street, under the wheels of a car. Hadn't that baby's mother called out to God?

Hadn't she begged Him for her child's life?

I saw the bird God had placed in my hand. I watched the small bird rise up and join the multitudes. And I heard the echo of God's message to me: *Can you care for your bird?*

Weren't millions of prayers going up to God now and in the last minute and the next? *God, save my child. God, don't let my wife find out. God, where are my car keys? Make the ball land on red. Lord, please let me get to class on time. God, bless my home, my marriage, my cat, my team.*

The image of floating on a calm sea, the fire blazing across it, the cold rainstorm, and the words of God had, one by one, come over me. It was easy to interpret.

God was telling me that my life was both heaven and hell on earth. It was mine to live. He loved me. But my life was my responsibility. All mine.

He had shown me the way again. *Take care of yourself, Brigid. Get Me?*

I was suddenly sick all the way through. The bed didn't move, but I felt as though I were falling nine floors to my death. The sense of falling was not a vision. It was abject shame and mortification in reality.

I had questioned God.

I had thought that I was so special, I could hold God to account. And why? I had never been promised, ever, that life would be safe and have a happy ending for myself and those I knew and loved, if only I had faith in Him.

A realization broke through my shame like a bright light. I *did* have faith. It had been shaken because I questioned it. But the fact that I was still asking God "why" was proof that I believed in Him.

I loved Him. I had never stopped.

As I lay there in the big bed, my skepticism and rage evaporated. I felt as though I'd been brought back to life, but for what reason? I had no idea.

I still didn't understand why people had to suffer, but God had made it clear that it was not for me to judge.

I was alive. I had to use my life well while it was still mine. I was on my knees, thanking God with the whole of my heart and soul, when my cell phone rang.

I heard it.

My hearing had returned and, with it, the clamor on the street outside the hotel, men shouting, horns blowing, heavy equipment scraping up metal.

And my phone.

Hardly anyone had my number. But Sabeena had it.

"Sabeena?"

"Are you all right?" she asked me.

"There was a bomb," I said.

"Brigid, I know. I saw the pictures on television after you texted me from Ben Gurion. I've been trying to reach you all night."

"I was near the explosion. I lost my hearing. But it just came back. My driver died."

There was a long silence.

"Sabeena?"

"There was a suicide bomber on the bus," she said. "Thirty-two people died, and many more are in the hospital. Brigid?"

"I'm here."

"That's a problem. Get the hell out of there."

"Where should I go?"

"I know where I would go," said Sabeena.

I'd gotten my answer from God. My life came without guarantees. I had to stop running and go back to what had driven me so far from home.

I needed to look into *myself*.

PART THREE

PART THREE

CHAPTER 64

I WAS sweating hard under my coat and so anxious that my stomach hurt.

When I got to the customs inspector's window, he asked me to lower my hood. Then he compared my passport photo to the actual me, standing in front of him.

The pictures didn't match.

My face was gaunt, and my head was shorn. I had deep circles under my eyes, and my hooded coat had only added to my appearance as a suspicious person planning to blow up a plane.

I was taken out of the line by two armed guards, brought to a small, windowless room where my bags were unpacked again, the linings pulled apart, my electronic devices turned on. I was shunted into a second room, and this time, I was strip searched. I was struck by the wretched memories of the last time I'd been publicly stripped, but I complied.

When the female guard told me I could put my clothes back on, I said, "My husband and baby died suddenly. I went to Jerusalem to pray. I was on Yafo Street yesterday when the bomb blew up."

She scrutinized my expression, looking to see if I was telling her the truth. She nodded. I was cleared for flight.

The only remaining empty seat was in the middle of a three-person row in the midsection of the plane. The overhead rack was full, so I balled up my coat, and when the man on the aisle stood up, I did my best to pack myself and my belongings into and under the narrow seat.

While we waited for takeoff, the news came over the individual media players in the seat backs. I don't speak Hebrew, but I understood enough. Hamas was taking credit for the bomb. The death toll had risen to forty-five. Pictures of the dead flashed onto the screen. One of them was of the woman I had tried to save with a strip of tire. One was of the precious five-year-old boy who'd had his legs blown off. And then there was Nissim.

I sucked in my breath, put my hands over my face, and shook as I tried to suppress my sobs. The woman in the window seat to my left asked me, "Dear, dear. Can I help you?"

I shook my head, and the tears came. I dug under the seat, went through my coat pockets, and found tissues. I clapped a wad of them to my face, but I couldn't stem the flow. I tried to stand so that I could get to the bathroom, but the seat-belt sign was on. The man in the aisle seat gave me an angry look, so I collapsed back into my middle seat, bent over, and just cried into my hands.

I'd gotten a brief glimpse of the woman beside me. She looked to be in her fifties, had silver-streaked blond hair, and wore a muted flower-print top over beige pants, and she smelled nice. She put her arm around my shoulder in the most welcome of awkward hugs and kept it there as the plane sped up the runway. When we were airborne, I mopped my face some more, then said, "Thank you. You are very kind."

"I'm Katharine Dunlop," she said.

"Brigid Fitzgerald."

"Are you American?" she asked.

"Yes. And you?"

"Yep. I'm going home to Boston."

"Me too."

"It's a long flight," said Dunlop. "I'm a good listener."

I didn't have to be asked again. I blurted, "My husband and baby died just last week."

She said, "Oh, my God, Brigid. I'm so sorry." She asked me what had happened, and I was ready, *more than ready,* to talk. I took Tre's rattle from my handbag and held on to it with both hands. We hadn't yet reached cruising altitude, and I was telling Katharine about my sublime marriage to Karl and about his and Tre's sudden deaths.

This woman didn't stop me. She didn't pull back or look at me as if I were insane. I kept talking.

I skipped back in time to Kind Hands, and when she asked, "What made you go to South Sudan?" I told her that I'd always wanted to be a doctor.

I explained that I had been only nineteen when I had graduated from Harvard. I had planned to go to med school there, but when my mother died, I couldn't stay in Cambridge any longer, and I got my MD at Johns Hopkins. I checked her expression to see if she was still with me.

True to her word, she was a good listener.

As we flew above the clouds, I told this stranger in the window seat about the bomb that had gone off in Jerusalem yesterday. That I had been right there.

"I'm lucky to be here, I know that. But I'm very depressed."

She said, "Of course. One tragedy compounding another and another. For this to happen while you're grieving—who has more right to depression than you?"

When the cart came up the aisle, I bought Katharine a drink. We talked about baseball over dinner, and we both slept for a full eight hours as the jet crossed a continent and an ocean.

When the plane was descending into Boston's Logan Airport, Katharine gave me her card.

I put it in my baggy coat pocket without looking at it.

She smiled. "Call me anytime."

I thanked her and hugged her good-bye, and after collecting my bags, I caught a cab and set out to see my father. I leaned back and took Katharine's card from my pocket.

Katharine Dunlop, Psychiatrist, MD.

My new friend was a professional good listener. She was a shrink. *Call me anytime,* she had said.

I held the card in my hand throughout the drive home.

CHAPTER 65

I DIDN'T want to see my father, but I couldn't move forward without going back.

I directed my cabbie to Harvard, where I had gone to college and my father had tortured his American-literature students from noon to two o'clock for the past thirty years.

I was glad for the long drive from the airport. I mentally rehearsed various approaches to speaking truth to my father and hadn't yet hit on the one that might open a fruitful conversation.

We took the Mass Turnpike and the Ted Williams Tunnel, which dove under Boston Harbor and the Boston Main Channel, and made our way toward Cambridge Street in Allston. The whole route was deeply ingrained in my memory of growing up in this city, driving on this road at night, wondering how much longer before I could move out of Cambridge and how far I could go.

We entered Cambridge, and as we wound through the Harvard campus, we turned onto Quincy. There was Emerson Hall, on my right. I gathered my travel-worn bags, paid the driver, and entered the three-story redbrick building through the main entrance that had a biblical quote carved in marble overhead: WHAT IS MAN THAT THOU ART MINDFUL OF HIM?

I was mindful of this one particular man, anyway. I continued down the faintly echoing corridor to the end. The door to my father's classroom was closed, of course, but I peeked through the window and saw that class was in session. The theater-style rows of blue seats were half-full and facing my formidable father, standing at the podium at the head of the room with a whiteboard behind him.

I couldn't read the board from where I stood, but I knew that it was a list of the chapters in Harold Bloom's *Western Canon*, the course outline for the first semester of my father's freshman class. I'd seen it before.

I opened the door and stepped into the room with my old carpetbag in my left hand, my leather hobo bag over my right shoulder. My father, George Santayana Fitzgerald, aka G.S.F., turned his head a few degrees and wrinkled his brow.

The hood of my coat was down around my shoulders, and he still didn't recognize me. And then suddenly he did.

I dipped my head in greeting and slipped into the back row and took a seat.

Too soon, Dr. Fitzgerald snapped out the assignment for the next day and reminded the students of an upcoming test.

"Every test is an opportunity to fail," he said. When there were no questions, he said, "Get out."

The room emptied quickly, the students grabbing a look at the bald woman in the back row as they streamed past.

My father stood across from and below me with a pointer in his hand. The look on his face was as cold as a blizzard in January. As if I had come here so that I could do him harm.

He spoke to me across the eighteen rows of seats.

"Well. You look bad, Brigid. Why did you shave your head and dress like a monk? What have you done now?"

"I want to stay with you for a week or so. We have a lot of catching up to do."

"The hot water is out. Your room is all file storage now."

"I'll sleep on the couch," I said. "I'll call a plumber."

"If you must," said my father.

He left the classroom, and I followed him. He didn't look behind him once as he walked through the parking lot, located the very old, baby-blue BMW that had belonged to my mother. Without being invited, I got into the front seat and sat with my hands in my lap as my father maneuvered the car out to Quincy.

"Have you been well?" I asked him.

"I had my gallbladder removed. I have arthritis. And my arteries are clogged. All that keeps me alive is pure meanness," he said.

"Whatever works," I said.

I knew that what worked for him was going to kill him, and that was a good reason to spend time with him while it was possible. I asked him about his medications, his exercise program, if he was writing his memoirs, as he had sworn he would do.

"Who are you? Barbara Walters?" he growled.

We were in our old neighborhood. The asphalt was still potholed. The shabby houses still needed paint, and the overhead lines sagged over the last nongentrified neighborhood in Cambridge. I remembered whipping around the potholes on my bike, staying out as long and as late as I could before going home to the angry house where I lived.

My father jerked the wheel into the driveway and drove the car up to the garage door and braked it a few inches before the hood went through the rotten wood.

I knew the signs.

My father needed his fix. And, as usual, I was getting in the way.

CHAPTER 66

ON THE inside, the old house where I had lived with my parents now looked a lot like the stacks in a college library or maybe a secondhand bookstore.

My father hadn't been lying about my room. Books were piled on the single bed, and the walls were lined with banker's boxes filled with papers. He was famous for flunking up to a third of his students, and it looked as though he had saved their records, possibly to amuse himself.

I found a pillow and a blanket in the hall closet and tossed them onto the sofa. My father was in the filthy kitchen making tea. For himself.

"Yes, I would like some tea," I said. "I just flew in from Jerusalem. Eleven hours direct flight."

He got a cup and saucer out of the cupboard and poured tea for me. "Anything else?" he said. He pulled out a chair, sat down at the table, and stared at me.

"My husband died. My baby, too. Your granddaughter."

He reared back a little in his chair, then settled back down.

"I never had a granddaughter," he said.

"I sent you a card."

"Goody. But she wasn't my granddaughter."

"I should know," I said. "I remember quite well that I gave birth to her."

"How about the DNA test? Did you get that?"

"How's your mind, Dad?"

"Still as sharp as ever. Want to test me?"

He grabbed a book off the toaster oven and dropped it on the table in front of me. Dante's *Inferno*. He said, "Open it to any page. I'll quote from it."

"I trust you," I said. That was a lie.

"You don't," he said. "You've hated me for most of your life, and I have no love for you, either. You can blame that on Dorothy."

"My mother, your *wife*, was a decent and loving person. I don't have to defend her. But isn't it bad enough that you killed her? You have to insult her memory, too?"

"I didn't kill her, Brigid. She killed herself."

"You were there when she OD'd. Why didn't you get her to the hospital? Were you so stoned yourself that you couldn't use a phone?"

He was drumming his fingers, looking past me. He got up from the table and went into the next room, returning a minute later with a framed family photo of the three of us with my paternal grandparents, taken when I was ten. George and Dorothy looked pretty good. Maybe they hadn't been using then.

My father cleared the table with his forearm, knocking tea out of cups and the book to the floor.

"Look at this picture."

"Yeah," I said. "I see it."

"Look at you. Do you see any resemblance to the Fitzgeralds in your face or your ears or anything else?"

Silence crackled around me, and it went on for a long time.

"What are you saying?" I finally asked him.

"This should please you, Brigid. You're not my flesh and blood. You're not my daughter. I wrung the confession out of your mother when you were only six weeks old. But she told me.

"Still, I gave you my name. I put a roof over your head. I put food on your plate. I put up with your shitty attitude. I made sure you got into Harvard. And I kept this to myself all these years because I loved your slut of a mother.

"As for *me* killing *her*? She was the first junkie. She got *me* hooked, not the other way around."

I wanted to say *I don't believe you,* but I did believe him. Maybe it wasn't entirely true, but it was true enough. My father picked Dante up off the floor. He rinsed out the teapot. There was a Red Sox pennant over the sink. My mother and I both loved our team.

I shouted over the sound of running water, "Who was my father?"

"No idea," he said, closing the faucet. "That's between your dead mother and her dead priest."

I got up from the table and gathered my belongings. As I walked through the kitchen, my father had his works on the table and was tying tubing around his arm, pumping his fist.

He looked up with his first smile since I'd arrived and said, "Let this be a lesson to you. 'You can't go home again.' Thomas Wolfe wrote that."

I walked through the doorway to the side yard, and the door slammed behind me.

I just kept walking.

CHAPTER 67

I STUMBLED out onto Jackson Street in shock. It was as if I'd taken a gut shot and my body didn't yet know that I was dead.

I passed the signs and touchstones of my childhood: the warnings about bad dogs, the rusted mailboxes, and a break in the sidewalk where my roller skates had caught, pitching me forward and skinning my knee to the bone.

In the black light of my titular father's vicious revelation, I was skating on broken sidewalks up and down the length of my life.

Who was I now?

The bitterness of my "father" had been explained, but it was still inexcusable. I had been a little girl. I had looked up to him. He had pretended to be my father, but he had never loved me. My pathetic girlish attempts to win his approval were appalling to me now. He was worse than I had imagined.

But I truly didn't understand my mother. She had praised me and loved me—but how could she let me grow up in the house of a man who hated me?

Was it because he had supplied her with the drugs that she needed? Was her husband her ultimate and fatal drug?

I'd been furious with him because I believed that he had first ruined her and then let her die. Now, I thought she was responsible for her addiction. And she hadn't done her best for me.

I knew that the Christian response was to forgive them for their deceit, but I was too raw and, at the same time, too numb to simply let this betrayal go. Everything I thought I knew about myself had changed into a stream of questions. Who was I? Who was my father? What traits of his did I carry? Had my mother loved him? Had he even known I existed?

Did any of this even matter at this stage of my life?

I walked the streets of Cambridge like a zombie and without a plan in the world.

And yet, my feet knew some of the way.

When I looked around to get my bearings, I was standing across the street from St. Paul's, the church where I used to go with my mother every Sunday.

I had loved everything about the redbrick church, with its rows of matching columns and the figure of St. Paul in the frieze above the central door. I teared up thinking of Father Callahan, the priest I had loved as young girl. He had kept my mother's secret. Maybe that was why he had been so kind to the funny-looking redheaded girl sitting with her mother in the front pew.

I went inside the empty church, walked down the aisle and under the barrel-vaulted ceiling with the rounded arches, and took my old place at the end of a front pew. I felt uplifted and expanded when I was in this hallowed place, knowing that God knew and loved me. Coming here with my mother, sitting close to her while we sang and prayed on Sunday, had been the highlight of my week, every week.

I clasped my hands in prayer and let my thoughts go out to God. I had a new understanding of Him. Whether my visions were God-sent or everyone had the ability to communicate with God if they were open to Him, I couldn't know.

But I had felt His presence here. And today I had brought my faith with me to St. Paul's, where I had always felt love and safety.

My bad father was wrong.

I *had* come home again.

CHAPTER 68

I WAS sitting in the front pew and was deep in prayer when a door slammed behind me. A priest came into the nave wearing jeans and a black shirt with a priest's collar. He was saying into his phone, "Let him know James Aubrey called. Thanks."

Then he saw me and said, "Oh. Sorry about that. I didn't mean to interrupt your prayers."

"Not a problem," I said. "I was nattering. God has heard it all before."

He gave me a big smile and said, "That's funny."

The priest was probably in his early thirties. He had a round face, sandy hair, and beautiful blue eyes. Despite the smile, his eyes were sad.

"I'm Father Aubrey," he said. "James."

He reached out his hand and I did the same, and we shook.

"Brigid Fitzgerald."

"Nice to meet you, Brigid. You're new to the neighborhood?"

"Not exactly. When I was a kid, my mom and I used to sit right here every Sunday."

He looked at me for a long moment, then said, "Forgive me for noticing, but you look a little lost, Brigid. No judgment. Just, do you want to talk?"

He was a pretty good read. I'd lost my loved ones as well as my father, my father's entire family, my trust in my mother, and pretty much my identity from the time I was able to say "da-da." Did I want to talk?

Apparently I did.

"I'm, uh, in mourning. I just lost my husband and baby girl in a terrible accident. I feel kind of dead myself."

James Aubrey told me that he was very sorry, then sat in the pew across from me and asked questions. I told him a little of the story, but it was hard to talk about Karl's and Tre's deaths without melting right down.

I switched the subject, telling him that I'd just come back from Jerusalem and had been yards away when the bomb went off.

"I'm a doctor," I said. "I tried to help. I couldn't do anything. It was just a bloody nightmare of a disaster, and after that, I came here. I'm kind of a homing pigeon, I guess."

"I'm sorry, Brigid. I can hardly imagine the horror you've been through."

I nodded, but I didn't want to talk anymore. My voice was splintered, and I thought I might just crack up entirely if I kept talking. I managed to say, "I have to go find a place to stay. I'll be back another time."

James Aubrey said, "Good. I'm almost always here. God be with you, Brigid."

Sometimes He was. Sometimes I carried on, on my own.

CHAPTER 69

A CAB was waiting for the light to change on DeWolfe Street, right outside the church. I grabbed the opportunity, threw myself into the backseat, and asked the driver to take me to the Dinsmore Motor Lodge, right off Route 2.

I knew of the Dinsmore, but I'd never been there.

The driver was a reed-thin man of indeterminate age wearing a knitted cap pulled down to his eyes and a Fitbit on his right wrist. He checked me out in the mirror, then he started the meter.

I watched without seeing as he drove us up Memorial Drive, along the Charles River, through North Cambridge, but I came back to the present when we closed in on my chosen destination, a skeevy motel in the worst part of the city, planted on the verge of a rumbling highway.

My driver stopped his cab in the motel's forecourt, beside the cracked plastic sign reading *Vacancies WiFi Coffee Shop. Happy B'day Sean.*

I asked my cabbie to wait, then bolted out of the cab before he could say no and fast-walked to the office.

I asked the towering teenage boy behind the desk if room 209 was available, and he nodded while staring at me.

I was getting a lot of strange looks these days, and I knew why. My black hooded coat looked like a storm cloud, and I was in the center of it, with my shaven head, my pale skin, and my generally deathlike appearance.

Never mind death*like*. I looked like the real thing.

I said, "May I see the room?"

Giant Teen unhooked the key from a board behind him and slapped it on the counter.

"You mind if I ask why 209?"

"Yes," I said.

I snatched the key.

The parking area around the Dinsmore Motor Lodge looked like a dumping ground for all the drug-addicted, jobless, homeless, hopeless people in Cambridge.

I said to my driver, "I'll be back in a few minutes."

"I can't wait more than five. I need to get back to the garage."

"Ten minutes, that's all. I'll give you a good tip."

He sighed, then shrugged. I took that to be a yes.

I jogged up the stairs to the second floor, found 209 three doors down from the landing, and opened the door to the room where my mother had died.

I'd seen police photos of the room and expected it to be a hellhole, but it was far worse than that. The windows were opaque with dirt. The bed was covered with a stained spread, the hard surfaces were grimy, and insects scurried when I turned on the bathroom light. The stink of smoke and fifty years of unwashed human beings clung to the carpets and curtains.

I stared at the revolting bedspread and thought of my mother lying there, half-naked, her heart exploding from a heroin overdose. And I saw my father lying next to her, watching her die.

The day after Dorothy Fitzgerald died at the age of forty-five, G.S.F. was arrested and charged with negligent homicide.

The prosecutor was young and determined, but this case was thin on facts, based on circumstantial evidence.

George S. Fitzgerald had signed for room 209 and charged it to his card, and the police had found him in this bed stoned out of his mind. A drug dealer admitted to selling him drugs, but said drug dealer was a very sketchy witness. And, even if he had been a font of truth, that G.S.F. had shared his H with my mother didn't make her death a homicide.

The case against G.S.F. came down to his statement to me the day before my mother died. He had been sitting on the stoop outside our house when I came home with take-out pizza.

"Your mother," he had said, "is a waste of oxygen. I wish to hell she was dead. I think I'm going to kill her."

I'd testified to that, but it was my word against his, and his attorney tore me into small pieces on the stand. Even if the jurors believed me, the proof against G.S.F. never rose above the level of reasonable doubt.

As soon as the case was dismissed, I fled to Baltimore, got my MD, and kept running.

Until now.

My driver was honking his horn, and there was nothing more for me to see. I slammed the door and left room 209 behind me. I had a moment of fright when I couldn't find my cab in the parking lot, but then I saw it parked on the street.

Giant Teen was trotting toward me.

I shouted, "I changed my mind!" and tossed him the key.

I got into the cab.

My driver said, "I was about to go. Where to now?"

"Portman House," I said. It was a small and decent boutique hotel about five miles from this spot and near the MIT campus. Parents of college kids stayed there.

"Good choice," said my driver. He turned the cab around, and as we headed back into the better parts of Cambridge, I wondered what I was going to do, where I was going to live, what my life was going to be like now and from this point forward.

I wondered if God was going to let me in on any plan He might have for me. Or if it was all up to me.

I knew the answer. Up to me.

CHAPTER 70

THE FRESH images of my mother's death, combined with the excruciating losses of Karl and Tre, washed over me like a tsunami, overwhelming me and leaving me gasping for meaning that just wasn't there.

I asked the driver to stop at the closest liquor store and wait for me. He gave me a look that told me he deeply regretted letting me into his cab, but he pulled up to Liquor World on White Street and kept the motor running.

I said, "Anything I can get you while I'm shopping?"

"Just hurry up."

I did that, and fifteen minutes later, I checked into Portman House. My room was clean. It faced the rear. It suited me perfectly.

I wanted to drink myself into oblivion, and I had a right to do it. I hung the Do Not Disturb sign on the doorknob and closed the curtains. I drank. I slept, and I wrote letters to Karl and to Tre in my digital journal. I spoke out loud to Karl as I wrote, and, of course, he didn't answer back.

After I'd saved my new pages, I unloaded my anger at my parents and held nothing back. There was a lot to unpack, spanning the first twenty years of my life, and the writing was exhausting. I drank and slept some more.

Three days after checking into Portman House, when I had nothing left to say or drink, I made arrangements for an evening out.

My new girlfriend and I agreed to meet on the corner of Lansdowne and Brookline Avenue in Boston, not far from Fenway Park.

"Let me reimburse you for my ticket," said Katharine Dunlop, the shrink I had met on the plane.

"No way," I said. "My treat. I'm so glad you could come."

It was a great night to go to a ballgame.

The sky was cloud-free. The stands were almost full, and the hotel's concierge had gotten me two of the best seats in the State Street Pavilion Club, behind home plate, near the press boxes, and with a great view of the game and the ballpark.

I'd never had such good seats in my life.

Katharine and I passed on the fine dining in the clubhouse and each put down two fully loaded hot dogs. I managed to get down a third. Heaven on a bun.

The game itself was a laugher. Despite playing barely .500 ball for most of the season, the Red Sox crushed the second-place Orioles 16–2. Third baseman Francisco Burgos and rookie shortstop Ted Lightwell both homered, while lefty Aaron Jenkins pitched a six-hit complete game, striking out nine. As I'd done at games as a kid, I kept score, which allowed me to stay focused on the action while I chatted with Katharine.

Night games always feel otherworldly, and tonight it was all that and more. The lights blazing down on Fenway Park encapsulated the game, separating it from the blackness of night and everything that had happened before the first ball was thrown.

The game was a great escape, a magnificent emotional release.

When I got back to my room that night, I emptied a bottle and a half of scotch down the sink and started a new journal entry about my mother.

Dear Mom, I wrote.

I wish you had told me about my real father. I guess you had your reasons.

Maybe you were protecting me from G.S.F. or from the man you'd been with. Maybe you thought that I'd never find out, but I have found out. And now I have a lifetime of questions that will never be answered.

I will never know if I look like my father, if he was good or bad, if he knew that he had a daughter, and if he would have loved me. I wonder if I have half siblings and a whole other family right here in Cambridge. That hurts, Mom, very badly.

I continued writing, but the secret of my conception made it very hard to close the book on my past. Still, I wanted to forgive my mother for her many poor choices.

I knew that she had loved me.

I had proof.

I made a list of the good stuff: the birthday parties with helium balloons tied to the shrubs in the backyard, and frosted carrot cupcakes, my favorite treat. I added racing skates to the list, the ones I had pined for that my mom gave me for Christmas when I was ten. Sometimes I had even slept with them. I wrote that one of her choices had been to live with a man who hated her. Maybe she had thought she was doing that for me.

I balanced off her high anxiety, inattention, sugar mania, and long zombie absences with the coziness of watching *The Late Show* under a blanket with her on Friday nights, falling asleep in a hug. And I loved when she braided my hair, as she did before we went to St. Paul's on Sunday mornings.

All those years of Sunday Mass with my mother had instilled in me the love of God.

I would always be grateful to her for that.

CHAPTER 71

PRISM WAS a drug-and-alcohol rehab center on Putnam Avenue, only two blocks from St. Paul's. The director, Dr. Robert Dweck, had run a help-wanted ad for a part-time doctor, and I made an appointment to meet with him.

Prism's storefront had a rainbow painted on the plate-glass window, and bells chimed when I opened the door.

A psychiatrist, Dr. Robert Dweck was a tall, bearded man in his mid-fifties, with thick glasses and a generous smile. He offered me a seat in his small office, read my résumé, whistled, then asked me, "You sure you want to work for a low-rent, city-funded operation like this?"

"Absolutely. I'm putting down new roots."

Dr. Dweck said, "You should know what you'd be getting into. Many of our clients are triple-whammied: physical disabilities, mental disorders, and drug or alcohol dependencies. You want to feel needed, Dr. Fitzgerald? This is the job for you. But I need you to know you'd make more money flipping burgers."

"Not a problem," I told him.

He said, "Okay, Dr. Fitzgerald. If your references check out, you've got yourself a job. Can you start on Monday?"

We shook hands, and I filled out some forms.

When I handed them back, Dr. Dweck smiled. "Is it Monday yet?"

"I'll see you then," I said.

After leaving the clinic, I called ahead to the real-estate company that had lined up a few properties for me to see. The agent said, "I don't know if you'd be interested in a handyman special. It's a good, old house, very cheap and in a great location. It needs tons of TLC."

The agent showed me the house, a narrow, two-story redbrick town house, built in the late eighteen hundreds. It hadn't been cared for in many years. The ceilings in the bathroom and kitchen were falling down. The doors were askew, and the floors sloped toward the street. But the bones were good, and the mechanicals were good enough.

It was equidistant between my church and new workplace. It honestly felt as though the house was calling to me.

I opened a bank account, and while I was still standing in the cool, marble lobby of Boston Private Bank and Trust, I phoned Heinrich Schmidt, Karl's lawyer in Berlin, and arranged for a fairly hefty wire transfer.

By the end of that week, I was a home owner.

It felt good. I was truly home.

The next three months went by fast.

I ran Prism's in-house clinic along with Louise Lindenmeyr, a top-notch nurse practitioner who had just returned from a stint of emergency care in hurricane-ravaged Haiti.

It was immediately clear to me that the staff at Prism did whatever was needed, no matter what their job titles. Dr. Dweck, "Call me Rob," was also a clinical psychologist. He ran group therapy sessions and also re-filled the copier's paper tray and took out the trash. I became proficient at fund-raising, administration, and making soup-and-sandwich lunches for forty people at a time.

When I told Rob about the falling plaster ceilings and iffy wiring in my house, he recruited skilled labor from among the clients at Prism. After that, my weekends were often spent making pasta lunches for the pickup painters and carpenters who buttoned up my little house.

I bought furniture. I hung photos of Karl and Tre in my bedroom and put a miniature one inside a locket that I wore on a chain around my neck. As I worked and feathered my nest, summer became fall.

My hair grew out with renewed vigor, and short curls flattered me. I cut way back on my alcohol consumption and didn't miss drinking at all. Rob gave me high fives for that.

I gave away my black hooded coat, bought new clothes. Louise said, "Let's go get your nails done. Maybe splurge for a pedi, too, while we're at it." Seeing hot-pink lacquer on the ends of my fingers and toes was unexpectedly hilarious.

I socialized with new friends and wrote to my old, far-flung ones, Sabeena, Tori, Zach. And I went to church every Sunday.

Occasionally, I went during the week at lunchtime.

That particular Wednesday, the church was almost as empty as it was when I stumbled into St. Paul's on my first day back in Cambridge. I went to "my" end of the first pew and had a one-way, silent conversation with God, and when I opened my eyes, I expected to see Father Aubrey.

I was disappointed that he wasn't there.

I crossed myself and left the church and almost walked right into him as he was coming out of the rectory.

"I'm heading out for a burger and beer," James said. "Care to join me?"

So far, I'd only had coffee that day, and I gladly accepted his offer.

CHAPTER 72

THE PICKLED Hedgehog was an Irish-style pub on Massachusetts Avenue, less than a ten-minute walk from the church. The interior was hunter green, and strip lighting sparkled around the ceiling's perimeter. Father James Aubrey and I sat down at a table with a view of the street.

James said to the waiter, "Heineken from the tap. Brigid?"

"Same for me."

When the waiter returned with beer, I told James about my new patient, a man who'd been living in his car until he found his way to Prism.

"Turns out he's my age," I said. "We went to middle school together."

"Meth user?" James asked.

"Yes, sorry to say."

The burger was perfect. The fries kind of sent me to the moon, and I was enjoying the company.

But James was distracted.

He kept his phone on the table, and when it buzzed, he said, "Excuse me," and walked outside. I saw him through the glass, looking agitated, and then he got angry. When he returned to our table, he apologized and said, "I have a confession to make."

"You're confessing to me? Maybe we should have another beer first?"

"Maybe an IV from the tap."

"That bad?" I asked.

"The absolute worst," he said.

The last time a priest had made a confession to me, I had been holding his hand when he died. I looked into James's sad eyes and said, "Talk to me."

"I'm about to go on trial for something I didn't do."

"What are you charged with?"

"I am seriously afraid of shocking you, Brigid."

"My shock threshold is pretty high."

"I'm accused of sexually abusing a boy ten years ago, when he was fifteen."

"Oh, no."

Father Aubrey slugged down some beer, then gave me a wry look. "I'm not a pedophile. My accuser is lying. My lawyer is good, but he says we don't have a bulletproof defense, and priests tend to lose child-abuse cases ninety-nine point eight percent of the time.

"He wants me to settle out of court. Save myself the stress of losing at trial. There's only so much money my accuser can get from me, but to settle is to admit I'd done something to him. Which I did not do. And if I settle to get this done with, very likely he'll go after the school and the archdiocese. I did nothing to him, and I can't let him get away with saying that I did."

I was shocked, after all.

In 2002, the *Boston Globe* uncovered a pattern of sexual abuse of minors by Catholic priests, which was followed by a nationwide scandal encompassing accusations in the thousands. The *Globe* revealed that the archdiocese had protected hundreds of priests, paying off potential litigants, passing the priests on to other parishes. When cases had gone to trial, the Church lost, and it was common knowledge that the Boston Archdiocese had paid out more than a $100 million in damages in the last twenty years.

"The man who is accusing me," said James Aubrey, "was in one of my classes when I taught history at Mount St. Joseph. He might have had a learning disability. I worked with him after school a few days a week. It was nothing but class work.

"He flunked high school, and when I was charged with sexual assault, I didn't actually remember him. I hadn't even thought of him in ten years.

"I called him. I asked him, what the hell? He said, 'You shouldn't have done it, Father.' He *lied* to me. To *me*."

"He may have been taping the call."

"Probably. These past months have been awful, Brigid. I say, 'I didn't do it,' and people I've known for years look at me like I'm filth. That kills me. This whole thing is really testing my faith."

James paid the check and asked, "Mind coming back to St. Paul's? I want to show you something."

CHAPTER 73

I MUST have hesitated at the entrance to the rectory.

"It's safe, Brigid," he said, opening the door for me. "I'm a pedophile, remember?"

He turned on the lights, scooped some magazines off the sofa, and put some food in a bowl for an orange tabby kitten he called Birdie.

He excused himself, leaving me alone in his living quarters. I liked the look of his clutter. I checked out his bookshelves and found books on a wide range of subjects ranging from ancient history to modern poetry. I was studying a primitive painting of Jesus carrying a lamb over his shoulders when James returned to the living room with an armload of books.

"Please have a seat," he said.

I sat down on the worn, blue sofa, and he sat next to me. He took a photo album off the top of the stack and put the rest of the books on the floor.

The cover page inside the photo album was inscribed with the name *Jennifer,* and inside were photos of a very young woman in a hospital bed holding her baby, grinning her face off, her dark hair forming long, damp ringlets.

She had just given birth.

"This is my sister, Cassandra. And this," he said, touching the picture of the baby, "this is Jenny. My niece and goddaughter.

"The point is," he said, "the worst thing about this phony scandal is that I don't want Sandy and especially Jenny to think that I'm the kind of person who would rape, touch, or mess with anyone, boy, girl, or anyone."

He showed me more family pictures, and then he picked up a Mount St. Joseph yearbook. He held the book in his lap and flipped to the pages that were signed by students who had penned notes to him when he taught there.

Dear Fr. Aubrey, I'm headed to Northwestern! Thanks for all your help. I'll always be grateful.

Yo, Father A. Thx for what I know about WWII and JC.

James opened a yearbook from two years earlier and found a picture of a boy with brown hair and a crooked nose. He said to me, "This is Wallace Brent, my accuser and a pretty convincing liar."

The page was signed, *Father Aubrey, Thanks for all your help. Anyway. Best of luck, Wally.*

James said, "Wally flunked out the next year." He clapped the book shut and paused to catch his breath.

"I did my best to help him, and now he's determined to destroy my life."

CHAPTER 74

I CALLED Karl's attorney at midnight my time, and he called me back in the morning with good news. He had contacted Kyle Richardson, one of the top criminal-defense attorneys in Boston.

Herr Schmidt said, "Brigid, he's interested in James's case. Are you quite sure you want to get involved? This type of case is media candy. The fallout could be messy."

I thanked Herr Schmidt for his help and concern. And I took his advice seriously. But I was having a gut instinct that I couldn't explain. I had just met Father Aubrey, but I had faith in him. I found him truthful and authentic, and he needed a friend. In the strongest possible way, I felt that I was that friend.

I called James.

"I have a connection to Kyle Richardson," I said. "He's expecting your call."

"*The* Kyle Richardson? Brigid, I can't afford that guy. His clients are all rich and famous."

"Don't worry about his fees. Richardson *wants* to defend you. Let's see if you like him."

The next day, James and I had a preliminary meeting at Richardson, Sykes and Briscoe's skyscraper office on Park Plaza, near Boston Common. Fifteen minutes into it, Richardson leaned across the table toward James and said, "If you want me, I'm taking this case. I believe in you."

I was moved when Richardson showed that he too believed in James. It felt like the UN choppers coming in. Like might had joined right. As we drove back to St. Paul's, James queried me about the bills from this expensive firm. He said that he didn't want to have "obligations to unknown benefactors."

When he wouldn't let it go, I said, "Can you just accept that God works in mysterious ways?"

"Fine," he said. "Who are you, Brigid? Who are you, really?"

"You're funny," I said.

We both laughed.

And, finally, he dropped the subject.

But we both knew that he needed first-class help to save his reputation. He was an honest man, a good priest, and he had to clear his name.

Over the next three weeks, James met often with his lawyers, and then, as the date for the trial closed in, Cardinal Cooney of the Boston Archdiocese called Richardson, asking for a meeting with James at his lawyer's office.

James asked me to be there with him.

The next day, six of us waited in Richardson's conference room, wondering why Cardinal Cooney had called this meeting.

James said, "I'm encouraged. I think he's going to tell me that the Church is going to fight this charge all the way. That I'm not being left to deal with this angry lunatic alone."

A half hour later, Cardinal Cooney, accompanied by three attorneys from the Boston Archdiocese, were shown into the conference room and took seats opposite me, James, and Kyle Richardson's team.

I have to admit that I was awed.

The cardinal was a strikingly good-looking man, silver haired, with refined features, and he simply radiated purity. He was well known in the very Catholic city of Boston for his active community outreach program on behalf of children molested by priests.

The meeting began, and James told the cardinal and his lawyers about his entirely innocent history with the accuser, Wallace Brent, who was now twenty-five years old and a bank teller.

The lead attorney for the archdiocese, Clay Hammond, spoke for his contingent.

"Father Aubrey. Even if there is no truth to this charge, the right thing to do is to put the Church's needs above yours. We're asking you to settle this dispute out of court. We will work with your attorney in writing a binding agreement with the plaintiff, offering him a cash settlement in exchange for his recantation of the charge. He will guarantee that he will never discuss the settlement or the charges again. This scandal will be snuffed out, and you can get on with your life."

"I'll be laicized," James said. "Defrocked."

"That hasn't been determined yet," Cooney said to James.

James said, "I never touched that boy. I'm not going to say that I did."

Cooney said, kindly, "James, I understand righteous indignation. And I understand honesty. But a sacrifice for the greater good is in order."

The cardinal went on to make an impressive speech about self-sacrifice, quoting Gandhi, St. Francis of Assisi, and John F. Kennedy. He closed by quoting Ralph Waldo Emerson, who had written, *Self-sacrifice is the real miracle out of which all the reported miracles grow.*

When the cardinal had finished speaking, James's attorney said, "You realize, of course, if my client were to admit guilt, it would be an injustice and an indelible stain on this good man's reputation. His accuser would not only profit; it would encourage him and others like him to bring false claims against the Church."

Cardinal Cooney said, "James, do you have any money?"

"Very little."

The cardinal said, "If you let this go to court, we won't back you. If you lose—and the odds are heavily against you—you will have to pay the damages, and if he comes after us, we will defend ourselves. You will lose your church and our friendship. We won't say a word in your defense."

My mounting fury was firing me up. I really couldn't listen quietly anymore.

"Your Eminence, Father Aubrey is *innocent*," I said. "God would want him to tell the truth."

The cardinal said to me, "Dr. Fitzgerald, what is your relationship with Father Aubrey, anyway? How do you know that he's innocent? Explain that to me, can you?"

I'd had enough.

I said, "I can't explain it, but I know it, and so do you, Your Eminence. In your zeal to defend the archdiocese, you've betrayed the Church and your conscience."

The cardinal's face went white. As if I had slapped him.

When James and I were alone in the elevator, he said to me, "Good of you to stand up for me, Brigid. Thank you for doing this."

CHAPTER 75

IT WAS the third day of Father James Aubrey's trial for child sexual abuse. I'd been sitting in the front row of the packed gallery from the first moment of the trial and had been in constant agony over what James had had to endure.

I had a clear view of the defense table, where James and his three attorneys scribbled notes. A few rows back from me, two of Cardinal Cooney's legal henchmen watched the proceedings with apparent disdain.

Up ahead, sitting at the bench between two flags, was Judge Charles Fiore. He was in his fifties, a Boston native, and a Catholic. So far, he had shown no emotion and had maintained order in his court.

On day one, I had listened in openmouthed disbelief as Wallace Brent, a young man with a cherubic face and a crisp, gray suit, told his horrible lies. He testified that when he was a sophomore at Mount St. Joseph high school, Father Aubrey had taken him for long walks in the woods behind the school, where he had fondled and kissed him and told him that he loved him.

He said, "Father Aubrey told me that he would deny it if I ever said anything to anyone. And now, that's what he's doing."

Brent concluded by saying, "I trusted Father Aubrey. I knew what he was doing to me was wrong, but I felt helpless to stop him. My grades crashed, and I flunked out of school. I can't live with the shame of it anymore. Not a day goes by when I don't think about what Father Aubrey did to me."

Brent swung his gaze to the defense table and leveled his charge at James. *"Father Aubrey. You ruined me."*

Murmurs swept the courtroom, interrupted by Judge Fiore asking Kyle Richardson if he wished to question the witness.

Richardson stood, gave Brent a cutting stare, and then did his best to discredit him.

Do you always tell the truth, Mr. Brent?

Did Father Aubrey write any notes to you?

Did anyone ever see the two of you together?

Did you ever tell anyone about this alleged sexual attention, either at the time or later?

No mention to a friend, a parent, another student, a nurse?

Is there anyone at all who can verify your unsupported accusations against my client?

Richardson was so good, most liars would have folded under his skillful cross. But there was only so much Richardson could do. It was James's word against Brent's. And Brent didn't have to prove what happened. He just needed to convince the jury that he was telling the truth.

If he did that, he stood to cash in, Father Aubrey be damned.

The plaintiff's attorney, Terry Marshall, was a woman in her thirties, trim, well dressed, with shoulder-length dark hair. She stepped smartly and pivoted like a circus pony as she questioned her next witness, Andrew Snelling, a former colleague of James's who had worked at Mount St. Joseph at the time of the made-up-for-profit crime.

Snelling was a beak-nosed priest of about forty who grinned inappropriately, his eyes darting around the courtroom as he told the court, "I always thought Aubrey was guilty of *something.*"

He was going for a laugh, but he didn't get it.

Richardson jumped to his feet and snapped, "Objection, Your Honor. Speculative, irrelevant, and improper character evidence."

"Sustained," said Judge Fiore. "Clerk, please strike the witness's last remark. The jury will disregard. Father Snelling, facts only, please."

It was one small point for our side, the first of the day. Terry Marshall had no further questions for Snelling, and Kyle Richardson cross-examined him, asking, "Did you ever see James act in a sexual way toward Mr. Brent?"

Snelling had to admit, "I never actually saw anything with my own eyes." But the tone and the sordid implications remained like the odor of rotting garbage.

"I have nothing further," said Richardson, and with that, Marshall stood up and told the judge, "We rest our case."

When James turned to his attorney, I saw from his expression that all of the plaintiff's blows had landed. I was worried for James and couldn't do a damned thing to help him.

That hurt.

CHAPTER 76

AT HALF past noon, court recessed for lunch.

I went down to the street and saw just how crazy it had gotten outside Suffolk County Superior Court. A restless, chanting mob filled Pemberton Square, clearly *enraged* by what they had read in the media. James Aubrey, yet another priest, was accused of committing obscene acts with a child. And they just *knew* he was guilty.

Signs with vile words and James's face scrawled in black marker pen bobbed over the heads of the riotous crowd. TV news outlets interviewed the loudest, angriest protesters.

I texted James: *Courage. The truth will out.*

He didn't reply.

I leaned against the courthouse wall and surfed the news with my phone. The stats of priests found guilty of child abuse were all there on the front pages, including one that claimed that 98 percent of sexual-abuse allegations against Catholic priests were found to be true.

The *Boston Globe* had scooped the original, shocking priest child-abuse scandal and had a proprietary interest in the subject.

Today, the *Globe* had profiled the "victim," Wallace Brent, peppering the piece with ugly quotes from Brent himself. It was disgusting, disgraceful, and the media found it irresistible.

At 2:15, I was back inside courtroom 6F, where the trial began again, this time with Kyle Richardson presenting James's case.

First up was a grade-school registrar who testified that Wallace Brent had lied about his salary and address in order to get his kids into their private school.

The next witness testified that Brent had lied about the extent of his injuries in a car accident, received a whopping settlement, and had later been photographed snowmobiling.

A third witness, a bank VP, told the court that Brent had forged a college transcript and that he was stunned to learn that, in fact, Brent hadn't gone to college at all.

Brent was being revealed as not just a liar, but a hard-core, long-term fabricator. At least, that was how I saw it.

Having taken a few shots at Brent's character, Richardson called character witnesses to speak for James.

Father Harry Stanton had been the dean of students at Mount St. Joseph ten years before. There was a respectful hush in the courtroom as the stately old gentleman took the stand.

When he'd been sworn in and seated, Dean Stanton detailed James's five years at the school, describing him as a highly regarded and inspirational history teacher. He was a good witness, but his testimony was dry, and the jurors looked bored.

Three sterling members of the St. Paul's congregation took the stand in succession to say that they would trust James with their money, their wives, their children, and their secrets.

I grew increasingly hopeful that these testimonies were helping James, but the plaintiff's attorney repeatedly responded, "No questions for the witness, Your Honor."

This dismissive rejoinder was meant to convey to the jurors that the testimonies of Richardson's witnesses were meaningless, as none of these people could support James's claim that he had never touched Wally Brent.

As promised by Cardinal Cooney, no one from the archdiocese testified for James.

The third day was coming to a close when James leaned toward his attorney and whispered to him from behind his hand. Whatever he was saying, Richardson wasn't going for it.

He shook his head and said, "No, I don't agree."

The judge asked what was going on, and Richardson stood up and said, "My client would like to testify in his own defense."

Fiore asked James if he understood that he was not required to testify and that the jury was not permitted to make any inference or draw any conclusion if he didn't testify.

James said, "I understand, Your Honor. I need to be heard."

"Well, Mr. Richardson," said the judge, "call your client to the stand."

CHAPTER 77

JAMES WORE a black suit with his priest's collar and had brushed his sandy-blond hair back from his face. When he got to his feet, he flicked his gaze toward me, and I nodded my encouragement. I saw the new creases in his forehead and tightness around his eyes and mouth.

He couldn't hide what this trial was doing to him.

He crossed the thirty-foot distance between the defense table and the witness box, placed his hand on the Bible, and, after being sworn in by the bailiff, took the stand.

Kyle Richardson approached James and asked preliminary questions. Then he said, "Father Aubrey, is it okay for me to call you James?"

"Of course."

"How do you know the plaintiff?"

"He was a student of mine ten years ago."

"Have you spoken with him since that time?"

"After I was notified that Wally was taking me to court, I called him and asked him why he was doing this."

"Did he answer you?"

"He told me to speak with his lawyer."

"Okay, then, James. Ten years ago, when Mr. Brent was in your tenth-grade history class, did you have occasion to see him after class?"

"I did."

"Could you describe the nature of these meetings?"

"Sure. Wally was having trouble with reading comprehension. We went over the assignments, and I showed him how the text was organized, how each part had a beginning, a middle, and an end, how the parts related to the whole. But he couldn't grasp it. He needed more than I could give him. I suggested he take a remedial reading course, but I don't believe that he followed through."

"And did you have any social relationship with him?"

"Absolutely not," James said.

"And his testimony that you had inappropriate physical contact with him about a dozen times during his sophomore year at Mount St. Joseph?"

James snapped, "There's no truth to it at all."

"Any idea why Mr. Brent would make up such a story?"

James said, "No idea at all. I've never had a personal relationship with Wally Brent, as God is my witness."

Richardson nodded and said, "Now, we all know you can't address Mr. Brent directly, but if you could, what would you say to him?"

Terry Marshall was on her feet in a flash, shouting, "Objection, Your Honor!"

"Speak only to your attorney," the judge said to James. "I'm allowing it for now, Ms. Marshall."

James leaned forward, directing himself to Kyle Richardson, who stood at an angle between himself and Wally Brent.

James said, "The first thing I would say is, 'Wally, to say that I've been alone with you outside the classroom, that we had any kind of personal relationship, is totally untrue, and you know that.

"'I cared about you, Wally, of course I did. You were a likable kid, and you were frustrated at Mount St. Joseph. I wanted to help you succeed. I did the best I could.'

"I would tell Wally that I am shocked and very angry that he would make up this vicious story that discredits everything I have done in my life and everything I might do in the future. And I would say, '*You can't do this, Wally.* I don't deserve it. Take it back.'"

Before the last word had left James's mouth, a woman in a blue checked dress sitting at the rail right behind the plaintiff's table jumped to her feet and screamed, "*God* knows what you have done to my son, James, you *snake! You LIAR!* You—"

The bailiff reached the woman at the same time Wallace Brent turned in his chair and shouted, "*Mom, noooo!*"

The courtroom went *crazy*.

Brent's mother shouted "*You corrupted my boy!*" as the bailiffs forcibly moved her out through the doors. The judge hammered his gavel, and the volume got even louder.

Brent's anguished features as his mother was ejected from the court-room kind of worked for him. It was as if James's speech and his mother's reaction to it had brought back all the suffering he had described to the jury.

I felt heartsick for James, but I also had a moment's doubt. That was how convincingly Wally's reaction gripped me. He had all my attention when he pressed his palms to the table and got heavily to his feet.

"Wait a minute, Terry," he said to his attorney.

"Mr. Brent," said the judge. "Sit down. You may not speak unless you are on the stand."

"Terry," Brent said. "I've got something to say."

CHAPTER 78

EVERY EYE in the courtroom was focused on Wallace Brent.

His posture was awkward, his face was red, and his breathing was labored. I thought maybe he was about to go into cardiac arrest.

He looked across the well toward the witness box and called out, "Father Aubrey, I have something to say."

Say what? Was he going to hurl more disgusting accusations at James?

Judge Fiore said to Ms. Marshall, "Counselor, control your client, or I will have him removed."

Ms. Marshall snapped, "Wally. Sit."

And, like the big dog he was, he did it—reluctantly.

Fiore asked Richardson if he had anything else for the witness, and Richardson said that he did not. Fiore told James to stand down and Wally Brent to retake the stand.

Judge Fiore said, "You are still under oath, Mr. Brent. Do you understand?"

"I do."

Marshall approached her client with a little less pep in her step.

She said, "Mr. Brent, what is it that you want to say?"

Brent wiped his boyish face with his jacket sleeve and then looked across the well to James.

"Father Aubrey," Brent said, "I'm the liar. When you flunked me, I held that against you. I didn't get into college, and it was easy to blame you for that, too. I make crap for money now, and I read that settlements in these kinds of cases can be over-the-top, and I thought, 'Yeah. Aubrey owes me.'

"But you don't. If I go to hell for doing this, that's not your fault, either. You never touched me. I'm sorry I made all this trouble for you. I don't deserve your forgiveness, but for what it's worth, I am truly, truly sorry. I mean..."

Brent sagged forward and, raising his hands to his face, broke into sobs so heavy, they echoed like an oncoming train.

The judge slammed the gavel, shouting, "Order! Everyone! *Quiet!*"

James spoke from his seat at the defense table. "Wally, I understand. I understand, Wally. I forgive you as a man of God."

The judge again made an attempt to establish order, but the commotion in the gallery overwhelmed even the sharp crack of his gavel. Fiore threw up his hands, and I heard him say over the noise, "Stand down, Mr. Brent. Case dismissed."

Chaos ruled as the jury was released through a side door and the spectators scrambled for the exits.

I opened the gate and ran to James. His face was bright with relief. He stretched out his arms, and I hugged him. I felt a rush of energy flow between us, unlike anything I had felt before.

Honestly, it scared me.

"James, you won," I said with my face pressed against his shoulder. "I'm so happy for you. Thank God this is over."

CHAPTER 79

JAMES PUT his hand at my waist and guided me through the surging throng inside the courthouse and out to the street. Gleaming black limos waited for us at the curb and minutes later delivered us to Kyle Richardson's office at Park Plaza.

There were buckets of champagne on ice in the glass-walled conference room in the sky where, only weeks before, Cardinal Cooney had tried to bully James into confessing to a crime he didn't commit.

The room filled with giddy lawyers and staff until there was standing room only. Richardson toasted James, and James returned the toast with a wholehearted thanks to the entire team for believing in him. And he thanked me, too.

"Friends, if you don't know her, this is Brigid Fitzgerald. She introduced me to Kyle and hung in, believing in me and supporting me throughout this awful ordeal. Brigid, you've done a wonderful thing here. I can't thank you enough."

I waved away the compliment as a young associate came into the room with the latest headlines on his phone.

"Everyone, listen up," he said. "This is the *Globe* quoting His Eminence Cardinal Brian Cooney. 'We thank the Lord that Father Aubrey was acquitted. We have always believed in his innocence and forgive his accuser. We pray Wallace Brent will seek forgiveness from God.'"

The hypocrisy was dazzling, and Richardson nailed it, saying, "What bullshit."

A hundred people applauded.

An hour later, James and I tripped down the stairs to St. Paul's basement, where the congregation had pulled together an impressive spread of food and drink in the brightly lit, low-ceilinged room.

James made a short, heartfelt speech about friends and faith and closed by saying, "Thank you all for believing in me. It means so much."

Men and women crowded him, hugged him, and told him that they never doubted him. We drank wine from Styrofoam cups and ate homebaked sugar cookies, and after the last well-wishers called out their good-byes, James invited me to the rectory.

"I really need to feed my poor cat," he said.

While James fed Birdie and changed out of his suit, I plopped onto the sofa. I kicked off my shoes and leaned back so that I could really take in the quaint painting over the mantel of Jesus carrying the lamb.

I must have dozed off, because I started when James came into the sitting room. He wore khakis and a blue shirt, and his hair was wet. There was a look on his face that I couldn't quite read.

He was nervous, I saw that, but I had no idea why. He pulled a chair up to the sofa, sat in it with his hands clasped in his lap, and said, "Brigid, now that I'm free of this trial, I want to tell you my plans."

Plans? What plans?

"Don't hold back," I said. "You know my shock threshold is quite high." I put my hand above my head.

He grinned.

"Okay. I'm leaving St. Paul's. After the way the archdiocese treated me, I just can't be their kind of priest any longer."

I stared at him blankly, finally managing to get out, "What will you do?"

"There may be a place for me in a little church near Springfield. It's a farming town. I like the authenticity of that. I want to try it out."

"You're leaving Cambridge?"

"As soon as I can. I have to ask you a favor. Will you keep Birdie for me? I don't want to leave her. And I don't know where I'm going to live. Everything is going to be in flux for a while and . . . Will you?"

"Okay," I said, still rocked by his news. "I've never had a cat."

"Thanks, Brigid. I really appreciate this."

James put the kitten in a carrier and toys and a bowl into a shopping bag, and then he walked me home.

For the first time, I felt awkward around James.

He was saying that he would notify the archdiocese in the morning, that he would tell the congregation the news on Sunday. I nodded, thinking that St. Paul's Church would feel so empty without him. That I would feel empty, too.

When we reached my front stoop, James bent to the carrier and stroked Birdie's face through the grille.

"You behave yourself, Birdie."

He stood up and smiled at me, wrapped me in a hug, and said, "Thanks again, Brigid. You'll be in my prayers."

I felt that rush again, both exciting and frightening. I held on to him, feeling everything: the pounding of my heart, the tears in my eyes, the sound of his breathing, and the warmth of his cheek against mine.

"You're doing the right thing," I said.

"I hope so. Be safe. I'll miss you."

He kissed my cheek before releasing me and headed off up the street.

I climbed my stoop, holding the carrier with a crying kitten inside, and when I turned to look after James and wave good-bye, he had already rounded the corner.

He was gone from my life. Just gone.

CHAPTER 80

AS THINGS turned out, I didn't have time to think about what James was doing in the next chapter of his life.

Birdie was a slippery, scampering handful. She thought my two-story house was built just for her and loved racing up and down the stairs, hiding in the laundry pile, pushing her tail in my face when I took to my laptop, and pawing the screen as my typing made the letters appear.

This orange pile of fluff made me laugh out loud, and at night, she slept on my pillow, right next to my face.

In the morning, Birdie woke me up by patting my nose and giving me a long, insistent meow.

"I get it, Birdie," I'd say.

I would feed her, turn on Animal Planet, set her up for her day before getting ready for my own.

I loved my job at Prism.

The brisk two-block walk to work was an excellent transition from the stability of my home to Prism, which was the center of a storm from the beginning to the end of the day.

Prism's clients needed medical care, psychological counseling, and breakfast, and everything we did for them had to be documented, filed, and printed out for the patient.

Over the next few months, my job responsibilities expanded, then doubled again. One of my grant papers got a hit, and we received a tidy windfall from an NGO. Four months into my employment, we opened a pharmacy in the empty storefront next door.

Our director, Dr. Dweck, was funny, expansive, and very loving. He used his platform at Prism to take our message about the dangers of drug use to schoolkids in our community.

"Synthetic marijuana isn't marijuana," he'd say. "It's two percent marijuana, ninety-eight percent unregulated components, which is as good as a hundred percent poison. This is a high that kills, get me?"

I volunteered often to go with Dr. Dweck to these schools. It felt good being with young kids who laughed and sang, weren't sick, dying, orphaned, tortured, or homeless.

Father Alphonse McNaughton took over at St. Paul's.

He was a traditional priest who stuck to the book, and his homilies were solid if not inspirational. I was asked to help with church benefits, and I always said, "Yes. When?"

Along with my job at Prism, good works were bringing me not just peace but joy, too.

Kyle Richardson took me on as a client, and together we set up a private foundation. I thought Karl would have approved of my anonymously donating his money to Boston clinics for the poor. My "father" and I had no contact, but when I learned that he had been admitted to an in-house drug rehab facility, I made sure that whatever Harvard's health insurance didn't cover was settled anonymously from my account.

When I came home at night exhausted from the activities of the day, unrest settled over me, and sadness rolled in like high tide beneath a full moon. James and I exchanged a few texts, but they were so impersonal, I felt worse after writing to him.

I prayed. I wrote in my journal daily, adding new stories of individual lives to my collection of hundreds. I entertained Birdie, and she did the same for me.

But I still felt less than whole.

I knew what was missing. I wasn't at the center of anyone's life. I was really alone, and midnight was the loneliest time of all.

That was when I thought of Karl and the best of our times, which had been spent lying together in bed, our sides touching, our fingers entwined, telling each other about what we had each lived through and felt since saying good-bye that morning.

And I ached for our baby. My instinct to check on her at night was still alive, even though Karl and Tre were not.

So every night, I draped my orange tabby cat over my shoulder, and I climbed the stairs. We got into bed, and I thanked God for all the good things in my life.

I closed my eyes, and then a paw would tap my nose, a yowl would ensue, as another morning arrived.

CHAPTER 81

ON A dark January morning, a blizzard fell on Boston and wrapped it in a cold, blinding hug.

When I arrived at Prism, homeless people bundled in rags were piled up three deep against the storefront. There were no lights inside the facility, and no one was home.

Rob called me. He was stuck in a snowdrift on Pearl Street. I had never needed a key to Prism, and I didn't have one now.

Louise, our nurse practitioner, had a spare, and she was on the way, but before she arrived, someone hurled a spanner through the glass of our new pharmacy. The opportunity to steal drugs was too good to pass up, and people poured in through the shattered plate-glass window.

I dialed 911 and was yelling to the operator that we needed squad cars, pronto, when a boy of about ten threw his arms around my waist and cried, "Don't let them take Mommy to jail. Please."

I hugged him back as people eddied around us and snow obliterated the curbs and hydrants along Putnam Avenue. Louise called out to me over the wail of sirens as she came up the sidewalk toward Prism, her head lowered against the driving snow. As squad cars streamed onto the street with red lights flashing, my phone rang in my hand.

"Rob? It's a mess. But Louise—"

"Brigid. It's James."

"What?"

It was too much to comprehend in one second.

The boy broke away from me, Louise struggled with the door lock, dark figures scattered with bags of drugs in their arms, and cop radios snapped and crackled around us.

"James!" I shouted into the phone. "I can't talk now."

"Call back when you can," he said.

It took all morning to sort out the chaos. Our clients were let inside. The young boy found his mother, and they came in for coffee and a good cry. Rob arrived by ten and shouted orders in the calmest possible way. When I finally got to my office, shed my coat, scarf, and mittens, I hit the Return Call button on my phone.

"James?"

"Everything okay?" he asked me.

"For the moment," I said. "How are you?"

"Can you take a break for a day or so? I want you to see what I'm up to."

"James. Tell me. What is it?"

"Telling you will spoil the fun. You have to see this for yourself. Expect the unexpected."

I was actually a little annoyed. I hadn't heard from James in months, hadn't seen him in more than a year, and now he was telling me to drop everything, and he wouldn't tell me why.

"Will you come?" he asked.

"There's a blizzard here," I said, "if you didn't know. A whopper. And I have a job. And a cat."

"When the blizzard moves on, see if you can take a few days off," said James. "And bring the cat."

CHAPTER 82

SNOW WAS still banked alongside the Mass Pike as I drove my rented Camaro two hours from Boston to the small town of Millbrook, Massachusetts, population just under two thousand.

The GPS directed me to the only traffic light in town, and I parked at my destination: a little old clapboard-sided church that had probably been built in the late eighteen hundreds.

Birdie was in her carrier in the front seat, next to me. She had been intermittently singing along with my playlist but had finally gone to sleep.

I got out of the car to get a better look at the church—and I liked it. It was definitely showing its age, but it had come through the years in classic form and with its dignity, bell tower, and spire intact.

Beyond the church was a two-lane road flanked by small shops and spiked with large, bare-limbed trees growing between them. American flags hung outside the fire department and post office, and pickups sat parked along the road.

Looking back again at the classic old church, I wondered if it held the surprise James had teased me with, and I wondered again what it could be. I told Birdie I'd be right back, then headed up a stone path to the church.

The door was ajar, and it creaked on its hinges when I opened it and stepped into the dimly lit nave.

James was standing at the altar, reading.

"Yo. James!" I shouted.

He looked up, peered down the center aisle, and shouted back at me, "Brigid, it's you! You're here!"

He stepped down from the altar, strode down the aisle with arms outstretched and a huge grin on his face.

"It's so good to see you," he said.

I went into his hug, again feeling that great surge of warmth when he held me. It felt *too* good. Oh, no. I stepped away, looked into his face, and said, "James! You look terrific."

"You too, Brigid. You too. Life is treating you okay?"

"The short answer is yes," I said, grinning up at him. I forgot that I'd been annoyed with him. I noticed that he was stronger and leaner than the last time I'd seen him, and that his gorgeous blue eyes were no longer sad.

"I saved your spot for you," he said.

He walked me back up the aisle, and I laughed when he offered me the end seat in the first pew. He sat down next to me.

"So, how do you like it?"

I took a good look around the church, which was so simple and unadorned, it reminded me of a chapel in a monastery. There was no stained glass. The altar and the floor were made of hand-hewn boards, and the pews looked as though they'd been polished by centuries of people sitting, standing, and sitting again.

"I love it," I said, getting some of my equilibrium back. "She reminds me of a dignified lady of a certain age."

"Very apt, Brigid. When I saw this church for the first time, I said, 'Jesus Mary Joseph.' So that's what I call it."

"Hah! And somehow that name just stuck?"

"Like crazy glue," James said with a grin.

He told me that the previous priest had died many years before and that the church had fallen into disrepair.

He said, "Some people in this town followed my trial and contacted me about their opening for a priest. When I said I was handy with a hammer and a saw, that cinched it. The job was mine. Small salary. Lots of work."

"Hah! Not everyone's idea of heaven," I said, laughing.

He grinned. "It's perfect for me. Like hitting a home run with bases loaded."

"I'm happy for you, James," I said.

"You brought Birdie?" he asked me.

"Did I bring her? I thought you gave me a direct order. *Bring the damned cat.*"

James laughed like crazy, actually cracked up with a full-on, whole-body laugh.

He was nervous, *too*.

"Well, let's get her, please," he said when he got his breath back. "I'll make you both something to eat before Mass."

CHAPTER 83

THE RECTORY'S old oaken kitchen was as rough hewn and handsome as the whole of the church. James fried eggs, made toast and tea, and set out cat chow for Birdie.

When he sat down across from me, James began telling me about his concept for Jesus Mary Joseph, which he called JMJ.

"The idea here is that, while we embrace Catholic traditions, we're way open to change. I didn't step away from Mother Church for nothing."

"What kind of change?" I asked.

"To start with, no one gets turned away," he said. "We are inclusive, not exclusive. God loves everyone."

"No argument from me," I said.

"I'll drink to that," he said, clinking his teacup against mine. Then, without missing a beat, he said, "So, get this, Brigid. Despite the threat of excommunication, women are being ordained outside the laws of the Roman Catholic canon. I'm all for that."

My mind kind of spun as I listened to James speak with passion and conviction about the role of women in the Church, same-sex marriage, and the inclusion of all people who wanted to know God. I saw that he was trying to bring at least *his* church into the real and modern world.

"I've been lecturing," he said. "Sorry, Brigid. And *look* at the *time*. Come to Mass. Or just make yourself at home."

James left the rectory, and a few minutes later, bells sounded out across the churchyard.

I washed my face, did the dishes, set Birdie up in the bathroom with a litter box. I fluffed my hair, straightened my pretty blue dress, and went to church.

My customary front pew was taken, but I was happy for once to sit in the back. I noticed right away that, unlike St. Paul's, JMJ was filled with young couples, many with small children. Those bright faces of the young churchgoers filled me with hope.

James came through the side door of the church and went to the altar wearing dress pants and a dark-blue long-sleeved shirt with a collar, but no vestments.

A few people clapped and whistled. Someone called out, "Good morning, Father."

He smiled and said, "Back at ya, Slade. But I'm no one's father. Um, Ms. Mary Jane, texting can wait."

Gentle laughter washed over the body of the church, and watching James begin the celebration of Mass his way gave me more of that hopeful feeling. The choir sang, accompanied by a boy playing an organ that was probably as old as the church. James led the service, praying in both Latin and English, tossing in his own commentary when he thought an explanation was in order. And, although the service was informal and very different from what I was accustomed to, praying to God in this place uplifted me.

Did God see all these joyful faces? Was He here?

I closed my eyes and opened myself to God without any hope of reaching Him. It had been a long time since I had floated on a burning sea from a hotel room in Jerusalem.

But He *was* with me. Soft rain misted my eyelids and my folded hands, a faint breeze ruffled my hair, and a single word came into my mind.

Home.

CHAPTER 84

THAT EVENING, James and I walked up through a wooded hillside behind the church. Leaves and residual snow crunched underfoot, and the three-quarter moon spilled pale light around us.

James was telling me about the angry letter he'd received from Cardinal Cooney's attorneys—but I couldn't concentrate on what he was saying.

I was in communication with God.

I put one foot in front of the other, following James under the milky moonlight and deep shadows thrown across the path by forest trees. The sensation I was having was unlike anything I'd felt before.

It was as if I were passing through the trees and they were also passing through me. I was insubstantial, and yet I was breathing, in the flesh and the moment, hearing James's voice as we climbed up a wooded path.

James said, "Brigid, take my hand. This part of the walk is tricky."

I took his hand, and I felt his solid grip. And at the same time, my fingers closed on my own palm. I thought, *Dear Lord, what does this mean?*

The air seemed to swirl around James and me.

God. Tell me, please. What is happening?

The sounds of the wind and the night birds and the crackling of sticks underfoot and God's voice were all as one.

Be with James.

"Be with James"?

I remembered a time when I was speaking with God, and He said to me, *Be with Colin.* And I had gone to Colin within that vision and spoken with him, and he had spoken with me—even though Colin had already died.

James was alive.

I was in that place deep inside my mind where somehow, I could hear God, and I asked Him, *Do you mean, be with James in the moment?*

James was saying, "See that hump over there? That rocky outcropping? That's where we're going. Okay?"

The sense of God's presence left me. I heard James's voice clearly, and when he squeezed my hand, my fingers wrapped around his.

"Cool," I said, in a voice that wasn't quite my own.

James showed me footholds and held my hand until we were seated on top of the smooth hillock of stone.

"I feel very close to God right here," he said.

I nodded. But I couldn't speak.

"Boston is that way," James said, pointing through a cleft in the woods. "Tell me about your job, how it's going for you. I want to hear it all."

"Will you hear my confession?" I asked him.

"Your confession, Brigid? Well. Not as your priest. I'm just James. And you can tell me anything."

"As James, then," I said. "It's been many years since my last confession. I don't actually remember the last time."

"Just talk to me, Brigid," James said. "I'm here."

Be with James.

CHAPTER 85

I WAS sitting close to James on that mound of stone, feeling the pressure of his body against mine. The breeze was faint but entirely worldly. An owl hooted. Two deer, twigs snapping under their feet, bolted across the path below the outcropping.

"I once killed a man," I said.

I credit James for not saying, *You did* what?

"Can you tell me what happened?" he asked me.

I didn't want to look back to that killing field in South Sudan, but I had to do it. I had never told James anything about Colin, the hospital, the last day, when Colin insisted that I stay in the camp. But I told him all of it now.

"I defied him," I told James. "And in doing so, I took a life and also became instrumental in Colin's death."

James said, "Brigid. Oh, my God. Poor Brigid. Go on."

I told him about the injured boy I had been trying to protect and that an enemy soldier had rushed us.

"I shot him, James. I shot him dead. I never thought in my life that I would kill anyone. I have never killed a chicken or a fly, but this man was going to shoot. I swear to you. I swear to God."

James put his arm around me and pulled me to him, and I pulled away.

"There's more," I said.

"Keep going," he said. "I'm here."

I told him about begging Colin to help me get the wounded boy off the field when a second helicopter had come in, firing down on us, and that bullets had gone through Colin's chest. That he had died trying to speak, and that I had never-ending guilt about his death.

"Good God, Brigid. Of course you feel guilt. You loved him."

"I did."

As the moon floated ever higher into the sky, I told James about flashes of anger that I have had toward Karl for Tre's death. "I know it wasn't his fault," I said.

James squeezed my hand, and I kept going. I told him about seeing my "father" the very day that I had met James for the first time. "He told me that he wasn't my father and that he never loved me.

"I hate him," I said. "He's no one to me, and that's the truth. But why am I still attached to him? I don't need him, and I don't want him, and I can't forgive him for what he's done."

"He was your father, even if he was not your biological father. Isn't that right, Brigid?"

I nodded, but I couldn't look at James anymore.

Had I shocked him? Had I told him too much? Or not enough? I was still holding back. I forced myself to look into his beautiful face, and I said, "James, I have spoken with God."

"Of course. Of course you have."

"No, not just in my prayers. He has given me visions. He comes into my mind and conveys thoughts and words. I swear to you, it's not a mental trick. I know this sounds crazy, but these—these *thoughts* that appear in my mind did not come from me. They came from God."

"Brigid. The day I first saw you huddled in the front pew at St. Paul's, hugging yourself, I knew there was something very"—he searched for a word—"godly about you," he said. "I believe you hear from God. It has happened before to others who believe in Him. Tell me more."

I told James about my God-given visions of the killing field and of Father Delahanty, about the multitude of birds and about the burning sea. But I didn't tell him that only moments ago, God had put three words into my mind: *Be with James.*

I said, "He has told me to live my life to the full extent of it. That He can't watch out for all of us all of the time. We have to take responsibility…"

My voice trailed off, and then James was saying, "How many lives did you save in that emergency room in South Sudan, Brigid? How many lives in Germany?"

"I never counted."

"In your heart, have you done your best for the people you've touched?"

"I don't know. Yes. I believe I have."

"God has forgiven you—if there was ever anything to forgive. Can you forgive yourself? Can you love yourself as God loves you?"

I blurted, "I have feelings for you, James. And you're a *priest*."

He said, "Oh."

He enfolded me in his arms, and I hugged him fiercely back, pressing my face to his jacket, not daring to lift my eyes and my lips to him. He held me for a long time before saying, "Do you trust me to get us safely out of these woods?"

"Yes."

"Well, I've never made this trip in the dark before. With the help of God and a little moonlight, let's give it a try."

CHAPTER 86

I SHOWERED while James prepared dinner, and as I stood under the tepid spray, I thought about my vision while walking through the woods.

I had been passing through the trees and the trees had been passing through me, which seemed to mean that I was part of the woods, and maybe the world, as they were part of me. Moving through the living forest spoke to me of my passage through time and perhaps eternal passage and unity with all things.

I washed my hair and meditated on *Be with James,* which God had said in the same way I remembered him saying *Be with Colin* when Colin was dead. And still, in that vision, Colin had spoken to me.

I wondered now if *Be with Colin* and *Be with James* were ways of saying *Be. Be aware. Be conscious. Be present. Absorb everything.* And, specifically, *Be with James as he leads you through the woods to a high place where you open your heart and he hears you.*

What did James think of me now?

I dressed in jeans and a sweatshirt and walked down the hallway to the kitchen, where soft lights shone on golden oak.

James was at the stove.

He turned, smiled, said to me, "I hope this is at least palatable."

He dished up an aromatic stew and even put a small bowl of it down for Birdie. I was so hungry that my awkwardness with James fell away. The stew, the bread, the wine, it was all delicious, and after dinner, we played with Birdie, who couldn't stop looking at James.

"She remembers you," I said.

"But of course. I took her out of a garbage can. Didn't I, Birdie? Fetch," he said, throwing a ball of paper, and she brought it right back.

James said, "Brigid, the dishes can wait. Let's go outside. Put on your jacket."

We sat together on the rectory steps watching the light traffic. A couple walking by waved to James.

I was conscious of all that, but my mind was on James. I had told him that I had feelings for him. He was a priest and had taken vows of celibacy. Clearly, he cared about me, but not in the same way I was feeling. He cared about me as a shepherd cared about a lamb in his flock.

I leaned away from him and said, "James, if I leave now, I can be in Cambridge by midnight."

He said, "No way, Brigid. What's the point of driving two hours at night when I have a perfectly good second bedroom with a semidecent bed? Will you stay? I'm not ready to say good-bye to you again. Okay?"

"Sure," I said.

He said, "Brigid, I'm not a priest as defined by Rome. Not anymore. I'm just James."

"What does that mean?"

He reached his arm around me, pulled me close, and then he kissed me. As I marveled at the feeling of that kiss, he kissed me again, and I kissed him back and I stopped thinking.

James said, "You're always in my thoughts, you know."

I blinked up at him. He was so familiar to me, and at the same time, I had never spent time like this with him before.

"Do you think you could love me?" he asked.

I blinked some more. Could I love him?

"Could I love you? Do you not see me staring at you with big moony eyes?"

He grinned. "How do my eyes look to you?"

"Moony," we said together. We laughed and then James released me.

He closed his eyes and folded his hands. And after a moment, he stood up, reached his hand down to me, and helped me to my feet. I didn't want to ever stop holding his hand.

When we walked through the door to his bedroom, I heard the words in my head.

Be with James.

With the help of God, that was what I would do.

PART FOUR

CHAPTER 87

SIX MONTHS had passed since the morning I drove into a church parking lot expecting to return home that night.

Since then, I had rented out my brick house in Cambridge, resigned from my job at Prism, and taken a new job at the Spring Street Women's Clinic, and I was living my new life to the fullest extent in JMJ's rectory with James.

His church was flourishing. There were overflow crowds that included people from other faiths, and clergy from other churches, who came to JMJ because they wanted to replicate what James had done in their own parishes.

On that high-summer morning, James wore plaid and denim. He held Sunday Mass on the wide deck he and other men and women in town who also knew how to use hammers and saws had built behind the church.

Rows of folding chairs were set up on the lawn. Daisies encroached from the field, and James and the choir had to compete with birdsong.

James spoke to the congregation about changes he saw happening in pockets of church communities across the country. Priests were getting married, women were becoming priests, and more liberal views on same-sex marriage and abortion were shifting people's view of what it meant to be Catholic.

"These changes will feel radical and worse to some, but those who believe that God is love will have an easier time understanding that anything that gets between a person and his love of God is wrong."

James was a soft-spoken but powerful orator. People nodded as he spoke to his ever-expanding flock. But he didn't tell them what I knew.

Cardinal Cooney had called James several times, making serious threats: excommunication for one, and a civil trial on the grounds that James was defiling the brand of the Roman Catholic Church by advancing "seditious ideas" and, in so doing, "undermining the Word of God."

How could Cardinal Cooney hope to succeed with these charges? James was doing God's work, not just in JMJ but in the community that surrounded Millbrook. He was helping the poor, finding jobs for the unemployed, visiting the jail in Springfield, and generally bringing out the best in people. Three other JMJ churches had sprung up in Massachusetts, and I thought *that* was what had inflamed the archdiocese.

JMJ was spreading.

The choir of young girls was singing when my phone buzzed from my skirt pocket.

It was Kyle Richardson.

"Brigid," he said, "I'm sorry to tell you this, but G.S.F. is in Mass General. He's been diagnosed with lung cancer. Stage four. He's asking for you."

"What?" I said stupidly.

Kyle said, "He wants to see you before he dies."

CHAPTER 88

MY FATHER wanted to see me before he died, but I didn't want to see *him*. I'd filed G.S.F. away in a box the size of a small bean in the back of my mind and almost never thought of him at all. But I remembered what he said when I'd seen him last: that he had put food on the table, pulled strings to get me into Harvard, and put up with my so-called crappy attitude.

True enough.

So it came down to duty. He asked for me, and I owed him for all the things he'd given his wife's bastard child.

The Clinton Family Home was a nursing home near the town of Westbrook, in an agricultural plain thirty-five miles north of Boston. The sprawling facility had roofs topped with cupolas, walls of windows and balconies looking over a western view of endless meadows and pasture land.

I entered G.S.F.'s private room as a nurse was leaving with his lunch tray. He was sitting up in bed, looking pale and thin and just as forbidding as ever.

"Dad," I said.

The word just jumped out of my mouth. I went to his bedside and kissed his cheek, and he said, "Take a seat."

"Sure." I dragged a hard-backed chair to his bedside, sat down, and asked, "How are you feeling?"

"They won't give me my drugs, Brigid. Why not? What's the difference at this point if it's heroin or methadone?"

"Heroin is illegal," I said.

"I think you can get me out of here," he said, plucking at the tape holding an IV in place in his arm.

The veins in his arm looked like major highways on a map of the Midwest. Must've been a nightmare to find a good one.

"Leave that alone," I said.

He sighed and looked at me with a question in his eyes.

I wondered if he was going to apologize to me for twenty years of tough love without the love. I wondered if he was going to ask for forgiveness.

But he said, "This is it, Brigid. I don't mind. Take it from the great Franz Kafka: 'The meaning of life is that it stops.'"

He went into a coughing fit that lasted three or four minutes and must have hurt like hell.

I stood and put my hand on his back, keeping my eyes on the IV line, making sure that he didn't yank it out, and finally he pulled himself together.

He sipped water, then launched another lofty quote from the dead writers' and philosophers' society. "As Socrates so wisely said, 'The hour of departure has arrived, and we go our separate ways, I to die, and you to live. Which of these two is better only God knows.'"

"You're thinking of God? Would you like to pray?"

"Hell, no."

He tried to laugh and was overcome with a coughing fit, spitting blood into tissues, and the chest spasms kept on coming.

A buzzer dangled from the side rail. I thumbed it hard.

A nurse came in, took a look at George, and left. She returned a minute later and gave him a shot.

"You need anything else?" she asked him.

"What else have you got?"

"I'll check in on you before I go off duty."

He waved her off as if he were flicking away a fly.

But he did settle down. I sat beside him, watching blue skies and fluffy clouds through his windows, and tried to call up a good memory of me and G.S.F. watching a movie, or a ballgame, or driving somewhere or dancing to something. I came up with no good memories. But I did remember the harsh criticism, rejection, and unapologetic neglect.

"Dad," I said. "You wanted to see me?"

"I did?"

"Didn't you? Kyle said you asked for me."

"Oh. I don't remember. I was just thinking of something Nathaniel Hawthorne once wrote. 'Death should take me while I am in the mood.' And I *am* in the mood, Brigid. My will is out of date, and I fired my lawyer. But stop off at the house. Take the books and pictures."

"Okay. Thanks. Feel better."

He fell asleep then. It was the drugs, not death. I stood looking at him, thinking of him, my mother, our small house on Jackson Street, his inability to forgive my mother for having me or forgive me for being born. And now he couldn't even say *I'm sorry* when he was close to death.

I should forgive him, right? But I didn't feel it. At all.

I waved to the nurse on my way out the door.

CHAPTER 89

JAMES HAD asked me to go with him up the steep and narrow staircase to watch the sunrise from the bell tower. The air was chilly, but we sat close together on a bench built inside the railing as daybreak lit the distant hills. I liked this little seat with a view so much. Like the rocky outcropping in the woods behind us, where I had opened my heart to James last year, I felt close to God here. I also felt part of this church, this village, and very connected to James.

We were holding hands. James looked deep in thought. I asked him what he was thinking, and I was prepared for him to say that he was rehearsing his homily, or that the tower needed painting, or that he missed Harold Noah, a parishioner who had moved away.

He squeezed my hand and said, "I didn't think I was ever going to be this happy."

"I know. I feel that way, too."

But the look on his face actually worried me. He was happy. Okay. Was there a *but?*

I flashed on the two of us making love last night on the sofa in front of the fire. I hadn't seen anything but love and ecstasy on his face. Had something changed after he doused the flames? Had he finally hit a wall of guilt? James was still a Catholic priest who was living with a woman and having unabashed unmarried sex inside a church. Priests had been excommunicated for less.

James hadn't spoken since I'd boarded this train of runaway thoughts. He sat still, looking past the big bronze bell, out to the timeless silhouette of the mountains.

"James? Is something wrong?"

"I never looked for anything like this," he said. "I thought I would get my happiness from serving God. From helping people. Maybe from a big plate of fried chicken and potatoes every now and then, and sometimes happiness is a good bed."

"Sure," I said. "Nothing wrong with that."

But?

"I'm so lucky, Brigid. That, despite all the bad stuff I was worried about the morning I met you in St. Paul's, you spoke to me. And that I recognized you for the good woman you are. I'm lucky. Or God really does love me."

"Both, maybe?"

"Both. Definitely."

But?

"I was thinking that we have an opportunity," said James. "Well, we have many opportunities, but one in particular."

"What kind of opportunity?"

My mind raced ahead. Opportunity to open yet another JMJ church? Go down separate roads? Take—or, in his case, *renew*—vows of celibacy? What?

"I want to build a life with you in God's grace. I love you, and I want to marry you, Brigid. I want to be your husband."

Tears were in his eyes.

Tears sprung into mine, too.

"Is it okay?" I asked him.

"Okay to marry? It's okay with *me*," James said. "Is it okay with *you*?"

I was laughing and crying at the same time.

"It's okay with me," I said.

"Thank you, God," James muttered, grabbing me into a hug. "You scared me for a minute, Brigid."

"I scared *you*? That's hilarious."

"Hang on," he said. He released me, dug in the back pocket of his jeans, pulled out a little black box. He opened it, and there was a ring winking up at me, with a cornflower-blue center stone and a diamond on each side.

"I bought it in Springfield," he said. "I liked the sapphire, but if you don't like it, we can return it."

"Are you kidding? I love it."

He told me to stick out my ring finger, and he wiggled the ring onto it. He took both my hands in his and said, "Brigid. Will you marry me?"

I said, "Yes. I will."

I collapsed into his arms, both of us laughing, hugging, rocking, nearly toppling off the narrow bench that was never meant for activity like this.

When we were somewhat composed, James took me over to the ropes, placed my hands around them and his hands over mine.

"Thank you, God," we said together, and together, we rang the bell. Our happiness could be heard all over the town.

"Amen."

CHAPTER 90

IT WAS my wedding day.

I was in the tiny second bedroom in the rectory with four new friends, my bridesmaids from JMJ, who were buttoning me into my ecru satin-and-lace vintage wedding dress and taking pictures. There was hardly room enough for the five of us to stand, so getting me ready for the big day was quite a riot.

I *hoped* I was ready.

Since our bell ringing seven months ago on that crisp February morning, James and I had planned a church wedding that would be true to us and would also approximate Catholic doctrine, which filled a book with rigid rules and rites that couldn't be personalized or amended.

We also took turns being scared.

I pictured my dear Karl, who had died three years ago. Ours was the only marriage I ever expected to have.

After Karl's and Tre's deaths, I was so devastated that even if God Himself had shown me that I would marry again, I would have been appalled.

James had talked about his little freak-outs, too. He had taken vows of celibacy. He had never planned to marry, and the intimate architecture of a married life wasn't in his mind. As soon as he married me, he would be laicized, meaning he'd lose his clerical rights and authority.

He was giving up a lot to be with me.

After weeks of planning and replanning, we threw the book away. Our love was deep and tested, and we had broken so many rules that crossing the line into a godly but off-road marriage ceremony was just our speed.

Everyone in Millbrook was invited to the wedding. James spoke to the *Millbrook Independent,* the town's online newspaper, saying, "Come to our wedding if you can hear the bells—or think you can."

Now, from upstairs in the rectory, I could hear organ music filling the stairwell. Soon I would be walking toward the altar and my new husband. I was humbled, excited, and scared half to death. I was having physical manifestations of all of that—sweating and light-headedness—and then I was falling.

When I opened my eyes, Dr. Foster was peering down at me, and James was peering over Doc's shoulder, looking more frightened than when he'd been on trial.

"What happened?" I asked.

Katherine Ross, my bridesmaid-in-chief, said, "You were buttoning your shoes..."

Dr. Foster had a stethoscope at my chest. He asked, "Have you eaten today?"

"Bread. Jam. Coffee."

"Have you ever had heart problems?"

"No, Joel, I haven't."

"How about panic attacks? Ever had one of those?"

"No."

"In that case, you just had your first."

Doc Foster and James had each taken one of my hands and had helped me into a chair when Louise Lindenmeyr, my dear friend from Prism, burst in with a bouquet she'd brought from Boston.

"Brigid. Are you ready? Hey. What's going on?"

"I fainted."

Louise said with total medical confidence, "James, she's okay. You get out of here, why don't you? Brigid? Ready or not, it's showtime."

CHAPTER 91

JAMES AND several men from our congregation were straightening up the church after our standing-room-only wedding, and I was doing the same for our living quarters inside the rectory. As I picked up and put things away, hung up my wedding dress and boxed my shoes, I tried to remember *everything* that had happened today. I wanted to make sure to commit it to memory.

The first thing I remembered was that when my bridesmaids and I crossed the yard from the rectory to the church, it began to snow. In *September*. A new weather record.

Snowflakes swirled around the steeple and the metal folding chairs on the deck, and the decision was made for us. Instead of having the outdoor wedding we had planned, we moved into the church. As Bishop Reedy said before the Mass, "I don't think this church has been this full since Lincoln was inaugurated."

The bishop was a wiry seventy-five-year-old with great strength and flyaway eyebrows and a very loud laugh. He had retired with the archbishop's permission and was now a full-time farrier, living above his feed store, Reedy's Feed and Seed.

Bishop Reedy had always been a bit of a renegade, but for now, at least, he was in good standing.

The processional to the altar was both hilarious and joyous. All the five-year-olds in town had been asked to be flower kids. They had picked roadside flowers—asters, goldenrods, and daisies—and they'd flung handfuls of them onto the wide board floors. Everyone laughed.

James looked staggeringly handsome as he waited for me at the front of the church.

Bishop Reedy beamed.

He led us through the customary vows: "To have and to hold . . . until death do us part."

Honestly, that one gave me pause. I'd been through the death of a beloved husband before, and, while it was absolutely true that we would die, I didn't want to think about that today.

James and I exchanged our own vows after that, each saying, "I promise to love you, to listen to you deeply, to support your passions, to stand with you even when there is chaos around us, to be a safe place for you, forever."

After we had pledged our eternal love, Bishop Reedy blessed our rings and said, "You two are married now. James, you may kiss your wonderful bride. Brigid, you may kiss him back."

Bishop Reedy had hitched a team of dappled gray draft horses to a farm wagon, and James, Bishop Reedy, and I led the snow-flecked wedding procession to the Candy Factory, a confectionery inside a huge barn on Route 283.

The snow was like icing on the cake.

My memory of the receiving line under the hayloft was something of a blur. I know I shook hands with and kissed the cheeks of several hundred well-wishers who showered James and me with blessings.

James also hugged and kissed me a lot, and we were grinning into each other's faces when I heard my name. I looked up to see a very tall, dark-haired man coming toward me.

It was Zach Graham, aka Yank, and I hadn't seen him since our scooter rides in Rome. I had spoken with him when he called after Karl and Tre died, and since then, we'd texted back and forth during baseball season.

But I never expected to see him at my wedding. And, frankly, I wasn't sure he should be here.

He took my hand in both of his and said, "Sorry for crashing, Brigid, but I could hear the bells in New York. At least, I thought I could. Actually, I read the invite online."

"You're too funny, Zach."

"I've very happy for you," he said. "James looks to be a very good man. And I gather you're kicking the Church in the butt."

"So they say. I'm glad you came, Zach."

"Be happy." He introduced himself to James and said, "Good catch. She's the best."

The sad look in Zach's eyes told me that he still had feelings for me and that this wasn't the happiest of occasions for him. Just then, James spoke into my ear.

"Look. Coming through the door. I don't believe it."

Father Peter Sebastian from the Boston Archdiocese had attended our pretrial meeting in Kyle Richardson's office, and he had also attended James's trial. Now, he was at our wedding reception.

Why?

Sebastian was slim and dark eyed, and he looked soulful in his formal vestments. He joined the line, and when he was standing in front of me and James, he said very loudly, "His Eminence Cardinal Cooney sent me to inform you that this marriage isn't accepted by the Church, and, similarly, your other activities are disgraceful and officially forbidden. This is a heads-up. There will be repercussions, James Aubrey."

James said, "Only those who wish us well are welcome here, Father."

"The cardinal will be in touch," he said. He nodded at me, a sharp, silent condemnation, and when he was gone, his black presence remained.

James had squeezed my hand hard and said, "That bastard. Brigid, he's the cardinal's spear carrier. Don't let him bring us down."

I said, "No, no, of course not," but I was so stunned by Sebastian's pronouncement that even the delicious meal and dancing with my husband failed to undo Cardinal Cooney's hand-carried warning that was now part of our history.

"He can't hurt us," James had said once we were in bed.

I wasn't so sure. Sebastian had come a long way to confront us in person. Cooney wouldn't deliver a toothless threat. After James fell asleep, I saw Father Sebastian in my mind. There he was, standing before us on our happiest day, and a feeling of dread came over me like a storm cloud crossing a sunny sky. I opened my mind to God, hoping for clarity or guidance. But I was alone, and not even prayer could drive that darkness away.

CHAPTER 92

THE STILLNESS of winter was ideal for hunkering down indoors, making a home, and making love with consequences.

I screamed when I saw the two blue bars on the home pregnancy test, and James shouldered open the bathroom door, afraid of—I don't think he knew what.

"James! Look."

I showed him the test strip, and I told him what it meant. He grabbed me, lifted me into the air, and told me what a wonderful woman I was.

It was a fantastic moment, and James's joy over the baby I would be having knit us even closer as we planned for our future family. We had met in a church, married in one, made a baby here, too. I felt triply blessed, and I wanted to try for a grand slam.

I knew that G.S.F. had a limited capacity to love, but we had been in touch. He was dying. I wanted to give him some good news.

I called. I told him, "I'm going to have a baby."

He said drily, "Congratulations, Dorothy."

I couldn't tell if he was being snide or if he actually thought that I was my mother. He may have been confused because of the drugs, or maybe he was just lost in the past.

"It's Brigid, Dad. I'll send you pictures after the baby comes," I said.

A week later, Kyle Richardson called to say he'd been notified that G.S.F. had died.

I sat for a long time at my desk in the rectory, remembering my father. The bean-sized place where I had quarantined thoughts of him burst open and flooded my mind. I was both in the rectory and in my house on Jackson Street as a teen. My mother was in a drugged sleep in their bedroom, and George and I were in the kitchen, where he was reading my essay on epic poetry.

His criticism was scathing. I was just fourteen, two grades ahead of other kids my age, still fearful of his enormous, condescending presence. But I stood up for myself that day.

"You're being too hard on me, Dad. Don't forget. I've been getting As."

He had taken a pen and written across the entire face of the paper, *C–. Sloppy thinking. G. S. Fitzgerald.*

I wouldn't be able to turn the paper in the next morning. I would have to retype and probably rewrite it again. I shouted, "I hate you!"

And he said, "Hate me all you want. Someone has to give you standards. You need something to push against, Snotface." And then he quoted Nietzsche, saying, "'What does not kill me makes me stronger.'"

I was furious. After telling him that I hated him, I shouted, "I wish you were *dead!*"

I didn't want to remember that, but now that he *was* dead, I had no defense against it.

I remembered that I rewrote the paper. I got an A+. I didn't tell him. George gave me plenty to push against until the day my mother died and I finally freed myself.

But had I?

After Harvard, I had gone to one of the most rigorous medical schools anywhere. I had achieved high grades, and I had gone to one of the arguably most savage places on earth to practice medicine. Not once but twice.

There was no denying it in this moment, when I was all alone with the memory of the man who had stood in for my unknown father. What hadn't killed me had indeed made me stronger. And now I missed the son of a bitch who had been the dominant influence in my life to this day.

Of course I forgave him. Why couldn't I do it when he was alive?

I folded my arms on my desk then, put my head down and cried. I cried for the caring moments we never shared, for the fact that he had never told me he loved me and that I understood now that he *had* loved me. I cried because he hadn't known Karl and he would have liked and respected him. He hadn't known Tre and would never know the child I was carrying.

I cried because my father was gone.

When I was all sobbed out, I washed my face.

Then I went down to the church and prayed for G.S.F.'s immortal soul.

CHAPTER 93

WINTER MONTHS flew by, and while unique and devastating weather patterns disrupted growing seasons around the globe, spring unfurled in western Massachusetts with leaves and buds and red-breasted robins.

The first Sunday in May, James presented a woman priest to our congregation. Yes, a woman priest. Her name was Madeline Faulkner, and we welcomed her at JMJ with applause and coffee and sugar cookies in the basement room.

Madeline was in her mid-thirties, had degrees in theology and law, and had missionary experience in the Amazon. She made a presentation to the congregation and was welcomed and well received. If the archdiocese knew or cared about this new priest, they didn't say anything to us.

That evening, Madeline, Bishop Reedy, James, and I had dinner in our oaken kitchen: chicken stew and honeyed tea and fresh apple pie.

Madeline asked me, "Have you seen the film *Pink Smoke over the Vatican?*"

I hadn't.

"It's about a movement that began back in 2002," she said. "Seven women were ordained in international waters, outside the reach and regulations of the Roman Catholic Church. Incredible, really.

"Women protesting the exclusion of women by the conclave that chose Pope Benedict released a cloud of pink smoke in front of U.S. cathedrals in Rome. Other women, in support of female ordination, did the same in the streets and from balconies throughout the world. Pink smoke, Brigid."

I said, "White smoke rises from the Vatican when a Pope is chosen..."

"That's it," said Madeline. "Pink smoke suggests that one day we could have a female pope."

"May we live so long," Bishop Reedy said.

Reedy, James, and Madeline proceeded to quote historic church elders who laid down Church law blocking women from the priesthood.

It was quite hilarious, really, to listen to the three of them snapping out quotes from ancient history that still lived today.

"Paul," said Reedy. "A woman should learn in quietness and full submission. I don't permit a woman to teach or to have authority over a man. She must be silent."

"Tertullian," James said, grabbing my hand. "Woman is 'the devil's gate.'"

"Timothy," said Faulkner. "'I permit no woman to teach or to have authority over men; she is to keep silent.'" She banged the table with her fist for emphasis, and we all laughed.

As for me, I counted my blessings: I had love. I had friends. I had a baby on the way, and I was helping clergy who came to JMJ seeking guidance on opening breakaway churches like ours. A dozen new JMJ churches modeled on ours had started up throughout the Northeast in this past year. Congregations had opened their minds and their doors. Under the name of the church, the acronym *JMJ* was posted on the churches' signs and doorways to let worshippers know that all were welcome.

I was excited to be at ground zero of this sea change in Catholicism. A woman priest. A married priest. Inclusiveness was catching fire. What next?

CHAPTER 94

WE NAMED our 110 percent healthy baby girl Gillian, and she became Gilly before we had even left the hospital. She was bright pink, had James's blue eyes and my red hair, a glass-shattering scream, and she was absolutely beautiful, made with love.

James beheld his daughter with such awe, handled her with such tenderness, that it felt to me that he couldn't believe that he had actually fathered a child.

He kept saying, "Brigid, *look* at her."

"I see her. I see her." I brushed her wispy hair with my fingertips. "Gilly, open your eyes."

I'd gotten to know and love this baby deeply while I carried her, but when she was inside me, she reminded me of the months I had carried Tre and how much I had loved that little girl.

But when Gilly was first put into my arms, my heart swelled so much, I could hardly breathe, and, while I would never stop missing my firstborn, I was overcome with love for Gilly, more than I could possibly say.

I didn't let Gilly out of my sight. And that was exactly how she wanted it. She slept in our room, and when I took a new job at the Maple Street

Clinic, only a few blocks from the church, I took Gilly with me. I commandeered an office next to mine, had a door installed between us so that I could watch her all day. Worse yet, I documented her waking and sleeping hours, her appetite and her bodily functions, in my journal. I was keeping a medical chart. I was that terrified that she might for some reason die.

It was nuts, but I forgave myself for being overprotective. And James forgave me, too. Gilly must have approved of the care she was getting, because she kept growing and thriving. I finally exhaled when she was six months old and I let James take her out of the house without my hovering over them.

Meanwhile, media storms continued to rage around our home.

The press knew of Gilly's birth, and James's being a married priest with a child added to his colorful history and mine, creating too much human interest to be ignored. It was as if the tiny farm town of Millbrook, Massachusetts, were outlined on the map in red marker pen and reporters had stuck innumerable pins in it.

We'd been married for just over a year and a half on the day I plucked our baby out of her bouncy seat and said to James, "Expect the unexpected."

"Wait. That's my line."

"Yep. I'm just borrowing it. You can have it back later."

We three dodged the ever-present media vans at the intersection, cut through a lane between two cornfields, and connected up with a side street where I'd parked my car overnight.

During the mystery drive, I told James that our landlord owed money to the bank and that our rent wasn't covering it. He had decided to sell JMJ.

"I can't believe this," James said.

"I negotiated with the bank, and if you agree, I want to pay off the mortgage. We'll own the church outright."

"How much is it?"

"I can afford it."

"Really? Oh. Wow. I should have guessed by now that you are loaded, Brigid."

He said that without judgment, but, still, he sounded wounded.

"I was waiting for the right time to tell you. Is this the right time?"

"This church. You want it, too?" he asked me.

"Yes, I really do."

Minutes later, we entered the Springfield Bank and Trust. Mrs. Stanford was waiting for us. She motioned us into chairs in front of her desk and asked to hold Gilly.

"Gilly," she said, "you are absolutely breathtaking."

Gilly pinched the nice lady's nose.

We signed the papers and bought a church, and on the way home, we took the truck into a car wash. Going through that watery tunnel just amazed and delighted Gilly. She laughed, waved her hands, and burbled, making her doting parents simply fall apart.

If I noticed the silver hatchback that seemed to be around the church a lot and that had been two cars in back of us on the way to Springfield, it didn't register enough for me to even mention it to James.

"We own our home, sweet home," James said as we headed back to Millbrook. "You're stuck with me now, girls. Lucky, lucky me."

CHAPTER 95

WHEN MADELINE Faulkner became the pastor of a church in Pennsylvania, she was barraged by every type of media attention, from blog articles on both sides of the controversy, to unrelenting network-news pieces. A woman priest was a huge story, and my old school friend Tori Hewitt sent me links to the Italian news coverage of American Catholic heretics.

I was amazed to see our names and faces: James's, Bishop Reedy's, Madeline's, and mine, all of us accused of blasphemy in top newspapers and glossy magazines.

Meanwhile, right here at home, protesters surrounded JMJ and shouted at our parishioners as they came to church. Being at the center of what could turn into mass hysteria made me sick. James was also distraught. He prayed for guidance, and he apologized to the town for the way our presence had disturbed the peace, and he thanked town leaders for their understanding.

In fact, I wasn't sure the town board had our backs.

One morning, Gilly and I were just yards from the entrance to the Maple Street Clinic when that silver hatchback that I'd noticed peripherally cruised up to the sidewalk and braked hard.

The man in the driver's seat buzzed down his window and shouted, "Hey! Brigid!"

He was square-faced and flushed, with thinning brown hair and a thick, workingman's build. I didn't know him, had never seen him before. I put Gilly behind me, stood between her stroller and the car, and asked the red-faced man, "Who are you? What do you want?"

"You're doing the work of the devil, Brigid. I know it. God knows it. We're not going to let you get away with this."

We? There was no one else on the street—no cars, no pedestrians— which was absolutely normal for Maple Street at nine a.m.

I said, "Are you threatening me?" And when he didn't answer, I dug into my enormous handbag, filled with baby things, and searched for my phone.

I felt ridiculous, but I said, "I'm calling for help."

"Yes, ma'am," he said. "Do it. Go ahead."

Then he stepped on the gas, and his car shot down the street like a missile. I memorized his license plate, and once I'd settled Gilly into her office crib, I called the sheriff.

"A lot of people are mad at you JMJ'ers, Dr. F.," said Sheriff Munroe. "Just avoid this guy. He's just shooting off his mouth."

My next call was to my attorney, Kyle Richardson. I told him that I'd been threatened by someone who had acted truly crazy. "I have his plate number."

Kyle made calls, and by the end of the day, I knew the name of the man who'd said I was working for the devil, and that he meant to stop me.

His name was Lawrence House, and he was a former town councilman, now divorced, but, according to police reports, he didn't consider the divorce to be valid.

Kyle told me, "His ex-wife has complained about him, but she didn't make it official. The cops went to her place a few times, walked him out, and warned him not to bother her or the children, and he backed off. He doesn't have a record."

That Sunday, JMJ was packed again. The young people in Millbrook weren't discouraged by the press gaggle lining the street. In fact, many of them waved at the cameras and even spoke with reporters before going inside.

James was giving his homily when a man stood up several rows back from where I was sitting with Gilly and shouted, "None of you are Catholics! You will be damned to hell. Especially you, James Aubrey. Especially you, Brigid Fitzgerald."

It was Lawrence House.

As ushers tried to escort House out of the church, he got away from them and pulled a gun. I saw the flash of metal in his hand. Adrenaline shot my heart into overdrive.

I yelled, "Everyone get down!"

The family in the pew in front of me dove for the floor. Pews tipped, making shocking cracks against the floorboards, and people screamed. I hid behind the pew and covered Gilly's body, but in my mind, I saw that lunatic level his gun at James.

James said calmly, "Guns don't belong in the house of God."

"I have a carry license!" House shouted. "I can bring it anywhere."

Pandemonium erupted as some people tried to hide and others broke for the doors. Everything happened so fast that when I looked up, I was surprised to see that James and several of the young men in the congregation had tackled House and were holding him down.

I scooped up the gun from where it had fallen as if I were fielding a bunt, and then I called the police.

This time, they came.

CHAPTER 96

THEY MET over drinks in the archbishop's office at the end of the day.

Cardinal Cooney was cheerful. The men assembled around the fine cherrywood conference table in the plain, white room were the best lawyers in the city and probably the state.

Cooney knew all four of them personally and well: Harrington, Leibowitz, Flanagan, and Salerno. He played golf with them and belonged to the same political party, banked in the same banks. There were two other people at the table, his right-hand man, Father Peter Sebastian, who was Harvard Law, and Fiona Horsfall, a public-relations heavyweight.

They had worked together and had contained most of the garbage that had come out about the Boston Archdiocese after James Aubrey had been exonerated. After Aubrey got off scot-free from the charges against him, Horsfall had fashioned a campaign to make both him and the Church look as good as possible.

That wouldn't be their goal today.

Cooney made sure everyone was comfortable, then said, "It starts with Aubrey. He's the match to the gasoline. Breakaway churches are bad enough, but a runaway trend is intolerable.

"Peter. You went to the wedding. Tell us about it."

Father Sebastian clasped his hands together in front of him on the table and talked about Jesus Mary Joseph Catholic Church.

"It's about three thousand square feet and almost primitive. I sat through the Mass, and Aubrey is charismatic in the modern sense of the word. He could have done well in politics. He's freewheeling. He does a credible job, but he makes off-handed comments. He answers questions during the service. He reads messages about headlights being left on in the parking lot.

"What he lacks in gravitas, he makes up in sociability. I think he can move people. Well, that's self-evident."

Cooney said, "Thank you, Peter. I guess Jesus had some of these traits, which is why I boil Aubrey's influence down to one word. 'Dangerous.'

"Right now, we have the upper hand," Cooney said to the group. "What's our best move? Can we sue him for abuse of the word 'Catholic' when he defies the legitimate doctrine of the Roman Catholic Church?"

The lawyers were prepared.

They told Cooney that the word "Catholic" couldn't be branded or protected, that Greeks and members of other Orthodox churches used the term "Catholic," but that it was possible to cast doubt on Aubrey's authenticity and credibility.

Said Flanagan, "Make him out to be a cult leader, not a priest. There's a reasonable basis for it. And he should be defrocked."

"Already done," said Cooney. "He's off the payroll."

"And excommunication?" asked Salerno.

"It's in the works," said Cooney.

Sebastian added, "I agree, Cardinal, when you say that Aubrey is dangerous, but he's not invincible. He was accused of sexual predation. Even though his accuser recanted, we could say publicly and loudly that Brent recanted not because Aubrey was innocent but because he couldn't take the pressure of what the trial was doing to his family."

"What else can we use?" Salerno asked Sebastian. Salerno was a big man who spoke sparingly unless he was in court. Cooney thought him to be a great litigator, one of the best.

Sebastian said, "He's in love with his wife and child. He won't let anything touch them. An attack on them could shut him down."

Cooney turned to his P.R. consultant. "Fiona, what have you dug up on the wife?"

Fiona Horsfall held up a thick file on Brigid Fitzgerald. "She's very well regarded. Has a huge reputation for her medical work in South Sudan. She was considered heroic. Saved many lives. Assisted our military in bringing down a paramilitary terrorist—or, as some say, our military assisted *her.*"

Cooney was pacing now, touching the backs of chairs as he walked around the table. "Go on," he said.

"She exhibited heroism again in a bombing a few years ago in Jerusalem. She has done a lot of work with the poor and disadvantaged. She's seen as pious but accessible and down-to-earth. She's working in a clinic now."

"Forget about her, then," said Cooney. "Concentrate on Aubrey. Full-court press. It will be easier and much more effective to cut Aubrey down—"

Horsfall interrupted.

"Your Eminence. I think Fitzgerald is a big influence on Aubrey. She has been and is currently instrumental in the expansion of this JMJ movement."

"Fiona. You've just said she's unassailable. Focus on Aubrey. He's the public face of his church. He's the pervert who is challenging Rome and canon law, defying two thousand years of Catholic doctrine.

"Bloody him. Put him out of business. I want his ratty little JMJ movement to die."

CHAPTER 97

JAMES WAS patching the roof when a slick, blue late-model sedan pulled up to our doorway.

He jogged downstairs and asked, "Are we expecting someone?"

I had Gilly in my arms when we opened the door to Father Sebastian of the Boston Archdiocese.

Why was he here?

The last time I'd seen him, he had crashed our wedding, given us the stink eye, and wished us a bad life.

The priest said, "I'm sorry to drop in like this, Dr. Fitzgerald, but I have an urgent message for James from the cardinal."

"Have a seat," I said, sitting down next to James.

"Cardinal Cooney wants you to know that your excommunication is in process, James. You will be severed from the Church, and you know what that means. You won't be able to conduct rites of any kind—not Mass, not marriages, not confession, none of it."

James said, "I get it. I won't be a priest under the auspices of Rome, but I will be a priest under the auspices of God. Which is all that matters. Is there anything else?"

"Yes. It doesn't have to go this way, James."

Sebastian wasn't speaking to me or even looking at me. I could have been a dust bunny under the sofa. That was fine with me, because it gave me a chance to observe the cardinal's emissary at close range. He was well dressed, crisply pressed, presenting himself as a messenger, but he was more than that. Sebastian was Cooney's chief of staff, with a degree in law from Harvard.

"You've lost me," James said.

James's expression was even, but I knew that this threat from the archdiocese felt like being kneecapped with a ball bat. James loved God *and* he loved the Church.

Gilly felt the tension in the room. She reached around my neck and held on to me fiercely, and I shushed her as she started to whimper.

"Let me clarify," said Sebastian. "Cardinal Cooney asks that you stop this destructive rebellion, James. Don't call this a Catholic church. It's not. Stop proselytizing. Stop undercutting the Church, and the cardinal will drop our public-relations offensive. Do you understand?"

"I'm sorry you had to come all this way, Peter," James said, getting up, displacing the cat. "Be careful when you back out that you don't hit the oak tree. It's been here for a hundred years."

Sebastian stayed seated.

"James, I must know if you understand me. The full force of the Boston Archdiocese is poised to launch a campaign against you. You will be painted as a pervert, as a tool of the devil, as a cult leader, and your followers will be tarred with the same brush..."

I had heard way too much of this crap, and I couldn't stay quiet anymore.

I jumped to my feet and said to the outrageous Father Sebastian, "Please understand *us*. James is a good man and a good priest, and there's nothing you can say that will stop the JMJ movement. The Roman Catholic Church's threats, rigidity, and exclusion are exactly why people are coming to JMJ. We will fight anyone who gets between people and their love of God, and we will *win*."

Now Sebastian was on his feet, too, and Gilly let loose with her signature, glass-breaking wail.

"I wasn't speaking to you," Sebastian said to me over the din.

James said, "Brigid and I are of the same mind. I've got work to do upstairs. Rain is in the forecast."

The priest made a gesture, as though brushing dirt off his hands. When he had cleared the threshold, James closed the door hard behind him.

Baby and I went into my husband's arms.

"You okay?" I asked.

"I expected to be excommunicated. But I *am* worried that Cooney will intimidate people and that they'll be frightened away."

"Some will. Many won't," I said.

I took Gilly upstairs to her room and soothed her as I looked out her window. I watched Father Sebastian get into his car, and I stayed at the window until that black cloud of a man drove away.

CHAPTER 98

AT FOUR in the afternoon, I was stitching a nasty head wound at the clinic when a patient called the front desk and I was called to the phone, stat.

"Doctor, it's Chloe." Chloe's voice trailed off, and I called her name several times until she came back, saying in a weak voice, "I've killed myself."

"Where are you?"

"Downstairs. Tell my mom."

Chloe Tremaine was one of my patients. At seventeen, she was a heroin addict, twelve weeks pregnant, and trying to clean up. I ran outside and found her lying on the pavement, curled into a ball. She wasn't dead, but a great amount of blood was soaking through her pink flannel pajamas.

She was just conscious enough to say, "I had to get rid of it. Tell... Mom... I'm sorry." I tried to keep her talking, but she had passed out.

Chloe lived with her boyfriend in his parked van behind the pizzeria where he worked, around the corner from the clinic. She had come in irregularly for checkups and had told me that she wanted the baby, but she was shooting up, horrified at herself for doing that, not eating or sleeping properly. She was a total mess with a sweet personality and a desperately dangerous and chaotic life.

Now, curled up at the intersection of Maple and the highway, she was close to death. Her pulse was thready, and she had a high fever, indicating a raging infection. But the loss of blood was going to kill her first. I wouldn't be able to save her in our low-tech walk-in clinic.

By the time the ambulance arrived, Gilly was under the care of our head nurse, and I had Chloe's medical records in my hands, including her pre-signed permission for procedures including surgery to save her life.

As messed up as she was, I was fond of Chloe. I talked to her nonstop as we tore down Interstate 91 at rocket speed, assuring her that everything would be fine.

Dr. John Nelson, the attending emergency surgeon at Springfield Metro Hospital that day, had booked an O.R. for us and was ready to assist. We scrubbed in and assessed Chloe's condition as critical. She was given a complete physical, a blood transfusion, and an MRI.

We were able to ascertain that Chloe had thrust a sharp instrument up her vagina, likely a coat hanger, hoping to hit something that would induce a miscarriage.

The fetus was dead, and the instrument Chloe had used had pierced the spongy walls of her uterus, clipping an artery on the way to puncturing her bowel, which had introduced a massive infection. She was septic, on the verge of shock, and I couldn't even give her Kind Hands' fifty-fifty odds. The very small chance we could save her was still dropping.

Over the next four hours, Nelson and I performed a complete hysterectomy and tried to stabilize our young, stupid patient. I felt stupid, too, that I hadn't guessed during those prenatal counseling sessions that she had considered doing *this*.

Chloe survived the surgery, and her condition stabilized. I was looking in on her in the ICU, waiting for her mother to arrive, when a nurse found me.

I asked her, "Is Chloe's mother here?"

The nurse had a very strange look on her face.

"Dr. Fitzgerald. Your husband is trying to reach you. It's an emergency. You're wanted at home."

"What *kind* of emergency? What *happened?*"

The nurse didn't know.

It had to be *Gilly*. Something had happened to Gilly. *Please, God. No.*

I called James. He didn't answer.

I'd come to the hospital in an ambulance, and I was going to have to return home the same way.

I went out into the hallway and shouted, "I need a bus to take me back to Millbrook. I need it *now.*"

CHAPTER 99

THE PARAMEDIC drove the ambulance as if it were *his* child's life on the line. We reached Millbrook's town limits after I'd gotten the message that James had called. During that drive, I was in a roaring panic. My God, it was so late. The clinic was long *closed*. I'd forgotten *Gilly*. What had happened to her? What had happened to my *child*?

James was with her, wasn't he? *Wasn't he?*

I prayed, asking God to please let my daughter be safe, but if He heard me, He didn't respond. I called James until I had jammed his mailbox with my messages, and we finally approached the rectory.

What I saw was so unbelievable, I thought I was in one of my open communications with God. But this scene was 100 percent real, in this time and place. While I was out, hell had come to our door.

The street fronting the church was clogged with cars, and four fire trucks were parked up on the grass. Fire burned behind the church's arched windows, and flames shot through the roof. The blaze looked like a living thing, an evil entity that was determined to destroy everything it touched.

Where is James? Where is Gilly?

The churchyard was pitch-black and raging orange at the same time. I searched the fire-illuminated faces of the bystanders and called for James. Water arced through the air, soaking the rectory's roof, our home, only fifty feet from the blazing church. The flames fell back, but the heat and roiling smoke made even breathing nearly impossible.

Where is James? Does he have Gilly?

A group of men with their backs to me were talking among themselves. I called out, "Please help me. I'm looking for my husband and child."

The men turned.

The one closest to me was the maniac Lawrence House. He'd pulled a gun in a church jam-packed with people, including dozens of children, and warned me that because of our message, there would be hell to pay. Had he done this?

"Sorry, Doctor. I haven't seen him," House said. "You know what this is, don't you?" He waved a hand toward the conflagration.

"What are you saying?"

I was looking past him, scanning the onlookers for my husband's face.

"Divine intervention," said House, with great pleasure. "Di-vine in-ter-ven-tion. And you earned it. In full."

I was staring at him, speechless with fury, when someone pulled at my arm. I spun around, ready to do violence.

It was Katherine Ross, my former bridesmaid, and she had Gilly in her arms.

I screamed my daughter's name and grabbed a double armful of Gilly and Katherine together. Kath was saying, "Gilly is fine. She's fine. My mom has your cat."

Gilly reached out her arms. "Where were you, Mommy?"

Kath handed my precious toddler to me, and I kissed her and held her so tightly that she yelped.

"I'm sorry, baby, I'm sorry. I was at the hospital. Kath, where is he? Have you seen James?"

She shook her head no.

I gave Gilly back to Katherine and said, "Please. Take care of her. I need to look for him."

I ran.

I rounded the church, and I saw a crew holding hoses on the western side, the side that faced the rectory. James was wearing a fire hat and aiming a hose at the roof.

"*James.*"

I ran to him and held on to him as he kept the hose trained on the flames.

"I couldn't find you!" he shouted over the crackle of fire, the roar of streaming water, and the grinding engines. "Katherine has Gillian. I was in the rectory when the fire trucks came. I called you."

"I was in a no-phone zone at the hospital. What happened?"

James waved his hand toward the church, taking in the blackened walls all the way up to what was left of the bell tower.

"Our wonderful old church. I can't believe this."

But I *could* believe it. I remembered an image of myself floating on a glassy sea with flames leaping around me. God had sent rain. And he had enveloped me in a ball of light.

James shouted, "We hosed the rectory down so that sparks can't set fire to the roof! Can you give me a hand with this hose, Brigid? My arms are wearing out."

I stepped in front of my husband, and we stood together with our hands on the line, dousing the fire.

"Thank God," he said to me. "No one was hurt. No one died."

CHAPTER 100

AT ONE in the morning, James, Gilly, and I opened the front door to the rectory. Our little home was smoke filled, water soaked, and uninhabitable. James left his phone number with the fire chief, and we drove to the closest motel on the highway.

We went to bed in our clothes, didn't sleep, and were back at the site of the fire at six a.m. Police arrived, as did the fire chief, an arson investigator, and an insurance adjuster.

The fire was out, but the nightmare continued.

I stared at what remained of JMJ and tried to picture what had happened since yesterday morning, when I kissed James good-bye, got into my car with Gilly, and drove to work. Sometime between taking Chloe Tremaine to the hospital and getting word in the ICU that there was a go-home emergency, this devastation had occurred.

I tried to picture that first spark. Had the wiring in the old church frayed and started the blaze? Or had someone deliberately torched our dreams?

The arson investigator, a man with a deeply lined face and a badge pinned to his jacket, stopped us from going into the church. He introduced himself as Walt Harrison and said, "It's not safe in there, folks. The rest of the roof could fall through. Same for the floor."

We stood just outside the dripping doorway as Harrison flashed his light around the scorched and ashen interior.

"Here's what I see. This fire started under the loft. A Molotov cocktail, or something like it, was tossed under there. Superheated smoke and poisonous gases traveled into the bell tower and steeple. As the gases ignited, the steeple, the tower, this section of the roof, collapsed."

Pale shafts of light came through the open roof and illuminated the ancient church bell, lying on its side on the floor.

Harrison took us to his mobile office inside a van. He asked, "Who do you think would do this?"

James told Harrison about the raging controversy surrounding JMJ, concluding, "Some people"—his voice cracked—"a lot of people think what we're doing is wrong."

"So I've heard," said Harrison. "I'd like you to look at some photos that were taken at the fire. Arsonists—if it is arson—are fascinated by the fires they set. They really cannot stay away."

Harrison turned his computer screen toward us and clicked through shots of the crowd watching our burning church. I skipped over the faces of neighbors and friends and stabbed at the face of a man who hated us.

"I ran into him last night, Walt. His name is Lawrence House, and he told me that the fire was 'divine intervention.' Months ago, he pulled a gun in our church. We got it away from him before he could hurt anyone."

James gave details to Harrison, and I thought ahead to the near future.

Our congregants would have to be interrogated.

The church would have to be rebuilt.

Even the rectory would require rescue.

I thought of my father quoting Nietzsche at my fourteen-year-old self: "What does not kill me makes me stronger."

This fire hadn't killed us. We would come back from this. And we would be stronger.

CHAPTER 101

I WAS painting the new cabinets in the rectory kitchen when Zach Graham showed up without warning, shouting, "Hello, Red!" Totally startled, I knocked over a paint can, which jumped off the counter and beyond the drop cloth, scared Gilly, who burst out crying, and sent Birdie racing across the spill, tracking powder-blue footprints across the ancient wide-board floors.

Zach laughed at the chaotic scene he'd caused, which was right out of a fifties Lucille Ball comedy, with me in the starring role. I didn't find it funny. He got that, loud and clear.

"Uh-oh. So sorry, Brigid," said Zach. "I woulda called, but I don't have your number."

"That can be remedied, Yank. Got something to write on?"

"Let me help," he said.

His help with paper towels was pretty hopeless, but Gilly became fascinated with Zach's attempts and stopped screaming.

"All done," he said. "The floor can be washed, right?"

I was glad to see Zach and, at the same time, a little freaked out that he'd just shown up in my house without warning. I moved the drop cloth, the bucket, and the brushes out of the way, put on the kettle, washed my hands in the big, old-fashioned sink, and after Zach did the same, I handed him a dish towel.

I sent Gilly out to the vegetable garden with a basket for peas. The garden was safe, fenced in, and I could watch her from the kitchen windows.

"So. How ya been?" I asked Zach.

"Well, I broke a wrist playing pickup hoops. All better now." He flexed to show me. "I'm taking Italian at the New School. And my girlfriend dumped me because, I don't know. She said it's not me. She likes someone else better. My best friend."

"Oh, man," I said. "Will you live?"

"In time. Every time a door closes, etc."

I poured tea, brought cookies to the table.

Zach said, "So, the door that opened is actually a great door. Tall. Wide. With an awesome view."

"Really?"

"I've been offered a book deal. Actually, I mentioned your name, but I didn't expect a publisher to jump over his desk and push a contract into my hands."

"Wait. My name?"

"Brigid, I had this idea. The Jesus Mary Joseph movement really is a phenomenon. By my last count, there are nearly a hundred JMJ churches now, is that right?"

"One hundred and two. I think. We're not always told."

"I stand corrected. One hundred and two in what? Three years? It's tremendous. It's controversial. It's dramatic, and with new records being set every day for the number of bad things happening simultaneously in the world, people are looking for ways to feel connected to God. You and James are providing answers. That's what makes this a story that must be told."

"Zach, you're not a Catholic. You're not religious at all."

"You're right. But this wouldn't be about me. I don't have to be Catholic to believe in all the good you and James are doing," he said. "You're on the right side of history. And think about this. If I write a book about the

JMJ movement, it would offset the cardinal's smear campaign. That would be good for you, wouldn't it?"

Before Zach walked in, I'd been thinking about the fire investigation, which had gone nowhere, but the fire was such a personal attack, it remained lodged in my mind. There was no evidence against Lawrence House, and he was still walking free. I saw him at the grocery store, the gas station, the pizzeria, the thrift shop. He wasn't on my tail, but he was always around. Sometimes he was accompanied by other men, all of whom looked at me as if I were dirty. There could be another attack. A worse one.

I didn't want to go far from home.

After the fire, I'd taken a leave from the clinic and was splitting my time between managing the church restoration, consulting with priests who'd come to learn about JMJ, and spending mommy time with Gilly. James had been traveling during the reconstruction, attending services in other JMJ churches, which, as Zach had noted, were sprouting up all over the country.

I really didn't want Zach to write about us. Our work was about making the Church accessible to everyone. And yet, we were in the public domain. Could I even stop Zach from writing this book?

I stared past Zach to the garden, where Gilly was chatting with the scarecrow. My eyes welled up.

Zach said, "Brigid. Brigid, don't worry. I won't do this book unless you and James are behind it."

"I'll talk to James," I said.

"Good," said Zach. "No pressure."

Zach was a powerful personality, and his *New York Times* byline lent authority to all his work. Zach was our friend, right?

He hugged me and kissed my cheek, and I waved good-bye to him from the doorway. A few days later, after a lot of thought and prayer, I forwarded my journals to him with a caution.

"This is just a loan."

"I'll take very good care of this," Zach said.

I hoped he would.

CHAPTER 102

IT WAS a gorgeous morning in May, and there was an overflow crowd at this, the first Mass in the restored JMJ church. We'd installed new double doors on the southern side that opened out to the large deck and the hay field beyond. I stood alone in the sacristy, listening to James speak to the congregation. I was wearing a simple, loose-fitting white dress with a hem to midcalf, a crucifix on a long, gold chain, and a white linen scarf that covered my head.

I heard James say, "No priest has ever been more moved to celebrate Mass than I. Brigid, please come out."

I had a nervous stomach, and I felt light-headed, too, but I refused to faint; nothing could ruin this remarkable day.

Last night Bishop Reedy had ordained me by candlelight here in our precious church. I was a priest now, and today, I would give my first Mass.

I assured myself that I could do this, and I prayed to God, saying, "I'll do my best, Lord. Thank You for my glorious life and for giving me this opportunity to do Your will."

I walked out to the altar and looked around at the packed pews, the standing-room-only throng that had spilled out into the sunshine. Every pair of eyes was on me, every face was expectant.

James was sitting in the first seat in the front right-hand pew, my usual spot, with Gilly beside him. They were holding hands.

I began the liturgy, speaking to everyone inside the church and to those standing within sight, to those just outside the walls, to all who had heard the bells or thought they had.

I knew every element of the Mass, and I hardly stumbled over the Latin words. I spoke in English, too. I forgot myself and became one with the congregation. I thrilled to the dialogue between us and was uplifted by the voices of our choir, coming from the strong, new loft.

I had not committed my homily to memory. There just hadn't been time, but I stood at the altar and told the assemblage, "I am so glad to be here. I feel so much love for all of you, and of course I've been worried that I might make some mistakes this morning. And then I reminded myself that there was no wrong here, with all of us together in the house and in the presence of God."

I spoke of the Resurrection and of the rebirth of this church. I said that sometimes change brought grief and sadness, and I saw the tears in James's eyes.

I said, "I've found that the greatest growth comes in times of change. And through this church, we are changing the way we think about God's love. He's here for all of us. All of us."

As the choir sang "Agnus Dei," I anticipated the Communion I was soon to receive from my dear James. I'd never felt as close to God and, at the same time, to another human being as I did then.

I offered Communion to the hundreds of people who had gathered in our church that day. Some of them were friends, and others were people who had come to Millbrook just for this celebration and to see a Catholic woman priest.

I said and repeated to each supplicant, "The body of Christ."

"Amen."

"The blood of Christ."

"Amen."

I gave the Prayer after Communion, speaking to the blessings of the Lord, and then I dismissed the congregation—who, against all reason but to my great, blushing delight, broke into applause.

I opened my mind to God, and I felt that special channel between us with an overlapping vision of the kind I had experienced before. I was both inside this old and beloved church, and I was with Him in an open field of pure light.

I thought, *Thank you, God, for this beautiful, blessed day.*

The light formed a sphere like the one that had enclosed me in Jerusalem. Now it surrounded me and James and Gilly and the entire congregation.

I had spoken to the congregation in a general way about changes that we might never see coming. I knew that what was happening *now* was profound. The blessings of this day, my first Mass, the hundreds of expectant faces, the love of God and my love for Him, the light encompassing every one of us—I knew that I had to keep these memories alive for as long as I lived.

Whatever came next.

CHAPTER 103

THAT NIGHT, James and I watched Cardinal Cooney on the eleven o'clock news condemning my "ordination." After he took shots at me, James, and our dear friend Bishop Reedy, he warned "true Catholics" not to be led astray.

The cardinal got so much airtime, we could switch from station to station and see him going after the "destructive" JMJ movement on every one of them. His latest spin was to call JMJ "Aubreyism," an affront to the Vatican.

In the weeks after my ordination, Cardinal Cooney defrocked Bishop Reedy and formed alliances with the archdioceses in other cities. He stirred up the Church's donor base with a fund-raising campaign, and I thought that it was only a matter of time before the pope weighed in with his own condemnation.

The cardinal was clearly unnerved by what we were doing, and his reaction scared me.

He said it again and again: The Church had been very clear about the role of women. Jesus chose twelve *men* to be his apostles. *Stand back, womankind. Don't even think of stepping up to the altar. Don't even* think *about it.*

James and I were mentioned in all of the cardinal's diatribes. Sometimes, the inflammatory image in the corner of the screen was of me, Aubrey's wife. Aubreyism's fake woman priest.

But as the weeks became months, it seemed that the cardinal's smear campaign had backfired. As appealing and omnipresent as he was personally, more renegade "Catholic" churches had come into being. Existing churches were transformed into JMJ churches. New churches were opened in people's homes, and by Gilly's fourth birthday, the movement had spread to South America and Europe.

The press continued to be fascinated by us, and Gilly had her own fans. A sparkly redhead, Gilly Aubrey was verbal and quite funny. And she could really ham it up when a camera was pointed at her.

Which was not good.

I remember a pushy reporter in a cute sundress and heels chasing Gilly up the walkway to the church, demanding, "Gilly, come and talk to me."

I got between my child and the reporter, and when I had the reporter's complete attention, I signaled to the others in the media van, and the three or four paparazzi I could see across the street, and waved them into the church.

When they had all assembled, I said, "Everyone, I understand why you're here, but Gilly is just a little girl. We need an agreement, all of you and me. I will be available right here every weekday at ten to answer your questions, but my daughter is off-limits. Seem fair?"

I gave the reporters my email address and invited them to church on Sunday. I started my weekday press meetings the next day, Monday, and they were actually good for all concerned. The reporters became normal people when we could talk one-on-one. And I got to know them: Jason Beans from the *Globe,* Arthur Glass from the *World Press,* Antonia Shoumatoff from the *Millbrook Independent,* and well-known reporters from cable and network news.

The aggressive attacks stopped. Susie Kennedy, the reporter who had chased Gilly up the path, was from *USA Today*. She started bringing brownies to the morning meetings. Often we all talked about world events having nothing to do with our church or religion at all.

Once in a while, Zach showed up. He was still with the *New York Times,* and he had questions, too. After the others left, we would sit together on the steps of the rectory and talk.

Sometimes I learned more about JMJ's progress from Zach than even James and I knew.

"And you, Zach? How are you?"

"Growing back my beard," he said in Italian, giving me a broad grin. "My editor likes my pages, and now I've got a dog."

"A dog?"

"Chihuahua named Jeter. He travels well."

We talked baseball for a while, and that was when I forgot that Zach was a reporter. He was just Yank. I told him that I was working on all cylinders and James was, too. That James looked tired, but he was doing what he loved.

"I get that," Zach said. "Me too."

Gilly came over and told Zach that she had had a dream about him. "You were Zach and the Beanstalk," she said.

When it was time to go, Zach hugged me, kissed my cheek, as always, and waved good-bye.

I asked myself once again if Zach's book was really going to be good for JMJ or if it would be just another punching bag for the cardinal.

I didn't know it then, but Zach Graham was the least of my worries. I was about to be blindsided by someone much closer to home.

CHAPTER 104

WHEN I took my seat opposite celebrity broadcaster Morgan McCartor on the *60 Minutes* set, I didn't have the slightest premonition that my secret life was about to be cracked wide open.

James was home sick with the flu, but the pre-taping of the show couldn't wait. McCartor was unconcerned about the programming change and introduced me to her TV audience of twenty-five million viewers. She sketched out the highlights of my life in glowing terms, from my work at Kind Hands, my near-death injuries on the battlefield, and the tragic loss of Karl and Tre, to my dramatic marriage to James Aubrey, my ordination, and the turmoil our movement had brought to Catholicism worldwide.

I almost couldn't take so much attention and fought the urge to squirm in my seat.

McCartor, on the other hand, was in her element.

She was beautiful and smart and was so familiar to me from her interviews of presidents and killers and rock stars, I almost thought of her as a friend. She tossed me some softball questions, and I got relatively comfortable, and then she hit me with her best shot when she said, "Brigid, take a look at this clip, will you?"

I watched as my darling Gilly's face filled the big screen. She was wearing a cherry-print jumpsuit with mismatched socks and shoes, her new favorite look this summer. An off-camera voice was saying to her, "Gilly, when you say your mom talks to God, you mean she prays, isn't that right?"

And Gilly, my dear daughter said, "Sure, she prays. But sometimes when she talks to God, He talks back to her. She told me so."

My face heated up. *Gilly. What made you say that?*

McCartor was saying, "Brigid, tell us what your daughter means. Do you converse with God?"

I had to decide right then, with cameras rolling, whether to tell the truth and risk whatever fallout ensued, or to deny my connection to God.

Morgan McCartor was saying my name.

"Brigid? Is it true that you not only speak to God, but He speaks to you?"

I was thinking fast, editing my own thoughts. How could I explain my personal experiences with God without sounding insane?

I gave it a try, relaxing my shoulders, speaking to my "friend" Morgan as if we were sitting together over coffee at a kitchen table.

I said, "Sometimes, on rare occasions and never on demand, my mind is filled with what I feel strongly is the word and presence of God. It's a momentous experience, and while it's happening, it's as if I'm both in the actual, physical present and, at the same time, in a metaphysical realm. I see moving images unlike anything I have ever seen or could ever imagine. I hear a resonance, *almost* like a voice, responding to a question in my mind. I have to interpret these visions and find the answers to my questions within them."

McCartor was right there, ready to ask, "What kind of questions, Brigid? What kind of answers? What can you share about this amazing phenomenon with us?"

"I can say that the first time I experienced this—this overpowering connection—was the day that I was shot. My heart *stopped,* and it took several minutes to bring me back. Technically—and by that I mean *literally*—I died. I've been neurologically cleared by the best doctors. I don't have brain damage, and I'm not crazy. So, what do I think? That through my death, a channel opened in my mind to the presence of God."

I conveyed a full stop after "God," and the TV interviewer got it.

"That's all you're giving us?"

I laughed. "Seems like an awful lot to me."

McCartor said, "Thank you, Brigid, for this most extraordinary interview."

She turned directly to the camera and told the audience what to expect in next week's show, and then hot lights went out, stagehands applauded wildly. McCartor leapt out of her chair and embraced me.

"You're an amazing person, Brigid. It's hard to believe what you've told us, but I *do* believe you. I've never had an interview like this. You're inspiring to so many people. You're the real thing. And, take it from me, I know the real thing."

CHAPTER 105

LAWRENCE HOUSE was on a bar stool at Cal's Roadhouse, watching *60 Minutes* on the TV over the bar, when Morgan McCartor signed off. Sunday-night drinkers crowded the far end of the bar, a group of rowdies crowded the dartboard, and a couple of kids were fooling around in a booth in the back.

Typical night in a one-saloon town.

House said to the bartender, "Bill. Did you see that?"

"See what?"

"Our lady priest was on TV again."

"Oh, her. Can I get you another one?" Bill asked House.

"No, I'm done."

A fanfare came over the TV, announcing a breaking news story. House grabbed the remote and turned up the volume as the on-screen reporter intercepted Cardinal Cooney leaving the Boston Archdiocese and heading to his car.

The reporter asked, "Your Eminence. Do you have a comment for us on the *Sixty Minutes* interview with Brigid Aubrey?"

The cardinal scowled at the camera, then said, "Brigid Fitzgerald Aubrey has said more about her loosely wrapped mind than anything I can say. She's delusional or blasphemous or both, but in any case, she took the Lord God's name in vain. She can answer to Him."

"YES," thundered House as he thumped the bar with his empty glass. "That's right, Cardinal. You got *that* right. Woman's a fraud and a heretic."

The bartender was mopping the bar. House shouted to him, "The backlash is coming, Bill! The tide is turning. God-loving people are getting fed up."

On screen, the cardinal disappeared into the backseat of his car, and the TV reporter turned to face the camera.

"Chet, I'll be outside the Millbrook JMJ church tomorrow, see if I can get Brigid Aubrey's comments."

House slapped some cash on the bar, said "Good night, Billy," to the bartender, then walked outside onto the street, empty except for the fallen leaves scudding across the pavement.

He unlocked his car and got in.

He sat for a few minutes, thinking about what Brigid had said, how disturbing it was to hear her sickening so-called experiences going out all over the country. It was good, what Cooney had said. But was it enough? Mrs. Aubrey had fouled the name of God with her sick mind. She and her predator husband were infecting true believers with their dangerous nonsense, and nothing seemed to stop them.

House started up the car and drove to the intersection of Main and the highway and parked under a tree where he had a good view of the lights coming from the upstairs windows of the rectory.

He switched off the engine and settled in to watch and to wait. While waiting, he prayed to God.

CHAPTER 106

JAMES WAS celebrating the second Mass of the day with a full church on a sunny morning in August.

He was in love with everything about this place, from the restored bell tower to the two-hundred-year-old floors and the new, hand-carved crucifix over the altar.

And he loved the people of this town.

He adjusted his stole and was beginning to receive Holy Communion when he felt a sharp stabbing sensation behind his right eye, more stunningly painful than anything he had ever felt before. The chalice jumped from his hand. He stepped back, lost his footing, and dropped hard to the floor.

What is happening? What is wrong with me?

He felt hands pulling at him, heard questions being shouted, but he couldn't comprehend any of it. The fierce pain obliterated words, his vision, and, struggling to get up, he realized that he had no control at all over his body. He vomited onto the floor.

James tried opening his mind to God as Brigid had described to him, but all he felt was the astonishing, unrelenting pain and the certainty that he was drowning. James heard himself say, "Not...going...to make it."

He didn't want to die. Not yet.

He lost consciousness and came back to the pain, still roaring through his head like a runaway train.

James heard his name shouted right next to his ear.

"Daddy!"

He opened his eyes and tried to smile at Gilly; then he rolled his eyes up and glimpsed Brigid's stricken face.

She said, "James, the ambulance is coming. Hang on to me. Hang on. Please. We'll get through this."

"I can't," he said. "Last. Rites."

She screamed "No!" but he knew she understood. He dropped away again, and when he opened his eyes, Brigid was there, making a cross on his brow, forgiving him for his sins, slipping a drop of wine between his lips.

The immense pain dragged James back again into nothingness. His last thoughts were, *Brigid has prepared my soul.* And, *The pain.*

CHAPTER 107

GILLY AND I were at Sloan's Funeral Home, sitting in the front row of the reposing room, empty except for my beloved James, lying dead in his open coffin before us. It was good that Gilly and I had this private time to say good-bye to him, to pray for him before his funeral.

But even prayer was knocked down and sucked under by my grief. Gilly, too, was devastated, switching back and forth between choked sobbing and long, sad silences. It felt as though my heart kept beating only so that I could be there for our daughter, who had watched her father die in agony.

I knew James's cause of death before we got the M.E.'s report. The suddenness and severity of his pain, the seizures and tremors, the dilated pupils and strangled speech, had told me that a brain aneurysm had ruptured, that his blood had rushed through and flooded the space between his skull and brain. If there had been time to get him into surgery—if only there had been time—maybe, maybe, he would have lived.

I looked at my husband in his coffin, with so many tall vases of flowers *banked* around him. Knowing that he was beyond pain gave me no solace or consolation. We had loved James so much. Gilly would grow up without him, and he had been deprived of so many things he had wanted to do. How could I sleep again in our house without him?

Gilly was lying across two chairs with her head in my lap. I dropped my hand to her head, buried my fingers in her hair. As she stirred, air rushed past my ears, and I saw a soft light arcing over James's coffin—*but he wasn't there*. The body lying on white satin was *mine*.

I was dead.

It wasn't James who had died, it was me.

What had happened to me?

Had I died in South Sudan?

Or was I immobilized in a hospital, my body paralyzed while my brain lived in a dream world? Had everything that had happened after I'd been shot been an illusion? I was more confused than during the times when I'd connected with God. I was no longer sure where I was, what was real.

It was happening now, the warmth inside my chest, the breeze from nowhere, the split locations and overlapping scenes.

There I was, sitting with Gilly on a folding chair, and *there* I was, enclosed in a wooden box with diffused light all around me, cool satin behind my neck. I smelled lilies close by. And I heard the indistinct sound of voices.

God. What is happening?

You know.

I know what?

I saw both dimensions in the round. Gilly and I were in chairs a few yards away from the casket. James was with us, too. *James.* He was *alive.* His cheeks were pink, his eyes were bright, and he seemed—happy. He took me into his arms, and I held him tight while sobbing into the crook between his neck and shoulder. I smelled his skin and hair. This was *reality. This was real.*

At the same time, I could see from where I lay in the coffin. I didn't have to sit up or even open my eyes as others came into focus. Colin knelt before my coffin and winked at me. I felt an indescribable pressure in my chest when I recognized the child sitting over there behind Gilly, kicking her seat—that was *Tre*.

Karl was beside Tre. He apologized to Gilly. I couldn't quite hear the words, but I saw the kindness and love in his face. My father approached the coffin. I heard him say, "You were a good girl, Brigid."

Tears streamed down my cheeks, and still the overlapping images persisted.

I saw refugees I'd known and who had died at BZFO, and the dead patients at Kind Hands, and soldiers who'd been massacred on the killing field. Father Delahanty knelt before my coffin and prayed, then he stood and crossed my forehead as I had crossed his.

He said, *God has a plan for you.*

That tore it completely. What was this plan?

I cried out, "God, why? Why did you let James die?"

When I'd asked God, "Why?" He'd given me birds. A baby who'd been run over in the street. The death of my own child. Of Karl. God had told me, *He lived the full extent of his life.*

Now the resonance came to me, the words, *Be with Gillian. Feel what it is to be alive.*

Gilly's voice cut through the vision, coming to me clear and strong at my side. She tugged my hand.

"Mom. Mommy. We have to go."

The vision dissolved. Sloan's dim reposing room was lit only by candles and sconces, not divine light. Earl Sloan Jr. walked stiffly toward me.

"We should be going. But do you need another moment?"

I was shaking all over. "Please."

I said to Gilly, "Let's say our good-byes to Daddy."

I put my arm around Gilly's waist as I knelt before James's coffin and said the Lord's Prayer. I was thinking, *What just happened? What am I supposed to understand from this? Was that really the Word of God? Why has He left me to suffer again?*

It came together as our car followed the hearse to the church. I had a lingering sense of what I'd experienced in the funeral parlor. I was sitting in the backseat of a hired car with Gilly beside me. And some vestigial part of me was lying in the coffin instead of James.

I understood.

God was showing me that life and death were transient states, indivisible parts of a whole.

I would see James again. I would be with my love.

PART FIVE

CHAPTER 108

IT WAS forty-five nippy degrees in New York City this Sunday morning in February, and I was excited that I would be saying Mass at the opening of the three hundredth JMJ church.

St. Barnabas was a stately, gray stone church in the East Village, built on a green in the eighteen hundreds, which over the last two hundred years had become a neighborhood.

The church had been closed by the Archdiocese of New York in 2008, along with more than two hundred and fifty other churches that had fallen into disrepair. A benefactor had bought St. Barnabas at auction, and it was now to be reopened as a JMJ church.

I walked anonymously through the throng of Sunday shoppers on East Fourth Street in my long, navy-blue coat and knitted hat and found the old church wedged between a Comfy Diner and an antique print shop, graffiti-free and perfectly intact.

When I entered the church through the red-painted doors, I had expected to be welcomed by Father Hubert Clemente. But the young priest was not alone. He seemed a little awed and off balance as he introduced me to Father Giancarlo Raphael, who wore his black vestments and cummerbund with European flair.

Father Raphael said in heavily accented English that he had just arrived from Vatican City to see me. He looked pleased and confident, but I didn't get it.

"Pardon me. Could you say that again?"

As congregants flowed past me into the nave, Father Raphael explained, "Forgive me. I should say I'm here on behalf of Pope Gregory. I hope to have a few words with you."

I was startled, to say the least. I managed to say, "Father Raphael, I am deeply humbled, but, as I have just enough time to get ready, can you wait? The congregation…"

"Of course. I am eager for your Mass."

After I finished a walk-through with Father Clemente, he introduced me to his rapt congregation.

"Good friends," he said, "you know all about our guest, who has become a guiding light to so many Catholics who have felt sidelined by the Church.

"She eschews any title but likes to be called, simply, Brigid. And that humility, that belief that we are all the same in the eyes of God, is the essence of JMJ principles that we will be adopting here."

I felt welcomed and at peace as I began the Mass, but I couldn't quite stop thinking about Father Raphael, the pope's messenger, sitting three rows back on the aisle.

He was waiting for me when I left the sacristy in my street clothes, as were dozens of congregants. I shook hands and exchanged kind words, and I signed scraps of paper to commemorate the occasion. Father Raphael stood to the side until I was finally alone.

And then he had all my attention.

"Brigid," he said, "I have a special invitation for you." He took an envelope from his coat pocket. My name was inscribed in calligraphy, and in the corner of the envelope was a coat of arms, the emblem of the Holy See.

Father Raphael held the envelope out to me, and when I took it, it felt warm to the touch.

"His Holiness Pope Gregory would like very much to meet you. These airline tickets are for you and your daughter, and my card is inside, too. Please let me know when it would be convenient for you to come to the Vatican."

CHAPTER 109

THE PEACEFULNESS of flight above the clouds gave way too quickly to the near riot that was waiting for Gilly and me at Fiumicino Airport.

We were met just outside customs by two very fit men wearing the smart blue uniforms of the Corps of Gendarmes of Vatican City State. Our driver was Alberto Rizzo, and our guard was Giuseppe Marone, who carried our slight luggage through the airport.

I gripped Gilly's hand and followed our assigned guards out under the swooping marquis, toward the street, when we were blocked by protesters who were shouting my name, calling me a heretic and the *devil*. One of them, a woman my age, was brandishing a cross. She said pleasantly, "I wish you to die."

Giuseppe strong-armed the woman out of the way. Alberto shielded us from behind, and we pushed forward through the loud and ugly crowd.

I was utterly shaken by the hatred.

I could stand up for myself, but this attack also affected Gilly. I kept my cool for my daughter's sake and held her close to my side until we were safely inside a black Mercedes with Vatican City plates.

Still, angry people, their faces bloated with hate, hammered on the car windows and roof with their fists.

"You are okay now," said Giuseppe. "No worries."

Two more black sedans joined us, one taking the lead, the other bringing up the rear, and we headed at top speed away from the airport and into the city. During the drive to the hotel, I tried to prepare myself for my upcoming meeting with the pope.

I liked what I'd seen and read about Pope Gregory. He seemed kind, a moderate with modern leanings, but he disapproved of everything JMJ stood for. And he had to be disturbed by the widespread growth of our breakaway churches.

I had a hard time imagining anything but a short, awkward meeting with Pope Gregory. I didn't see it ending well. At all.

Gilly was having a different experience entirely. She was absorbing everything: the wide avenues and historic landmarks, the police escort, the crazy Roman traffic. She had her hands pressed against the windows and said, "Mom, are we staying here?"

Our car pulled up to the Hotel Hassler, a five-star hotel at the top of the Spanish Steps, overlooking the ancient city. Our bodyguards escorted us through the teeming and gilded hotel lobby to the front desk. All the while, her head turning from side to side, Gilly stared around in a state of subdued wonder.

"Mommy, *look*. Mommy, Mommy, Mommy, *look*."

I looked at the beautiful people, at the grand scale of the famous hotel lobby, at the rich appointments, and I laughed, delighting in my seven-year-old little girl's innocence and astonishment.

Gilly wasn't in Massachusetts anymore.

Our suite, like the lobby, was appointed in ruby red and gold, hung with Venetian mirrors and crystal chandeliers. There was a terrace the length of the suite with a fireplace and endless city views. On the table in the sitting room was an extravagant floral arrangement and a note from Father Raphael.

It read: *Welcome, Brigid and Gillian. I will come for you tomorrow morning at nine and bring you to the Apostolic Palace. Pope Gregory is very eager to meet you.*

We kicked off our shoes, and I was looking at the room-service menu on the video monitor when the room phone rang.

Gilly answered, "Heyyyy."

Then, "Mom. Guess who?"

CHAPTER 110

I PEERED through the peephole and saw his face.

"Open up, Red. It is I, your humble scribe."

I opened the door and told our bodyguards that Zach was a friend. I was so excited to see him—and yet puzzled. Zach insisted on making surprise drop-in visits. Why? He had a phone. I hugged my tall, journalist, book-writing friend, and Gilly flew across the room and jumped up into his arms.

"I'm a royal princess," she said. "Would you like to see my domain?"

"I absolutely would," said Zach.

As Gilly took Zach away, I shouted after him, "Why are you here?"

"Easter week at Vatican City. I was available to cover it."

"Are you having dinner with us?"

"Uh. Sure. Thanks."

I'd seen Zach every few months since he signed his book contract, and I knew him well enough by now that I could read between the lines on his face. Something was bothering him.

But Gilly had Zach under her spell. She gave him the grandest of tours.

He taught her the waltz while I signed for room service that was delivered after scrutiny by our guards outside the door.

We tucked into a six-course gourmet dinner on our terrace overlooking the Spanish Steps, and after Zach pointed out the visible ancient landmarks, Gilly provided the entertainment.

"I wanted kittens for my birthday," Gilly was telling Zach.

"Kittens and rodents are off the table," I said.

Ignoring me, Gilly went on. "After I got turned down for hamsters and kittens, I asked for Jesus to come to my birthday party."

I rolled my eyes. "She did not."

"Oh. How did that turn out?" Zach asked her.

Gilly reached down into the front of her dress and pulled up a gold chain. "Look," she said, showing off her new crucifix.

"Beautiful," said Zach, looking over Gilly's head at me.

I said, "Gilly, do me a favor? Get me my sweater? The pink cardigan."

While Gilly was gone, I said, "Zach, something is bothering you. What is it?"

"Why don't I just get right to it," he said, looking miserable. "Maybe you caught it on CNN."

"What? No."

"There's been a credible threat of violence against a JMJ church here in Rome."

"Oh, *no*. I hadn't heard. When did this happen?"

"Early this morning."

"That's *horrible*. Was this because of my visit?"

Zach forced a smile.

"Don't know."

"Why does the pope want to see me?"

"Don't know that, either. But, whether he wants to or not, he'll like you. Even if he's made of marble, he'll like you."

Zach looked at me for a moment too long.

I cleared my throat, refilled his wineglass.

"I want you to take this seriously. Look at me, Brigid. It's not safe for you here. This is Rome. It's Easter week. You're a woman priest going against the Catholic Church. These are unsettling times. You know what I mean?"

Of course I knew. The deepening planetary crisis—rampant terrorism, mutating disease, dramatic weather patterns every year...none of these patterns were good. Science-fiction fantasies of a self-driving car in every garage and a top doctor on the other end of every phone had not come true on this ravaged planet, which was one downed airplane away from an apocalyptic war.

Even clean air and water and food, basics that people had once taken for granted, were in short supply. People asked why. Some answered that this was because of lack of faith in God.

Lifelong believers and the newly faithful were coming back to religion, and some saw JMJ as an attempt to overthrow the two-thousand-year reign of the Roman Catholic Church.

That had never been our goal. Never. We only offered an alternative to those who felt excluded by canon law.

"I hear you, Zach. I understand. But I couldn't refuse an audience with the pope, could I? He's assigned bodyguards to us. I'll be back in Cambridge before you know it."

Gilly brought me my sweater, and after a barely tasted chocolate-and-peanut "exotic passion" dessert, Zach said he had to go. Cheek kisses were exchanged all around, and then, with a tight smile, he left our room.

Gilly asked, "Is Zach okay?"

"Yes, of course. You don't think so?"

"I think he loves you, Mommy."

"He loves you, too, Gilly. Hey. Let's unpack. Hang up our clothes and go to bed. Tomorrow we have an audience with the pope."

For once, she didn't argue with me.

CHAPTER III

I WOKE up four or five times that night.

Each time I looked at the bedside clock, it was an hour closer to my private audience with His Holiness Pope Gregory XVII.

I tried on worst-case scenarios: he would say that I wasn't a priest. He would tell me that none of the sacraments I had performed were valid: not marriages, Communion, last rites. He would tell me I was endangering mortal souls.

Was I doing that?

I groaned and shifted in the bed that I shared with Gilly. Along with having concerns about meeting with the pope, I was shocked at the anger we'd touched off with our breakaway church.

Zach was right. It was dangerous here. I should never have taken Gilly with me to Rome.

Gilly poked me with her elbow and told me to stop flopping around on the bed, to stop sighing. "Just think of fluffy clouds or something and calm down."

"Thanks, peanut."

"If Daddy were here, he would say exactly the same."

We slept, and in the morning, we dressed in black, which was definitely a new look for my little girl and me. Thanks to my father, from whom I'd heard it, I remembered what Henry David Thoreau had written: *Beware of all enterprises that require new clothes.*

Still, black dresses and headscarves were proper protocol for women meeting with the pope.

Giuseppe and Alberto, our dedicated gendarmes, picked us up outside the hotel without incident, and soon our sleek car, flying triangular, yellow-and-white Vatican flags from a pole on the hood, was speeding toward Vatican City.

During the time I'd lived in Rome, I'd learned the city, but to Gilly, this was all new, and it was grand.

Our car took us on Viale della Trinità dei Monti, passing the Villa Borghese gardens on the right. From there, we crossed the Tiber on the Ponte Regina Margherita, and not long after that, we turned onto Via della Conciliazione toward St. Peter's Square, where preparations were being made for the expected millions on Easter Sunday.

And that was when my apprehension vanished, leaving behind something like sunny optimism.

I realized that I had been imagining the pope as another version of my supercritical father. But the pope had invited me to the Vatican. He had made me very comfortable and welcome and safe. Meeting with him was an honor, a privilege, and an extraordinary opportunity to tell him about my experience as a priest. I would tell him about my overwhelming acceptance and could cite examples of other woman priests in the many breakaway churches who were having a positive effect on their congregations.

The air was crisp and the temperature fair when we arrived at the Apostolic Palace, where Pope Gregory spent his days.

This was it.

Gilly and I were going to meet the head of the Catholic Church, the man who represented Christ on earth to more than a billion Catholics.

I was ready.

CHAPTER 112

FATHER RAPHAEL met us at the car and took us into the Apostolic Palace through the Portone di Bronzo. It was a true palace of enormous scale and breathtaking grandeur. I knew that it had a thousand rooms—fish ponds, conservatories, museums and chapels, including the glorious Sistine Chapel, and other rooms that were not open to the public.

But the priest didn't give us a guided tour. Rather, he led us without comment through frescoed rooms and long, gilded corridors hung with ancient religious paintings and, from there, up three tall stories of marble staircase, the most direct route to the pope's office.

As we climbed, I became aware of a tingling sensation across my cheeks, as if water were drying on my skin. A slight breeze ruffled my hair.

I held tight to Gilly's hand as Father Raphael showed us into the office where Pope Gregory worked. The walls were ecru patterned with gold. Gold damask hung at the windows, and the pope, wearing white vestments, sat at his desk facing the door.

Pope Gregory looked in real life as he did on screen. He was white haired and a bit stooped, with genial features and an exceptionally warm smile.

When we entered the room, he rose to his feet, stepped out from behind his desk, and came toward us, extending his hand. I dropped a practiced curtsy and kissed his ring. Gilly stared up at Pope Gregory and said, "You're so—radiant."

He smiled widely and said, "Thank you, Gillian. You're also very radiant, and so pretty."

Father Raphael stepped forward and asked Gilly if she would help him feed the fish.

"We have big fish that you can feed by hand, signorina, and conservatories where very tall trees grow under glass."

"May I go, Mom? Please?"

When Gilly had skipped off with Father Raphael, the pontiff directed me to a seating area across the room from his desk. After he took a seat in an ornate white upholstered armchair, I dropped into a similar but simpler chair across from him, with a low, wooden table between us.

He said, "I've been told that you speak Italian."

"Yes."

That sparkling sensation on my cheeks and forehead seemed to intensify. It reminded me of the dusting of snow on my face when James and I sat with Bishop Reedy in his horse-drawn carriage on our way to our wedding reception.

God. Are You here?

I accepted coffee and tried to be just normal Brigid while sitting opposite the Supreme Pontiff. He made small talk, and as he asked about the flight and accommodations, the tingling on my face extended to my folded hands and my crossed ankles, and I felt that special warmth inside my chest. The breeze circled the white furnishings, riffling the skirts on the pontiff's chair.

Could the pope feel the breeze? I couldn't tell.

He was saying in Italian, "I wanted to meet you, Brigid, because so many people are drawn to your church. Tell me, please, about what I think you call your 'communications' with our heavenly Father."

When he said *"il nostro Padre celeste,"* present reality cleaved in the same way it had for me before, during enormous stress and in the presence of God.

I was looking directly at Pope Gregory and also looking down on the two of us from overhead. I saw the particles that I had only felt before. They were like flecks of gold floating away from me, swirling within a vortex around the pope and me like the fallen autumn leaves eddying around the feet of Bishop Reedy's dappled horses.

God, are You here?

The resonance, almost like a voice, came to me.

Be with Gregory.

I was with the pope, seeing *myself* through his eyes. I saw my long, curling hair, my hazel eyes, and my mother's heart-shaped face. I saw the details of my dress: the darts, the tucks, the stitches in the hem, the cutouts in the lace of my scarf.

My view swiped to the left and flowed past the centuries-old gold-framed painting of Jesus's resurrection on the wall behind the pontiff. And then my view locked in.

I was back in my own body, looking at the pope in minute detail. But the most striking thing was, I saw that Pope Gregory was seeing me. He saw what I looked like, but also, I felt that he was reading my heart.

He asked, *"Sei in presenza di Dio in questo momento?"* Are you in God's presence now?

I said, "Yes. I feel Him here."

"Please describe this feeling."

I had to tell him. At least, I had to try. I started out haltingly, but as I spoke, the words came out simply and truthfully.

"It is a feeling that I must call exalted, Your Holiness. I feel that God is with me and I am being directed by Him. I remain in place, and, simultaneously, I leave my body and can see things that don't exist in stationary

332

reality. I have an expanded awareness of myself, and of the moment, and of other people who are with me. Sometimes I am powerfully aware of people who have died, and I feel that they are aware of me—as if they were living.

"Right now, Your Holiness, I have an expanded awareness of you."

"Do you feel a slight breeze?"

He waggled the fingers of his ring hand beside his face.

I swallowed hard and said, "Yes."

He placed his hand over his heart. "Do you feel warm inside?"

"Yes, I do."

The pope nodded and said, "I too. I see a very soft light around you. And I hear an intonation in here." He touched his temple. *"Be with Brigid."*

I gasped. I had never told anyone about the directives: *Be with Colin. Be with James. Be with Gilly.* I had told no one at all. And now Pope Gregory had said, *"Be with Brigid."*

He was also with God, both of us were, together. I felt almost consumed with love for him.

I said, *"Be with Gregory."*

His face crumpled with emotion. He crossed himself and kissed the plain cross he wore on a heavy chain around his neck. As I struggled to stay with Gregory, His Holiness said, "Will you pray with me?"

We prayed, the pope in his ornate armchair and flowing vestments, I in the more austere seat and black clothing, across from him. I folded my hands and kept my feet flat on the ground as the pope asked God for peace and unity in the world. A breath of air whispered through my clothes and hair and whirled around my ankles.

We said "amen" in unison, and just then, Gilly ran into the room, her shoes clattering on the polished floor, her face flushed with excitement.

The pope stood and reached out to her, and Gilly went directly to him and threw her arms around his waist. He gave her a hug she would never forget for the rest of her life.

She said, "Thank you for letting me see your wonderful home."

The pope looked down at her fondly and said, "I love having you and your mother as my guests. God's blessings on you both."

Father Raphael took photos, and then the pope kissed the top of Gilly's head and put his hand on my arm.

"Please keep me in your prayers," he said. "Go safely with God."

CHAPTER 113

THE CHURCH of the Sacred Heart was at the juncture of two narrow, winding cobblestoned streets. The street was choked by protesters and some who supported JMJ.

I was torn. I didn't want to bring Gilly into this chaos, but, at the same time, it was Maundy Thursday. I felt compelled to go to this church that had received an unspecified but still credible threat.

"Gilly, stay in the car with Alberto, okay?"

"Not okay," she said. "Mom. I'm coming, too. No one is going to hurt us. I'm sure of it. Besides, the pope has given us his protection."

"Gilly, stay."

"No."

Giuseppe and Alberto, big men with guns, were still with us. They cleared the way as we waded into the constricted, crowd-filled Via di Santa Maria Maggiore. I was recognized immediately. There was just nothing subtle about my tall frame, my flame-red hair, and my mini-me, tripping along beside me. People gathered around us.

I squeezed outstretched hands and said *"Buongiorno"* and "God bless you" as our bodyguards urged us forward.

We entered the church, an architecturally perfect ninth-century basilica with Byzantine mosaics in the apse and granite columns forming the side aisles. Behind the high altar was a magnificent oil painting of the Crucifixion.

Gilly and I genuflected before the altar, and then Sacred Heart's priest, Father Vincenzo Mastronicola, introduced himself.

I said, "Father, I only heard about the threat last night. I am so sorry."

"Thank you for coming here to say Mass. So many people have come to receive Communion from you."

Within a few minutes, the crowd on the street filled the church out to the walls. After I was introduced, I spoke to the congregation about how much it meant to me to be with them during Easter week.

I had just begun Mass when a cracking *boom* reverberated throughout the church. People screamed and hit the floor. I ran down to where Gilly sat in a front pew and covered her body as I had done at JMJ Millbrook when Lawrence House had pulled his gun.

As I crouched on the floor, waiting for bullets to puncture flesh and ricochet off stone, I feared for Gilly and for myself. Had we lived the full extent of our lives? Was this the meaning of the visions I had experienced in the presence of the pope and of God? Was I ready to die?

I felt no breeze, no vortex, no shifting of place or time. The creaking of rusted door hinges cut through the moans and frightened sobs. Giuseppe had come through the sacristy doorway into the transept.

He shouted, "Everyone! A bomb exploded on Via San Giovanni Gualberto. This exit is the safest way to leave the church."

Giuseppe helped Gilly and me up from the floor and out the side door, saying, "A car will pick us up on the next street. We have to get you out of here before all traffic is detained."

As the big man led us out, people touched me, kissed my scarf. Tears wet their cheeks.

I said, "God protect you," but I thought, *I'm Brigid. Just Brigid.*

"*Vai con Dio,* Brigid," Father Mastronicola called out to me. "Go with God."

CHAPTER 114

ZACH WAS pacing near the curbside check-in at Alitalia. Once I was out of the car, he hugged me, hard, and he picked Gilly up into his arms. Zach and Giuseppe accompanied the two of us to the flight lounge, where we sat with our backs to the wall until our flight was called.

Both men walked us to the check-in desk, Zach saying, "I'm glad to say good-bye to you, Red. Do you hear me? I'm happy. Keep your head down, will you, please? Call me when you get home."

The flight to Boston was scheduled to leave on time.

We stowed our luggage overhead and buckled in, and I noticed that my normally energetic Gilly was quiet and thoughtful.

"What are you thinking, peanut?"

"About the pope, Mommy. See if Father Raphael sent the pictures."

I turned on my phone and saw that, yes, he had.

Actually, it was a little video of the pope hugging Gilly and putting his hand on my arm, asking me to pray for him.

"We should do that now," Gilly said.

We prayed for Pope Gregory, and moments later, the plane sailed down the runway and lifted smoothly into the air. Once we'd reached cruising altitude, Gilly fell asleep. I pulled down the window shade and tipped my seat back. There was some chance I could sleep. If only.

But I couldn't stop examining and replaying the remarkable events of the past thirty-six hours. We had slept in a hotel suite fit for royalty. We had survived an attack that may have been directed at the JMJ church.

Between those events, I had spent the most precious time with Pope Gregory XVII, who had astounded me with his—how else can I say it?—his holiness.

Be with Brigid.

I dropped off to sleep with the hum of engines in my ears, thoughts of Pope Gregory in my mind, and my beloved child sleeping peacefully beside me.

When I awoke, we had landed. Dawn was backlighting the wing tips, and my cell phone was buzzing in my pocket.

I had a text from Zach.

Brigid, he wrote. *I'm sorry to tell you. Pope Gregory died in his sleep.*

CHAPTER 115

THE PRESS was waiting for us when Gilly and I went through customs at Boston's Logan Airport. Even from fifty yards away, I could see that the reporters were charged up, bordering on frenzied, and there were a lot of them.

I had a hope that they were on our side. I knew so many of these people from the morning press meetings I'd held on the front steps of the rectory at JMJ Millbrook.

But, still, the sight of the mass-media scrum was daunting.

I needed time to absorb that Pope Gregory had died in his sleep as memories of being with him just two days ago flashed through my mind. I had even more questions than before.

Why had the pope summoned me to the Vatican? To learn if I had a genuine connection to God? Did he know that he was going to die? Was he giving me a message when he asked me to pray with him and for him?

As the gang of reporters thundered toward us, I said to Gilly, "Stay close." We had no bodyguards, and I didn't see a hired driver with a sign bearing our name. Gilly and I were about to be mobbed.

I pushed Gilly awkwardly through the revolving doors and got into the next compartment as the reporters powered through the swinging doors beside us. When we were all on the sidewalk fronting the departure lane, Tonia Shoumatoff, a firebrand reporter and writer from the *Millbrook Independent,* came in close.

"Brigid. See this?"

She held up the front page of her paper. A quick glance showed a still shot from the video of Pope Gregory enclosing Gilly and me in his farewell embrace. The photo had to have been released by the Vatican. The headline read, POPE GREGORY MEETS WITH LOCAL WOMAN PRIEST.

Tonia made eye contact and spoke urgently. "Brigid, please say a few words about your meeting with the pope. What did you talk about? How did he seem to you?"

I said, "Tonia, and everyone, I just learned the news about fifteen minutes ago. I still can't believe it. Pope Gregory looked *fine* when I saw him two days ago, just *fine.*"

My voice caught in my throat, and as the reporters, mics and cameras in hand, waited, I saw satellite trucks parked in the bus lane. This curbside interview was going live.

Randy Norman from the *Times* asked what we had spoken about, and I answered, "We talked about the meaning of God in our lives."

More shouts: *"Did he criticize JMJ?" "Where is he on woman priests?" "Did the pope give you any indication that there would be any progress in the Church's positions on divorce and remarriage?"*

I reached for Gilly, but she was no longer at my side. Where had she gone? Where was she?

"Gilly? Has anyone seen Gilly?"

I frantically searched the crowd—and then she poked through the ring of reporters, saying, "Our ride, Mommy. He's right there."

A man in livery was holding a card with my name on it over his head. I grabbed Gilly into a hug and kept her beside me as I apologized and worked my way through the thicket of reporters, out to the curb.

Our driver opened the door, and still the press mobbed us. Their faces were shining with emotion and passion and ambition. They shot endless photos and lobbed more questions.

I boosted Gilly into the backseat and followed her in, saying, "That's all, everyone. We need to get home."

We buckled up, and I locked the door.

"Ready," I said to the driver. And he stepped on the gas.

After a long and jerky ride through morning rush-hour traffic, at last we were climbing the stoop to our home.

After James died, I handed the JMJ Millbrook keys to Bishop Reedy. A week later, Gilly, Birdie, and I moved back to my small brick house in Cambridge. By the congregation's unanimous vote, I became pastor of St. Paul's, the very church I'd attended with my mother as a child and where I had met James. St. Paul's was now JMJ St. Paul's, and to serve God in this, my lifelong church, was a many-layered happiness.

Now, I jiggled a key in the stubborn lock and opened the door fast, before we were spotted.

Birdie was at the church being minded by the deacon, and Gilly begged to go get her.

"She can wait, Gilly. Please."

The milk in the fridge was still good after our three-day absence. I made cocoa for Gilly and myself, and we got into my bed, covering ourselves with a handmade quilt. I palmed the remote and turned on the TV news. It was all about the death of Pope Gregory. Millions were grieving around the world.

I was overcome with sadness and couldn't help sobbing into my hands.

Gilly tried to comfort me, but she was crying, too.

We had only just met him, but we had loved him. And I was missing him as if I had known him my whole life.

I kept seeing myself through the pope's eyes, seeing him in a many-dimensional view through mine, feeling God's presence surrounding us. And then, he died.

What would happen now?

CHAPTER 116

I SLEPT in ragged snatches and woke up for real before sunrise on Easter Sunday.

Everything that had been in my mind overnight rushed back to me. I thought about the way Pope Gregory touched my arm and asked that I pray for him. My train of thought was derailed by the buzz of my phone. It was on my dresser, across the room.

It had to be a reporter, and that was an outrage. I kicked off the bedding, crossed the floor, and grabbed the phone.

It was Zach.

He had actually used the *phone*.

I croaked, "Zach. Where are you?"

"I'm in St. Peter's with a couple million other people. Can you hear me okay?"

"Loud and clear."

"There are always educated guesses and wild rumors, but never have there been rumors like this, Brigid. The cardinals are locked up until the vote is in, but there's been a leak. Your name is being circulated in the College of Cardinals."

"*My* name? What are you talking about?"

"Brigid, your name has come up as a candidate for *pope*."

My legs went out from under me as if I'd been slammed behind the knees by a two-by-four, and I dropped to the floor in a state of stunned shock and denial. There was no way the church would want a woman pope. And I entirely lacked the background to qualify. This story was crazy, frightening, and I didn't get it. I sat down hard at the foot of the bed, pressed Redial, and heard the ring tone.

Zach answered.

"Brigid," he said.

"Wait. What you just said? It's absurd. It's some kind of bad joke."

"You don't understand, Brigid. Something is happening here in Rome. My sources are reliable."

A tremendous roar came over the phone. The only thing that sounded even close was a game-winning homer at Fenway. This sounded ten times louder.

Zach shouted, "Brigid! I think news is breaking. Keep your phone with you and charged. I'll call you."

And the line went dead again.

I tried to blank out what Zach had said. I had to say Easter sunrise Mass in an hour. I had to get ready.

I went to wake Gilly, but she was already sitting up in bed with her iPad. She flashed the screen toward me. "Zach sent this clip."

"Let me see."

I sat next to Gilly and watched the images of a roiling mass of people within the confines of St. Peter's Square.

"What's happening?" Gilly asked. "It looks *crazy*."

"St. Peter's is always filled like that on Easter Sunday because the pope goes onto his balcony—somewhere in here—and gives a blessing."

"But the Pope *died*."

"That's right. And now, there's a vote going on in the Vatican to elect a new pope."

"A new pope? Today?"

"Could happen. But sometimes it takes a few days for the cardinals to reach an agreement. Hey. Are you as hungry as I am? Five minutes until breakfast. And then we've got to hustle.

"Let's go, Gilly. We have to beat the sun."

CHAPTER 117

THE STREET outside our front steps had been closed to traffic and was jammed with people out to the very walls of the houses. The crowd was chanting my name, holding up babies to be kissed; their expressions were ecstatic, pleading, expectant.

"Brigid, is it true? Don't forget us when you go to Rome."

This was how I learned that the rumor in Rome had flashed across the "pond" and that I had become the flesh-and-blood manifestation of hope.

But I had no answers. I opened my mind to God, and I felt a slight breeze that moved around me so faintly, I couldn't be sure that it was anything but the natural movement of air.

I looked out from my short stoop at the field of people who'd gathered to see me. For a moment, I was paralyzed, but Gilly loved this. Dressed in her second-best dress, blue and embroidered with daisies, and with a bandage over the cut on her hand, she thrilled to the attention. She waved from the top step and was rewarded by people calling out to her.

"Yo, Gilly, did you meet the pope?"

Gilly was still small enough to get trampled. I picked up my little girl, and she gripped her legs around my hips, tightened her arms around my neck. She was getting heavy, but once I had a good hold on her, I stepped down into the street.

Reporters assailed me with questions from all sides. One of them, Jason "Papa" Beans of the *Boston Globe,* was wearing a button on his jacket, the universal question *Y* in bold red on a yellow ground.

"Have you gotten the call from the Vatican?" Beans asked.

"Aww, Papa. It's a rumor, nothing more. And that's the really big scoop. Now, pleeease pardon me. I have to go to church. I have a Mass to say."

"Bri-gid! Bri-gid!"

Beans did the gallant thing. He walked ahead of me, parting the crowd so that I could go through. Still, people threw flowers and grabbed at my sleeves and even my hem, and they blew kisses as we moved slowly up the block.

By the time we reached the entrance to St. Paul's, thousands were funneling from the broader avenues down the narrow streets, toward the entrance to the church.

Only a small number of these people would fit inside, and as this became apparent, panic began. They all wanted to see me.

My vision started to blur. I was walking behind Beans through the crowd, and I could also see myself with Gilly and the restive mob from a great height. It reminded me of the view of St. Peter's that Zach had sent Gilly this morning.

It was Jason Beans who brought me back to earth. Having cleared a path for me and Gilly right to the sacristy door, he shot his last, desperate questions at me.

"Brigid, has the Vatican contacted you? Have you been told that you're in contention for pope?"

"No and no. Thanks for the escort. I'll see you after Mass, Papa, I promise."

I closed the sacristy's street door behind me. As I caught my breath, Gilly embraced Birdie and fed her, and when I told her to go into the church, she said okay.

I opened the door to the nave, and Gilly scooted through. I watched her squeeze into the aisle seat in the front right pew, my seat for thirty years. I had been sitting exactly there when I met her father. It was Gilly's seat now.

I looped my stole around my neck and looked out over the congregation. The air was supercharged with expectation, and I was pretty sure that the congregants were more interested in what had transpired in Rome than they were in St. Paul's thoughts about the resurrection of Christ.

I would read the First Epistle to the Corinthians anyway.

I felt a draft at my feet and at my cheeks.

God, are You here?

I smiled at the congregation, and I began to speak.

CHAPTER 118

THAT WAS a pretty rough scene out on DeWolfe Street," I said to the congregants. "But I'm glad we're all together now on this momentous Easter Sunday. We have a lot to reflect upon and much to pray for."

As I spoke, I felt that strange sensation of water drying on my skin, the same one I had first felt when climbing the imposing marble staircase in the Apostolic Palace.

Now, as then, I felt a soft breeze in my hair.

Could anyone see it?

I reined in these thoughts and focused on the faces before me. I knew, *Be with them.*

But something was going on inside me. I felt woozy and warm, maybe feverish. I rationalized that it was jet lag and stress, lack of food and sleep. Or maybe the channel between me and God was so flexible now from use, it had become like a window that could open at any time.

I anchored myself to the altar with both hands. I very much wanted to celebrate this sunrise Mass, and I didn't think I could do that if I was both *with* the congregation and *watching* them from under St. Paul's barrel-vaulted ceiling.

I was reaching for my next words when a commotion broke out, back in the shadows at the rear of the church. A bearded man jumped to his feet and called my name, *demanding* my attention.

"Look here, Brigid. Look at me."

I looked, but I couldn't make out his face. Did I know him? He walked up the aisle toward me, and when he reached the rail, he dropped to one knee and made the sign of the cross, smoothly slipping his hand inside his jacket. I was focused on his square, bearded face—it was the beard that threw me off. And then I got it: he was Lawrence House, the man who had threatened our family and who had likely burned down our church.

Gilly shouted *"Mom!"* from her seat in the front pew.

Her face was contorted with fear, but before I could react to her, I felt a punch to my shoulder. I dropped, reached out toward Gilly, and heard, as if from a distance, the second of two sharp cracking sounds.

I toppled backward, grabbing at the altar cloth, pulling it and everything on the altar down around me.

I fought hard to stay in the present. I tried to get to my feet, but I was powerless. The light dimmed around me. The screams faded. I was dropping down into a bottomless blackness, and I couldn't break my fall.

CHAPTER 119

ZACHARY GRAHAM signed off from his call to the international desk at the *Times* and exited the media van. His cameraman, Bart Buell, was leaning against the hood.

"You ready?" Bart asked. "It's starting to break."

"Follow me," Zach said.

They went back the way Zach had come, up Via della Conciliazione, cutting around St. Peter's Square, waiting in line for the small elevator to discharge its half dozen passengers and for the next group in line to get in.

After five or six minutes, Zach and his cameraman were riding the creaking lift up fifty feet to the top of Bernini's colonnade, with its full view of St. Peter's Square and the backdrop of Vatican City.

The two men blocked out their shot, and while Buell erected the setup and tested the equipment, Zach went over his notes. When he felt good to go, he put on his shades and peered out into the blazing sunshine bouncing off the ancient cut stones of the venerable buildings and the extraordinarily beautiful dome of St. Peter's Basilica.

The people in the square were in a spiritual frenzy. The millions moved as one, looking almost like a single-celled organism under a microscope.

The sounds coming from the crowd, the shouting, praying, and keening, were like nothing Zach had ever heard before.

These people had wanted to see and be blessed by the beloved Pope Gregory. Now they were waiting to be blessed by his replacement.

Who would it be?

Would Brigid be elected the head of the Roman Catholic Church? If so, she would have powerful enemies inside the Vatican and without. Would she ever be safe?

Zach tried to make out the chimney atop the Sistine Chapel, at the far end of the square. When a conclusive vote was confirmed, the ballots would be burned, and the rising white smoke would signify that the Church had elected a new pope.

Zach asked his cameraman, "Do you see that?"

The cameraman was zooming in with his long telephoto lens when Zach's phone buzzed. He slapped his shirt pocket and retrieved it. The caller ID read *Brigid*.

He pressed Receive.

"Brigid, I think I see smoke. I have to go on air right now. We may have a new pope. I'll call you back... *Who is this?* Gilly? You're breaking up, Gilly. Take a breath. Say it again. What's wrong?"

The undulating rumble coming from St. Peter's Square took on volume and pitch as the wisp of smoke thickened and rose in an unmistakable column. Cheers and weeping became a thundering roar.

Zach crouched down and pressed his phone hard against his ear.

"Gilly?"

"Zach!" the little girl cried. "It's Mommy! My mommy was shot!"

CHAPTER 120

THE JUBA Line bus from Juba Airport to Magwi was the same bus I'd taken so many years ago. The chassis had been repatched and painted over, and the sign in the front window reading *God Is Good* had been replaced with a new sign, same message.

The people of South Sudan had little except their faith in God, but they still had that.

In contrast to the torrential rains that had been drowning Magwi when I'd last been here, this was drought season, and so the air was dry and the heat oppressive. Brown dust blew away from the wheels of the bus and swirled in golden vortices around the trunks of parched trees.

Gilly pulled at my arm as the bus slowed.

"Is that him? Is it, Mommy?"

Kwame's old, brown junker was parked by the bus shelter. My grin was so wide, my cheeks hurt. I couldn't wait to see him.

The hydraulic brakes squealed. I held Gilly back so that the men and women and children and chickens and the one goat could leave the bus. We stepped down to the ground, and finally I had to let my daughter go. She ran toward the old Dodge, and the driver's door opened.

I couldn't make sense of what I saw. The driver wasn't Kwame. I gasped as I realized that the man wearing the panama hat, black pants, and black shirt with white collar was Father Delahanty, the priest I had met at Kind Hands. I had given him his last rites and heard his confession, even though I was a doctor at the time. I had been with him when he died.

I knew then that I was dead.

And Gilly?

Please, God, no.

I thought hard, desperately trying to remember the moment of my death. I kept walking, gripping my old leather bag, feeling the weight of Gilly's backpack, strapped across my shoulders. When I got near the car, Father Delahanty reached out his arms to me.

"Ah, Brigid. I've been waiting to see you."

I couldn't say the same, but I hugged him. He was as substantial as ever. He smelled good. His eyes sparkled. He was so—alive.

I asked him, "Is this God's plan for me, Father? The plan you were always rattling on about?"

"What do *you* think?" he asked me. He was grinning like a fool. "Brigid, get into the car. Do you know where we're going?"

"I guess you'll tell me."

"You have a very dry sense of humor," he said.

"And an enormous confusion about what the heck has happened."

I got into the backseat with Gilly, and she turned her bright, always curious gaze to the countryside, the goats tied to trees, the meager shops lining the streets of the town. Beyond the town, the long dirt road cut through the open plains and over the dusty hills. It all looked solid and real.

I was hardly surprised when we pulled up to Magwi Clinic at sunset. The clinic was lit up from within, and I heard the loud hum of the generator. This had been a very good place for me. Perhaps Gilly could be happy here, too.

As I got out of the car and looked around, I took in the tent village under the red acacia trees outside the clinic, much bigger than it had been before. I heard babies crying and the braying of donkeys and saw a new structure beyond the tent city and opposite the clinic.

It was a church with the name *Jesus Mary Joseph, Magwi,* on a hand-painted board affixed to the siding. The doors were painted red, symbolizing the phrase *To God through the blood of Christ.*

My eyes welled up. Tears spilled over. And when I heard my name, I turned. I recognized her voice before I saw her, and there she was.

Sabeena, her hair wrapped in colorful fabric, was running down the steps from the clinic, and two tall girls were running right behind her. Sabeena, Jemilla, and Aziza all reached Gilly before they reached me, and they hugged her and danced her around as if she was a long-lost sister as well as my baby girl.

Sabeena screamed my name again, and when she got to me, she almost knocked me off my feet with her full-body hug.

"Oh, Brigid, I've missed you so much. Come inside. Albert has been cooking all day. Father Delahanty," she called over my shoulder, "you come, too. Dinner is served."

Were we all dead, living on a parallel plane alongside the living? I said, "Sabeena, I don't understand."

"Don't worry. You are off duty, doctor."

I began the climb up the steps to the long porch, my mind racing in circles inside my skull, my arm around Sabeena's waist. We had just reached the old screen door when a horrible racket cut through the night sounds of babies wailing, young girls laughing, insects chirping.

"Dr. Douglass. You are needed in room four forty-one. Dr. Douglass. You're needed—"

And that was when my reality split.

God. Are You here?

I was standing on the the long porch of Magwi Clinic, Sabeena's arm around my waist and mine around hers.

And at the same time, I watched myself lying in a hospital bed. My eyes were closed. There were tubes in my arms, and a doctor was sitting on the edge of my bed, saying and repeating my name.

Sabeena was saying, "We'll take the night shift, Brigid. Just like old times."

I stopped on the stairs and looked out past the JMJ church, the cross at the top of the steeple silhouetted against the cobalt-blue sky. I saw long lines of people streaming toward Magwi Clinic with baskets on their heads, babies in their arms, their bare feet stirring up the golden dust as they made their way down the road. I couldn't see the end of the line. There were so many people, and there was so much to do.

The doctor sitting near my feet adjusted the valve on the IV line.

"Brigid. Dr. Fitzgerald. This is Dr. Douglass. Can you hear me?"

God. What should I do?

There was a vibration inside my mind, the hum that was almost a voice. *You know.*

I was so warm, I thought I had a fever. A hot wind came up and blew at my clothes.

I opened my eyes and gasped.

I hurt all over.

CHAPTER 121

I WAS in a hospital bed with needles in my arms and a cannula in my nose. I ripped that out and blinked.

"Okay. Good," said the doctor. He looked to be in his sixties. The name tag on his white jacket read *J. Douglass.*

He asked, "How do you feel?"

"On a scale of one to ten?"

"That's right," said the doctor.

"Five. It hurts to breathe. What happened to me?"

"You took a couple of bullets, doctor. One passed through your left shoulder and your back and exited under your shoulder blade. The second bullet was a doozy."

"New medical term?"

"Just coined."

"You're my surgeon?"

He nodded, told me to call him "Josh."

"After you were shot in the arm, you dropped to your knees and put out your hand to stop the bullet. It didn't stop. It went through your palm, traveled along your humerus, broke rib number three, missed your heart by a millimeter. After that, this misshapen lump of lead zigzagged as it hit several ribs and came to a stop at your right hip bone. Your major organs were spared. I call this both a doozy and a kind of miracle. I take it you pray."

"I do."

"Don't stop. You came through the surgery beautifully. I've kept you moderately sedated in the ICU, and, although you've opened your eyes a few times, you didn't want to wake up.

"I had you moved to this private room a couple of hours ago and turned down your Versed. I'm going to take a look at you, okay?"

Dr. Douglass examined me, and when he was finished looking at my wounds, listening to my heart and my lungs, flashing a light into my eyes, he said he'd be back in a few hours to check on me again.

Then he opened the curtain with a flourish.

He said, "Your friend has been waiting for you to come out of it."

I stared around at the flowers around the room, enough of them to fill a flower shop. My quilt from home covered my bed, and there were balloons tied to the foot rail with a sparkly ribbon and a note reading *Get Well, Mommy*. The TV was on. I looked up. Baseball. Sox versus the Yankees. Fourth inning. Sox were up by two.

The TV went black.

That was when I saw Zach sitting in a chair against the window, backlit by sunshine coming through the glass. He had the remote control in hand and tears in his eyes.

"Welcome back, Brigid. You made it," he said. "I knew you would."

CHAPTER 122

IT WAS coming back to me. Easter Sunday. The bearded man in the back of the church shouting, *Look here, Brigid. Look at me,* followed by Gilly's scream. Lawrence House had shot me.

"Zach, where's Gilly? Is she all right?"

"She's perfect. Congregants are fighting to take care of her, and she's been here to see you every day and twice on Sunday."

I let out a huge sigh. Then, "What happened to House?"

"Three guys slammed him to the ground before he could empty his gun. He's in jail. No bond. He's not going anywhere."

"Thanks for being here, Zachary."

"Of course."

He reached over and squeezed my hand.

"How long have I been out?"

"A week. You breezed through the surgery. Well, this wasn't your first rodeo, was it?"

I laughed. It hurt. "No jokes, please."

Zach said, "Okay, no joke: I'm sorry to inform you, you're not Pope Brigid the First."

I couldn't help laughing again. Pain racked my chest and shot through my right arm. Even my head hurt. When I finally got my breath, I told Zach that I could not adequately express my relief that his reliable sources were wrong.

"They were wrong. But you were right. The new pontiff is a Frenchman. A progressive. Bishop Jean-Claude Renault is now Pope John XXIV.

"And you're going to love this," Zach went on. "In Pope John's first public speech to the world, he made a big announcement. He said, 'I've long been aware of certain inequities.' He was quite sincere."

"Zach! What inequities?"

"He said he was inspired by Pope Gregory—and by a woman priest from America. You, Brigid. He said your name."

Zach looked proud and a little choked up.

He pushed on, saying, "The pope believes that the Catholic Church should allow—no, he said 'welcome.'... He said the Roman Catholic Church should welcome woman priests."

"Nooo."

"Yes. And Pope John believes that priests should be allowed to marry. That God would be glad for this. It would be *très bon*."

"You're not making this up?"

"I'll send you the link to his speech. Okay, Brigid? Happy?"

"Very happy. It is sooo *très bon*."

I must have fallen asleep.

When I opened my eyes, Gilly was sleeping under my good arm. I said, "Gillian. Gilly, are you awake?"

She cuddled in closer and made little kissing sounds. When I opened my eyes again, Gilly was gone. Dr. Douglass looked into my eyes, wrote on my chart. "How do you feel, Doctor?"

"Chest pain."

"Your ribs?"

"*Yesss*. Will I be able to use my arm?"

I thought I heard him say, "Yes. You're doing fine."

CHAPTER 123

IT WAS morning when I came out of a drugged sleep again.

There were more cards and flowers in the room. The balloons were touching the ceiling, and the nurse who had changed my dressings said, "You're healing well, Doctor. Your little girl said to say that she loves you to pieces."

"Oh, thank you."

She said, "I'll be back to read you your cards in a little while," and she drew back the curtain.

Zach was wearing different clothes, and he was back in the chair in front of the window. He had a box in his hands.

"I brought you a little something," he said.

"Aw, you shouldn't have."

"Actually, yes, I should have. I'll open it, okay? Stay right where you are."

"Hah. Okay."

Zach ripped through paper and cardboard and pulled out a thick sheaf of paper. He said, "This is the manuscript. You can go over this and mark it up to your heart's content."

He held it at an angle so that I could read the title page: *Woman of God*.

The words under the title were *By Brigid Fitzgerald Aubrey, as told to Zachary Graham*.

There was a slight shimmer in the air. I was no longer in pain, but I was surely in a hospital bed, looking at a manuscript for a book about my life. It had started with a boy telling me about his beloved grandmother, Joya, who had been murdered in South Sudan.

I thanked Zach. I lifted my hands and wiggled my fingers toward him. I said, "Hug, please, Zach. Gentle one."

He leaned over me, bracing his arms on the side rails. I hugged him. I remembered sitting behind him on a red scooter in Rome, my arms around his waist, and our talks about this book while sitting on the rectory doorstep. Now, he was here, bringing this tremendous gift, hugging me gently with tears in his eyes.

I said, "Zach, Thank you so much."

"No," he said, releasing me from the hug, grinning like crazy. "Thank you. You really know how to give a book a good ending," he said, waving his hand to take in the bed, the flowers, the vital-signs monitors, the photo on the side table of Pope Gregory embracing Gilly and me.

He sat back down and asked, "So, what's next for you, Brigid? When you get out of here?"

I twiddled the edge of my quilt, drawing out the silence as flecks of gold wafted upward in the sunlight behind my dearest friend.

I thought about my first tour in South Sudan, twenty years ago. Those of us who had fought to be assigned to the hard duty at Kind Hands admitted to ourselves and each other that we were all running away from something. We just hadn't known what it was.

Well, I had known. I had been running from my father and the void left by my mother's death, and I wanted to practice good medicine for people who had nothing. Kind Hands had been more than a job. The work had called upon the best in me. It had been so fulfilling that even after nearly dying, I had gone back.

Since my first days in South Sudan, my life had taken so many unexpected, unpredictable turns. I thought of those beautiful and wrenching years in Berlin with Karl and the too-short time we'd had with Tre. I had looked for meaning in the Holy Land and, afterward, met my extraordinary James, who had brought love into my life again and Gilly into the world.

I had become a woman of the cloth and opened myself to the Lord. I was washed over with gratitude for that and was in awe at the sheer magnificence of God.

When I had asked God what to do, I had heard, *You know.*

And, at last, I did know.

I wanted to heal people as a doctor and serve God in His house. Both—body *and* soul.

I turned my head so that I could look at Zach and said, "I'm going back to Africa."

"Wow, really?"

A soft breeze blew tears from the corners of my eyes. Red Sox fans cheered over a radio in the O.R., and a generator kept the lights on. Patients waited, and I knew what I was meant to do.

I was already halfway there.

ACKNOWLEDGMENTS

Our thanks to these good friends who shared their time and expertise with us in the writing of this book: Dr. Humphrey Germaniuk, Coroner and Medical Examiner, Trumbull County, Ohio; Chuck Hanni, IAAI-Certified Fire Investigator, Youngstown, Ohio; Thomas D. Kirsch, MD, MPH, Johns Hopkins University School of Medicine; and Christopher J. Finley, MD, FACEP, PeaceHealth Southwest Medical Center. Thanks also to top attorneys, Philip R. Hoffman and Steven Rabinowitz of Pryor Cashman, NYC, for their wise legal counsel. Our great appreciation to the home team, John Duffy and Lynn Colomello for their many contributions, to Mary Jordan for managing all the moving parts, and a big round of applause to our amazing researcher, Ingrid Taylar, West Coast, USA.

IT'S EASY TO GO MISSING IN THE MIDDLE OF NOWHERE.

CHAPTER 1

"IF YOU reach the camp before me, I'll let you live," the Soldier said.

It was the same chance he allowed them all. The fairest judgment for their crimes against his people.

The young man lay snivelling in the sand at his feet. Tears had always disgusted the Soldier. They were the lowest form of expression, the physical symptom of psychological weakness. The Soldier lifted his head and looked across the black desert to the camp's border lights. The dark sky was an explosion of stars, patched here and there by shifting clouds. He sucked cold desert air into his lungs.

"Why are you doing this?" Danny whimpered.

The Soldier slammed the door of the van closed and twisted the key. He looped his night-vision goggles around his neck and strode past the shivering traitor to a large rock. He mounted it, and with an outstretched arm pointed toward the northeast.

"On a bearing of zero-four-seven, at a distance of one-point-six-two kilometres, your weapon is waiting," the Soldier barked. He swivelled, and pointed to the northwest. "On a bearing of three-one-five, at a distance of one-point-six-five kilometres, my weapon is waiting. The camp lies at true north."

"What are you saying?" the traitor wailed. "Jesus Christ! Please, please don't do this."

The Soldier jumped from the rock, straightened his belt, and drew down his cap. The young traitor had dragged himself to his feet and now

3

stood shaking by the van, his weak arms drawn up against his chest. *Judgment is the duty of the righteous,* the Soldier thought. *There is no room for pity. Only fury at the abandonment of honor.*

Even as those familiar words drifted through his mind, he felt the cold fury awakening. His shoulders tensed, and he could not keep the snarl from his mouth as he turned to begin his mission.

"We're greenlit, soldier," he said. "Move out!"

CHAPTER 2

DANNY WATCHED the Soldier disappear in the brief, pale light before the moon was shrouded by clouds. The darkness that sealed him was complete. He scrambled for the driver's side door of the van, yanked it, pushed against the back window where a long crack ran upwards through the middle of the glass. He ran around and did the same on the other side. Panic thrummed through him. What was he doing? Even if he got into the van, the keys were gone. He spun around and bolted into the dark in the general direction of northeast. How the hell was he supposed to find anything out here?

The moon shone through the clouds again, giving him a glimpse of the expanse of dry sand and rock before it was taken away. He tripped forward and slid down a steep embankment. Sweat plastered sand to his palms, his cheeks. His breath came in wild pants and gasps.

"Please God," he cried. "Please, God, please!"

He ran blindly in the dark, arms pumping, stumbling now and then over razor-sharp desert plants. He came over a rocky rise and saw the camp glittering in the distance, no telling how far. Should he try to make it to the camp? He screamed out. Maybe someone on patrol would hear him. Danny kept his eyes on the ground as he ran. Every shadow and ripple in the sand looked like a gun. He leapt at a dry log that looked like a rifle, knelt, and fumbled in the dark. Sobs racked through his chest. The task was impossible.

The first sound was just a *whoosh*, sharper and louder than the wind.

Danny straightened in alarm. The second *whoosh* was followed by a heavy *thunk,* and before he could put the two sounds together he was on his back in the sand.

The pain rushed up from his arm in a bright red wave. The young man gripped his shattered elbow, the sickening emptiness where his forearm and hand had been. High, loud cries came from deep in the pit of his stomach. Visions of his mother flashed in the redness behind his eyes. He rolled and dragged himself up.

He would not die this way. He would not die in the dark.

CHAPTER 3

THE SOLDIER watched through the rifle scope as the kid stumbled, his remaining hand gripping at the stump. The Soldier had seen the Barrett M82 rifle take heads clean off necks in the Gaza Strip, and in the Australian desert the weapon didn't disappoint. Lying flat on his belly on a ridge, the Soldier actioned the huge black rifle, set the upper rim of his eye against the scope. He breathed, shifted back, pulled the trigger, and watched the kid collapse as the scare shot whizzed past his ear.

What next? A leg? An ear? The Soldier was surprised at his own callousness. He knew it wasn't military justice to play with the traitor while doling out his sentence, but the rage still burned in him.

You would have given us away, he seethed as he watched the boy running in the dark. *You would have sacrificed us all.*

There was no lesser creature on earth than a liar, a cheat, and a traitor. And bringing about a fellow soldier's end was never easy. In some ways, it felt like a second betrayal. *Look what you've forced me to do,* the Soldier thought, watching the kid screaming into the wind. The Soldier let the boy scream. The wind would carry his voice south, away from the camp.

The cry of a traitor. He would remember it for his own times of weakness.

The Soldier shifted in the sand, lined up a headshot, and followed Danny in the crosshairs as he got up one last time.

"Target acquired," the Soldier murmured to himself, exhaling slowly. "Executing directive."

7

He pulled the trigger. What the Soldier saw through the scope made him smile sadly. He rose, flicked the bipod down on the end of the huge gun and slung the weapon over his shoulder.

"Target terminated. Mission complete."

He walked down the embankment into the dark.

CHAPTER 4

IT WAS Chief Morris who called me into the interrogation room. He was sitting on the left side of the table, in one of the investigator's chairs, and motioned for me to sit on the right, where the perps sit.

"What?" I said. "What's this all about, Pops? I've got work to do."

His face was grave. I hadn't seen him look that way since the last time I punched Nigel over in Homicide for taking my parking spot. The Chief had been forced to give me a serious reprimand, on paper, and it hurt him.

"Sit down, Detective Blue," he said.

Holy crap, I thought. *This is bad.* I know I'm in trouble when the Chief calls me by my official title.

The truth is, most of our time together is spent far from the busy halls of the Sydney Police Center in Surry Hills.

I was twenty-one when I started working Sex Crimes. It was my first assignment after two years on street patrol, so I moved into the Sydney Metro offices with more than a little terror in my heart at my new role and the responsibility that came with it. I'd been told I was the first woman in the Sex Crimes department in half a decade. It was up to me to show the boys how to handle women in crisis. The department was broken; I needed to fix it, fast. The Chief had grunted a demoralised hello at me a few times in the coffee room in those early weeks, and that had been it. I'd lain awake plenty of nights thinking about his obvious lack of faith in me, wondering how I could prove him wrong.

After a first month punctuated by a couple of violent rape cases and three or four aggravated assaults, I'd signed up for one-on-one boxing training at a gym near my apartment. From what I'd seen, I figured it was a good idea for a woman in this city to know how to land a swift uppercut. I'd waited outside the gym office that night sure that the young, muscle-bound woman wrapping her knuckles by the lockers was my trainer.

But it was Chief Morris in a sweaty grey singlet who tapped me on the shoulder and told me to get into the ring.

Inside the ropes, the Chief called me "Blue." Inside the office, he grunted.

Here in the interrogation room there was none of the warmth and trust we shared in the ring. The Chief's eyes were cold. I felt a little of that old terror from my first days on the job.

"Pops," I said. "What's the deal?"

He took the statement notepad and a pencil from beside the interview recorder and pushed them towards me.

"Make a list of items from your apartment that you'll need while you're away. It may be for weeks," he said. "Toiletries. Clothes. That sort of stuff."

"Where am I going?"

"As far away as you can get," he sighed.

"Chief, you're talking crazy," I said. "Why can't I go home and get this stuff myself?"

"Because right now your apartment is crawling with Forensics officers. Patrol have blockaded the street. They've impounded your car, Detective Blue," he said. "You're not going home."

CHAPTER 5

I LAUGHED, hard, in the Chief's face.

"Good work, Pops," I said, standing up so that my chair scraped loudly on the tiles. "Look, I like a good prank as much as anyone, but I'm busier than a one-armed bricklayer out there. I can't believe they roped you into this one. Good work, mate. Now open this door."

"This isn't a joke, Harriet. Sit back down."

I laughed again. That's what I do when I'm nervous. I laugh, and I grin. "I've got cases."

"Your apartment and car are being forensically examined in connection with the Georges River Three case," the Chief said. He slapped a thick manila folder on the table between us. It was bursting with papers and photographs, yellow witness reports, and pink forensics sheets.

I knew the folder well. I'd watched it as it was carried around by the Homicide guys, back and forth, hand to hand, a bible of horror. Three beautiful university students, all brunettes, all found along the same stretch of the muddy Georges River. Their deaths, exactly thirty days apart, had been violent, drawn-out horrors. The stuff of mothers' nightmares. Of my nightmares. I'd wanted the Georges River Three case badly, at least to consult on it due to the sexual violence the women had endured. I'd hungered for that case. But it had been given to the parking-spot thief Detective Nigel Spader and his team of Homicide hounds. For weeks I'd sat at my desk seething at the closed door of their case room before the rage finally dissipated.

I sank back into my chair.

"What's that got to do with me?"

"It's routine, Blue," the Chief said gently. He reached out and put his hand on mine. "They're just making sure you didn't know."

"Know what?"

"We found the Georges River Killer," he said. He looked at my eyes. "It's your brother, Blue. It's Sam."

CHAPTER 6

I SLAMMED the door of the interrogation room in the Chief's face and marched across the office to the Homicide case room. Dozens of eyes followed me. I threw open the door and spotted that slimeball Nigel Spader standing before a huge corkboard stuffed with pinned images, pages, sketches. He flinched for a blow as I walked over but I restrained myself and smacked the folder he was holding out of his hands instead. Papers flew everywhere.

"You sniveling prick," I said, shoving a finger in his face. "You dirty, sniveling...dick hole!"

I was so mad I couldn't speak, and that's a real first for me. I couldn't breathe. My whole throat was aflame. The restraint faltered and I grabbed a wide-eyed Nigel by the shirtfront, gathering up two fistfuls of his orange chest-hair as I dragged him to the floor. Someone caught my fist before I could land a punch. It took two more men to release my grip. We struggled backwards into a table full of coffee cups and plates of muffins. Crockery shattered on the floor.

"How could you be so completely wrong?" I shouted. "How could you be so completely, *completely* useless! You pathetic piece of—"

"That's enough!" The Chief stepped forward into the fray and took my arm. "Detective Blue, you get a fucking hold of yourself right now, or I'll have the boys escort you out onto the street."

I was suddenly free of all arms and I stumbled, my head pounding.

And then I saw it.

The three girls, their autopsy portraits beside smiling, sunlit shots provided by the families. A handprint on a throat. A picture of my brother's hand. A map of Sydney, studded with pins where the victims lived, where their families lived, where my brother lived, where the bodies of the girls were found. Photographs of the inside of my brother's apartment, but not as I knew it. Unfamiliar things had been pulled out of drawers and brought down from cupboards. Porn. Tubs and tubs of magazines, DVDs, glossy pictures. A rope. A knife. A bloody T-shirt. Photographs of onlookers at the crime scenes. My brother's face among the crowd.

In the middle of it all, a photograph of Sam. I tugged the photo from the board and unfolded the half of the image that had been tucked away. My own face. The two of us were squeezed into the frame, the flash glinting in my brother's blue eyes.

We looked so alike. Detective Harry Blue and the Georges River Killer.

CHAPTER 7

I'VE HAD two cigarettes in the past ten years. Both of them I smoked outside the funeral home where a fallen colleague's body was being laid to rest. I stood now in the alleyway behind headquarters, finishing off the third. I chain-lit the fourth, sucked hard, exhaled into the icy morning. Despite the chill, my shirt was sticking to me with sweat. I tried to call my brother's phone three times. No answer.

The Chief emerged from the fire exit beside me. I held up a hand. Not only did I not want to talk, I wasn't sure that I could if I tried. The old man stood watching as I smoked. My hands were shaking.

"That...that rat...that stain on humanity, Nigel Spader, is going to go down for this," I said. "If it's my last act, I'm going to make sure he—"

"I've overseen the entire operation," the Chief said. "I couldn't tell you it was going on, or you might have alerted Sam. We let you carry on, business as usual. Nigel and his team have done a very good job. They've been onto your brother for about three weeks now."

I looked at my Chief. My trainer. My friend.

"I've thought you've been looking tired," I sneered. "Can't sleep at night, Boss?"

"No," he said. "As a matter of fact, I can't. I haven't slept since the morning the Homicide team told me of their suspicions. I hated lying to you, Blue."

He ground a piece of asphalt into the gutter with his heel. He looked ancient in the reflected light of the towering city blocks around us.

"Where is my brother?"

"They picked him up this morning," he said. "He's being interrogated by the Feds over at Parramatta headquarters."

"I need to get over there."

"You won't get anywhere near him at this stage." The Chief took me by the shoulders before I could barge past him through the fire door. "He's in processing. Depending on whether he's cooperative, he may not be approved for visitors for a week. Two, even."

"Sam didn't do this," I said. "You've got it wrong. Nigel's got it wrong. I need to be here to straighten all this out."

"No, you don't," he said. "You need to get some stuff together and get out of here."

"What, just abandon him?"

"Harry, Sam is about to go down as one of the nastiest sexual sadists since the Backpacker Murderer. Whether you think he did it or not, you're public enemy number two right now. If the press gets hold of you, they're going to eat you alive."

I shook another cigarette out of the pack I'd swiped from Nigel's desk. My thoughts were racing.

"You aren't going to do yourself any favours here, Harry. If you go around shouting in front of the cameras the way you did in that case room just now, you're going to look like a lunatic."

"I don't give a shit what I look like!"

"You should," the Chief said. "The entire country is going tune in for this on the six o'clock news. People are angry. If they can't get at Sam, they're going to want to get at you. Think about it. It's fucking poetry. The killer's sister is a short-tempered, frequently violent cop with a mouth like a sailor. Better yet, she's in Sex Crimes, and has somehow managed to remain completely oblivious to the sexual predator at the family barbecue."

He took a piece of paper from the breast pocket of his jacket and handed it to me. It was a printout of a flight itinerary. He untucked a slim folder from under his arm and put it in my hands. I opened it and saw it was a case brief, but I couldn't get my eyes to settle on it for more than a few seconds. I felt sick with fear, uncertainty.

"What's this?" I asked.

"It's an Unexplained Death case out on a mining camp in the desert near Kalgoorlie," the Chief said.

"I'm sex crimes, Pops. Not clean-up crew."

"I don't care what you are. You're going. I pulled some strings with some old mates in Perth. The case itself is bullshit, but the area is so isolated, it'll make the perfect hideout."

"I don't want to go to fucking Kalgoorlie! Are you nuts?"

"You don't get a choice, Detective. Even if you don't know what's best for you right now, I do. I'm giving you a direct order as your superior officer. You don't go, I'll have you locked up for interrogative purposes. I'll tell a judge I want to know if you knew anything about the murders and I'll throw away the key until this shitstorm is over. You want that?"

I tried to walk away. The Chief grabbed my arm again.

"Look at me," he said.

I didn't look.

"There is nothing you can do to help your brother, Blue," the old man said. "It's over."

JAMES PATTERSON

To find out more about James Patterson
and his bestselling books, go to
www.jamespatterson.co.uk

JAMES PATTERSON
BOOK**SHOTS**

stories at the speed of life

BOOK**SHOTS** are page-turning stories by James Patterson and other writers that can be read in one sitting.

Each and every one is fast-paced, 100% story-driven; a shot of pure entertainment guaranteed to satisfy.

Under 150 pages
Under £3

Available as new, compact paperbacks, ebooks and audio, everywhere books are sold.

For more details, visit: **www.bookshots.com**

BOOK**SHOTS**
THE ULTIMATE FORM OF STORYTELLING.
FROM THE ULTIMATE STORYTELLER.

Also by James Patterson

ALEX CROSS NOVELS

Along Came a Spider • Kiss the Girls • Jack and Jill •
Cat and Mouse • Pop Goes the Weasel • Roses are Red •
Violets are Blue • Four Blind Mice • The Big Bad Wolf •
London Bridges • Mary, Mary • Cross • Double Cross •
Cross Country • Alex Cross's Trial (*with Richard DiLallo*) •
I, Alex Cross • Cross Fire • Kill Alex Cross • Merry
Christmas, Alex Cross • Alex Cross, Run • Cross My
Heart • Hope to Die • Cross Justice • Cross the Line

THE WOMEN'S MURDER CLUB SERIES

1st to Die • 2nd Chance (*with Andrew Gross*) • 3rd Degree
(*with Andrew Gross*) • 4th of July (*with Maxine Paetro*) •
The 5th Horseman (*with Maxine Paetro*) • The 6th Target
(*with Maxine Paetro*) • 7th Heaven (*with Maxine Paetro*) •
8th Confession (*with Maxine Paetro*) • 9th Judgement (*with
Maxine Paetro*) • 10th Anniversary (*with Maxine Paetro*) •
11th Hour (*with Maxine Paetro*) • 12th of Never (*with Maxine
Paetro*) • Unlucky 13 (*with Maxine Paetro*) • 14th Deadly Sin
(*with Maxine Paetro*) • 15th Affair (*with Maxine Paetro*)

DETECTIVE MICHAEL BENNETT SERIES

Step on a Crack (*with Michael Ledwidge*) • Run for Your Life
(*with Michael Ledwidge*) • Worst Case (*with Michael Ledwidge*) •
Tick Tock (*with Michael Ledwidge*) • I, Michael Bennett
(*with Michael Ledwidge*) • Gone (*with Michael Ledwidge*) •
Burn (*with Michael Ledwidge*) • Alert (*with Michael Ledwidge*) •
Bullseye (*with Michael Ledwidge*)

PRIVATE NOVELS

Private (*with Maxine Paetro*) • Private London (*with Mark Pearson*) • Private Games (*with Mark Sullivan*) • Private: No. 1 Suspect (*with Maxine Paetro*) • Private Berlin (*with Mark Sullivan*) • Private Down Under (*with Michael White*) • Private L.A. (*with Mark Sullivan*) • Private India (*with Ashwin Sanghi*) • Private Vegas (*with Maxine Paetro*) • Private Sydney (*with Kathryn Fox*) • Private Paris (*with Mark Sullivan*) • The Games (*with Mark Sullivan*) • Private Delhi (*with Ashwin Sanghi*)

NYPD RED SERIES

NYPD Red (*with Marshall Karp*) • NYPD Red 2 (*with Marshall Karp*) • NYPD Red 3 (*with Marshall Karp*) • NYPD Red 4 (*with Marshall Karp*)

NON-FICTION

Torn Apart (*with Hal and Cory Friedman*) • The Murder of King Tut (*with Martin Dugard*)

ROMANCE

Sundays at Tiffany's (*with Gabrielle Charbonnet*) • The Christmas Wedding (*with Richard DiLallo*) • First Love (*with Emily Raymond*)

OTHER TITLES

Miracle at Augusta (*with Peter de Jonge*)

FAMILY OF PAGE-TURNERS

MIDDLE SCHOOL BOOKS

The Worst Years of My Life (*with Chris Tebbetts*) • Get Me Out of Here! (*with Chris Tebbetts*) • My Brother Is a Big, Fat Liar (*with Lisa Papademetriou*) • How I Survived Bullies, Broccoli, and Snake Hill (*with Chris Tebbetts*) • Ultimate Showdown (*with Julia Bergen*) • Save Rafe! (*with Chris Tebbetts*) • Just My Rotten Luck (*with Chris Tebbetts*) • Dog's Best Friend (*with Chris Tebbetts*)

I FUNNY SERIES

I Funny (*with Chris Grabenstein*) • I Even Funnier (*with Chris Grabenstein*) • I Totally Funniest (*with Chris Grabenstein*) • I Funny TV (*with Chris Grabenstein*)

TREASURE HUNTERS SERIES

Treasure Hunters (*with Chris Grabenstein*) • Danger Down the Nile (*with Chris Grabenstein*) • Secret of the Forbidden City (*with Chris Grabenstein*) • Peril at the Top of the World (*with Chris Grabenstein*)

HOUSE OF ROBOTS SERIES

House of Robots (*with Chris Grabenstein*) • Robots Go Wild! (*with Chris Grabenstein*) • Robot Revolution (*with Chris Grabenstein*)

OTHER ILLUSTRATED NOVELS

Kenny Wright: Superhero (*with Chris Tebbetts*) • Homeroom Diaries (*with Lisa Papademetriou*) • Jacky Ha-Ha (*with Chris Grabenstein*)

For more information about James Patterson's novels, visit
www.jamespatterson.co.uk

Or become a fan on Facebook